That Thing about Bollywood

ALSO BY SUPRIYA KELKAR

American as Paneer Pie

Ahimsa

Bindu's Bindis

The Many Colors of Harpreet Singh

Strong as Fire, Fierce as Flame

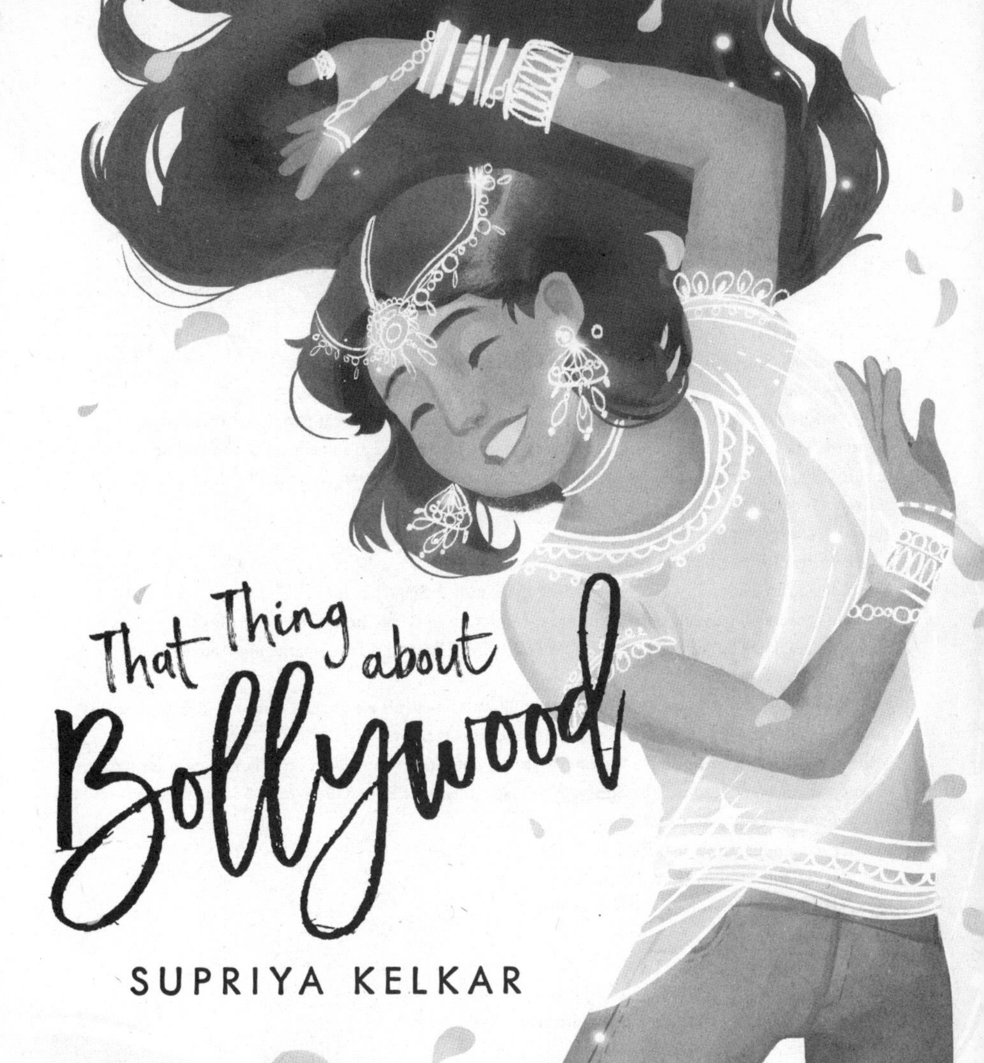

That Thing about Bollywood

SUPRIYA KELKAR

SIMON & SCHUSTER BOOKS FOR YOUNG READERS
New York London Toronto Sydney New Delhi

SIMON & SCHUSTER BOOKS FOR YOUNG READERS
An imprint of Simon & Schuster Children's Publishing Division
1230 Avenue of the Americas, New York, New York 10020

Interior design by Laura Lyn DiSiena
The text for this book was set Amiri.
Manufactured in the United States of America
0421 FFG
First Edition
10 9 8 7 6 5 4 3 2 1
Library of Congress Cataloging-in-Publication Data
Names: Kelkar, Supriya, 1980– author.
Title: That thing about Bollywood / Supriya Kelkar.
Description: First edition. | New York : Simon & Schuster Books for Young Readers, [2021] | Audience: Ages 8 to 12. | Audience: Grades 4-6. | Summary: Middle-schooler Sonali cannot bring herself to share her feelings, but when she wakes up one day and begins to involuntarily burst into Bollywood song and dance routines that showcase her emotions, she realizes she has to find her voice and share her feelings.
Identifiers: LCCN 2020038928 (print) | LCCN 2020038929 (eBook) | ISBN 9781534466739 (hardcover) | ISBN 9781534466753 (eBook)
Subjects: LCSH: East Indian Americans—Juvenile fiction. | CYAC: East Indian Americans—Fiction. | Emotions—Fiction. | Bollywood—Fiction. | Divorce—Fiction. | Magic—Fiction.
Classification: LCC PZ7.1.K417 Th 2021 (print) | LCC PZ7.1.K417 (eBook) | DDC [Fic]—dc23
LC record available at https://lccn.loc.gov/2020038928
LC eBook record available at https://lccn.loc.gov/2020038929

To the filmi magic that shaped my childhood,
and the family and friends I got to share it with

CHAPTER 1

You know how in Bollywood movies, people sing and dance on mountaintops when they're in love? I wonder if they do the same when they're splitting up.

I walked my dinner plate to the kitchen sink, searching for the answer as I thought about all the Hindi movies I'd seen. The rules of classic Bollywood, from way back in the '80s and '90s, were pretty easy to remember: everything was loud, exaggerated, and colorful.

I scrubbed the miniscule remnants of green-bean shaak and daal bhaat off my stainless-steel plate. As the specks of spices, lentils, and rice slipped down the drain, I made a mental list of what you do when you're feeling a certain way in an old Hindi movie:

When you're happy, you sing, sometimes from a mountaintop.

When you're sad, you sing.

When you're really into what you're wearing, you sing. Seriously. There are songs about scarves, bindis, bangles, anklets . . . any accessory will do. I'll bet one day there will be a song about thermal underwear.

When you're mad, nope, you don't sing. But you can do an angry instrumental dance or scream while shaking in rage, and the soundtrack behind you will be full of *dishoom dishoom* as you beat up the bad guys and save the day.

And when you're jealous, you can sing or take part in a bonus dance-off.

Basically, anytime you are feeling something, you show it. So, I guess, yeah, you would sing in a Bollywood movie when you were breaking up.

I dried my hands and walked past the window with the swaying jacaranda trees in our backyard. I glanced at the white house behind ours with the clay tile roof crawling with purple bougainvillea vines, my friend Zara's house, and I headed into our family room. My grandparents' four pictures hung on the light-gray wall there with dried sandalwood garlands around them, symbolizing that they had passed away. Across from the pictures,

Mom and my little brother, Ronak, were already snuggled under a blanket on our long gray sofa.

"What are we watching tonight, Sonali ben?" Ronak asked, adding on the respectful Gujarati word for "big sister."

"Something funny," I replied, accidentally bumping into the stack of dusty books about the history of Hindi films on the end table. I straightened them out and opened the wooden armoire in the corner, which was covered in family pictures of us whale watching and at Sequoia National Park. I was extra careful not to knock over the new framed photo of my aunt Avni Foi, grinning with her fiancé, Baljeet Uncle, at their engagement party.

The armoire was stuffed to the max with old VHS tapes from when my grandfather owned Indian Video, a little store in Artesia that used to rent Hindi movie videotapes to people, before switching to DVDs. When Dada passed away last summer, he left all the store's retired videotapes to me, because he knew how much I used to love watching them with him when I was little. Luckily, Dada had passed his old VHS player down to me too, or I'd have no way to watch the tapes at home. And now every Sunday, my family got together and watched an old Hindi movie.

I wasn't sure how long this tradition was going to last, but I was going to enjoy it while I could. I moved the red, plastic, convertible-car-shaped VHS rewinder and grabbed a movie off the top shelf of the alphabetically sorted tapes. It was fun and silly, and from the lines in my mom's forehead, which seemed to be permanent these days, it looked like she could use the laughs.

I put the videotape into the rewinder so it wouldn't wear out the VHS player, popped it into the VHS player when it was back to the beginning of the movie, and settled in under the blanket next to Ronak as the ancient commercials that always played before these movies began. One was for a turmeric cream and featured a bride getting turmeric paste all over her legs before her wedding and a catchy song. Ronak sang along, tapping his toes. The next one was for a pain balm and also had a catchy song, of course, so Ronak kept singing. And then the censor certificate flashed, showing the movie's rating.

"Wait." Ronak reached for the remote in my hand and pressed pause. "What about Dad?"

"What about him?" I asked, swiping my silky black locks out of my eyes.

"We always wait for Dad."

I sighed. "And he always works and makes us wait forever."

Mom's fingers were clenched tightly around one another as she squeezed her hands in her lap like she was trying not to say something. "I block my whole evening schedule off at the hospital for this every week. But clearly he doesn't prioritize—"

Whoops. It seemed she didn't squeeze her hands hard enough and something slipped out. Ronak's eyebrows furrowed with worry, but Mom gave us a tiny smile with her chapped lips.

"Why don't we start the movie, and if Dad wants to see what he missed, after his client dinner, we can always rewind it for him?" she asked.

"But you always tell us to think about how we would feel in someone else's shoes, and I would feel sad if you started the movie without me," Ronak replied.

Ronak was sensitive and kind and not afraid to show the world how he felt. He would be a perfect fit in a Bollywood movie.

"Well, we don't wear shoes in the house," I said. "So don't pretend you're in anyone's shoes right now and just enjoy the movie."

I clicked play on the remote that Dada had always kept wrapped in plastic to keep it clean. It may have saved the remote from sticky fingers, but it meant I had to press extra hard to make the buttons work.

"You have no feelings," Ronak muttered as the colorful titles began.

"You have too many feelings," I retorted.

"Shh," Mom said as the opening scene played. She smiled as Ronak giggled uncontrollably at Aamir Khan's antics.

I let out a puff of air through my nose at a particularly hilarious line. "That's funny."

Mom raised an eyebrow at me. "Is that your laugh? 'That's funny'?"

"Wouldn't want anyone to see your emotions or anything," Ronak said, before laughing loudly at the next line.

"Stop fighting, you two," Mom said gently, leaning into us.

I gave Ronak a small look out of the side of my eye. He was two years younger, but even at nine, he understood the irony of Mom telling us not to fight when she and Dad fought all the time. His eyes glistened, and I was afraid he was going to start crying.

I poked his arm. "This is the funniest part, remember?"

"Yeah." Ronak smiled, wiping his eyes. "You might even actually laugh out loud instead of just saying, 'That's funny.'"

But I didn't, even as Juhi Chawla made the most hysterical expressions at Aamir Khan on-screen. "That's funny." I said, and smiled with a small puff of air.

Ronak was holding his belly and laughing as loudly as Mom when we heard the garage door open, and Dad walked in, his briefcase full of papers from work.

"Hey, Rony-Pony and my little Soni," he said to us, setting his briefcase down and taking a seat on the other side of me without a word to Mom.

Mom suddenly stopped laughing, and those laugh lines that were on her face were outnumbered by the frown lines between her eyebrows as she stared hard at the screen.

I guess, unlike in Bollywood, in real life, people don't sing when they're growing apart. Nope. They're just silent.

CHAPTER 2

The next morning, with the late-January air still heavy with mist, Zara and I waited at the top of my driveway, backpacks on, passing a basketball back and forth.

"Do you think if this acting thing doesn't work out for me, I could be a choreographer?" Zara asked, chasing after the ball as it bounced into the garage around my parents' white sedans.

My belly did a nervous twitch. It was not only the start of the new school week. It was the start of the new semester, which meant new electives. So Zara was about to get a lot of acting practice in, because today we started drama. "You're an awesome actress," I replied, skipping over how having to act in front of everyone made me want to hurl. "It will totally work out."

Zara gasped from the garage. "Oh my god. Whose are these?"

She emerged with a dusty pair of roller skates with faded red wheels and teddy bears painted on the sides.

I grinned. "They're . . . my dad's."

"Your dad wore these? As an adult?" Zara slid her shoes off and slipped into the skates that were way too large for her. And then she immediately fell forward.

I dived and grabbed her arms, steadying her.

"That was so Suraj of you," Zara laughed, referencing the old Hindi movie hero who roller-skated to defeat the bad guy and save the day.

A cool breeze swirled past us, fluttering through my long black waves, and Zara flipped her own curly black hair like she was in a Hindi movie. "*Hawa ke saath saath,*" she sang. It was a line about going along with the wind, from an old roller-skating song.

I glanced around us. Our street was empty.

"No one's looking. You know the rest." Zara put her hand to her ear. "I'm waiting."

"Ghata ke sang sang." I said the line about going along with the clouds, in monotone.

Zara dramatically kicked herself back, rolling toward the garage with her hands outstretched. "*O saathi chal!*" she sang loudly, telling me to go along with her.

Just then the door slammed and Dad and Ronak rushed out. The gust from the door caused Dad's thinning hair to fly up off his bald spot.

"I think we have everything," Dad said, patting his hair down while glancing at his briefcase, a stack of papers, and Ronak's bag. "Come on, everyone. We're late!"

Zara bugged her eyes out at me, mouthing, "Busted," as she pointed to the skates.

I stifled my laughter, grabbed Zara's shoes off the driveway, and got into the car.

Dad opened the other door for Zara. She gave him a big, goofy grin to distract him from his skates on her feet, and tumbled in. Dad was too busy reading a work email on his phone to notice, so Zara hurriedly kicked off the skates as I passed her shoes across Ronak.

"You're not going to be driving any clients around today, are you, Kirit Uncle?" Zara asked, pointing to the skates for me and Ronak to see as we all buckled up.

Ronak laughed, despite trying not to, as Dad said no and put his phone away. He then gave us a brief but boring overview of his day as he pulled out of the driveway and headed for Oceanview Academy, which, despite its name, did not have a view of the ocean.

"Do you think Ms. Lin is going to have us sing and dance in drama?" Zara asked, throwing the back of her hand to her forehead and making over-the-top Hindi movie faces as the two gold bangles from her last trip to Pakistan jingled against each other. "Bollywood-style?"

The reporter on the car radio began talking about a squirrel stuck in the tar pits, and Dad quickly switched to the LA traffic station.

"No way. There's no way she would do that." I sank in my seat. *Would she?*

"Why? We just had an awesome Bollywood performance," Zara said, making the roller skates dance out of Dad's view, trying to make me laugh.

"No matter what, Sonali, you have to do your best, right?" I saw Dad's eyes look my way in the rearview mirror. I bit the inside of my cheeks. I knew he was trying to remind me to get good grades this semester, after my last report card was less than stellar.

"Speaking of dance," Dad continued, "Avni Foi called this morning. She wants you and Ronak to do a dance at her sangeet with all your cousins, Sonali."

Zara squealed in excitement for me. A sangeet was an event

before a wedding where everyone sings and dances. Her black curls caught the light from the window, turning a golden brown. "Oh, that's going to be so awesome!" She gasped. "You could totally do 'Dil Le Gayi Kudi Gujarat Di!' You know, since he's Punjabi . . ."

". . . and she's Gujarati," Ronak continued, as excited as Zara. "This is going to be so cool."

"Not really." I frowned, pressing down hard on the button to lower the window, letting in the sounds of the sparrows and warblers and traffic from outside. I always felt a little bit of motion sickness in cars, but this dancing-in-public talk made me feel even more nauseous than normal. I loved watching all the songs and dances in Hindi movies but felt ridiculous dancing to them in front of witnesses, grinning super cheesily at a romantic line or exaggerating my eyebrows at a sad one.

"You're as good a dancer as Parvati," Zara replied, talking about my super-talented cousin, who would be choreographing us just like she always did at family party performances. "You should totally practice when we're on the mountain for our field trip next week. Sridevi-style."

The thought of dancing on the little fire-scarred mountains over the 405 in front of everyone was mortifying, and a far cry from the snowcapped mountains or lush green mountains peppered with bright wildflowers that Hindi movie stars danced on. "You know I hate dancing in front of people," I replied as we waited forever at a red light on Wilshire. "And it's for sure going to be a medley at the sangeet. I'll bet Parvati will cram in, like, ten songs. My cheeks will hurt from smiling that long."

"Your cheeks can handle a ten-minute smile," Zara laughed.

"She's right, robot-sister." Ronak grinned just as the car speakers began to ring.

Dad pushed a button. Before he could say a word, Mom started talking, and I could hear her frown in every syllable.

"Tell me you remembered to pack Ronak's water bottle and didn't forget again?"

"Oh no." Dad groaned as he turned toward our school. "I have a morning meeting."

"Yeah. I know. So now I'll have to leave the hospital between patients, go home and get it, and take it to school. Because you can't be responsible and complete a simple job."

"Speakerphone on chhe." I saw Dad's ears turn red as he switched to Gujarati, letting Mom know she was on speakerphone. "Jara relax tha, okay? Mhari meeting bhaley chuki jaaye, hoon kari daish. Taari eklinij nokri bahu important chhe ne?"

Zara, who couldn't understand Gujarati but could definitely understand the tone being used, looked out the window, pretending the white-barked fig trees next to the sidewalk were the most fascinating things in the world. I looked at Ronak, who was staring at the cheerful teddy-bear roller skates on the floor as my dad told my mom he would miss his meeting and take care of it because she was the only one with an important job.

"Relax?" Mom snapped.

My ears burned, and I hoped the rest of my face wasn't as twisted as I felt. Why did Mom have to start this fight when she knew Zara would hear it? Didn't she realize how embarrassing this was?

"I'll call you later. I'm turning in to the school," Dad replied, hanging up. He pulled to a stop in the drop-off line for middle school.

"Bye, Ro. Bye, Kirit Uncle," Zara said as she got out of the car. "Thanks for the ride."

"Of course," Dad replied warmly, even though I could tell he was still mad from the call by how red his cheeks remained.

"Bye," I said softly, following Zara as my dad headed down the road to take Ronak to the elementary school on the far end of campus.

"Smile," Zara said to me, linking elbows as she practically bounced. "New semester New beginnings. In just a few hours we will be in drama!"

I clearly had enough drama at home, so I wasn't sure why I had let Zara convince me to sign up for drama at school. But I took a breath and faked a smile as we entered the building, pretending, like always, that everything was going to be okay.

Maybe I would be good at this acting thing.

CHAPTER 3

With English and history having gone by way too fast, I walked down the hall to the amphitheater by the cafeteria, my feet dragging. Each step was a huge effort, because I knew I was going to be miserable in class. And it wasn't just because of what I was going to have to do there, losing my cool to act ridiculous with over-the-top tears for everyone to see. It was also because I knew Zara was going to be acting ridiculous in there too.

Despite our love of Hindi movies, lately Zara had been more interested in Hollywood than Bollywood. Well, one particular member of the Hollywood family: Airplane O'Neil.

A lot of kids at our school had famous parents. This was LA., after all. But Airplane, who went by "Air" because there was nothing "plain" about her, was different: after being partnered up for a history project and hitting it off last month, Zara had zeroed in on Airplane for co-best-friend status.

I wasn't sure I was willing to share that title. It was like when two people tied for a category during the movie awards shows in India, awkwardly sharing one trophy, and one person always got less time for their speech. Who wanted awkward sharing and less time to talk to each other? Not me.

I entered the round room full of familiar faces, kids I had gone to school with since elementary school. Zara was giggling on the side with Air. I walked past the props to the side of the dark-gray stage, made my way around a large, plastic jacaranda tree with purple flowers always in bloom, and took a seat next to Zara.

"Hey." Air smiled politely, noticing me a split second before Zara.

"Oh, phew!" Zara exclaimed. "I was afraid you weren't going to show up!" She handed me a neon-green sticker. "Here. I got your name tag for you."

I stuck it on as Zara squealed. "This is going to be amazing." She squeezed my hand.

Air looked down at her feet. Clearly, she wasn't into sharing Zara either.

A loud clapping stopped me from focusing any more on the BFF drama, as Ms. Lin entered the room. She brushed her graying bangs off the black frame of her glasses and took her spot on a big *X* in the center of the stage. "Greetings, future Broadway stars, future Academy members . . ."

Zara nudged me. "Like Air's mom," she whispered.

I nodded as Ms. Lin continued. ". . . and future amazing kids who are in touch with their feelings and not afraid to show it." Ms. Lin added a flourish of the hand. "I want to let you know how this semester is going to work. Each week we are going to do little exercises to loosen up and get comfortable emoting."

Zara raised her hand. Ms. Lin pointed at her. "Will we be doing the show in spring?"

Ms. Lin shook her head. "I'm afraid the spring musical is for eighth graders who have had lots of drama classes. But you will be putting on a solo show for your midterm."

My throat felt dry. If I wanted to put on a show, I'd join Ronak in crying or saying I was sad every time our parents got into a little argument.

"You'll be doing a monologue," Ms. Lin continued.

My legs felt a little weak. A monologue meant it would be just me onstage. I had done school presentations before and it was fine. But school presentations didn't require emoting. They didn't require showing your feelings to the world. I had sworn off that years ago.

Ms. Lin grinned like this awful assignment was a little puppy to be adored. "For your midterm, you'll each be taking on the role of a mythical creature and showing us, through your expressions, gestures, and words, what that creature is feeling."

Ms. Lin approached us with a glittery purple top hat. "I want you to know now what character you're going to become, so you can think how to apply every lesson to that midterm. It will be worth a quarter of your grade. The rest will be based on class participation and the final."

Air reached in and unfolded the yellow piece of paper. "A unicorn."

Zara reached in next. "Mermaid." She nodded. "I can work with that."

"I hope I get narwhal," said Landon, a tall kid who played violin in the school orchestra.

"A narwhal isn't mythical." Air frowned.

"What?" Landon's eyes went wide.

I smiled. Despite how clearly jealous Air was about me being friends with Zara, I kind of liked her. Maybe Zara was right, and we did have some stuff in common. I pulled out a slip of paper from the hat. "Werewolf." I forced a smile on my face for Ms. Lin. "Neat," I lied, like I was thrilled to pretend to be a furry wolf-person, as the rest of the class picked from the hat.

With all characters assigned, Ms. Lin came back to the *X* on the floor. "Now let's make a circle."

I joined the herd around Ms. Lin, like a good sheep.

"Acting is sometimes over the top," Ms. Lin proclaimed.

"Like in Bollywood," Zara said.

Ms. Lin nodded. "Some Bollywood films are over the top, aren't they? But that's why we love them."

"Over the top?" Landon asked. "They're so out there, they're hilarious."

I looked at Zara, my eyebrows narrowing at Landon's words. "It's not okay to make fun of someone's culture," I snapped. I turned to Zara for some support, but she was busy giving Air an annoyed look at how ridiculous Landon was. A look she would normally share with me.

"Sonali is right," Ms. Lin said, reading my name tag. "Let's be kind and respectful. No matter what kind of style an actor performs, be it Bollywood, Broadway, or a TikTok video, the emotions actors portray are based on real-life emotions. You have to be able to channel that by reaching into something real and connecting to your audience. So let's start connecting right now by digging deep inside and playing . . . 'The One Thing You Don't Know about Me.'"

I didn't like the sound of this game. There was a reason Zara and I worked so well together. She liked to talk. She loved to share and overshare. And I listened. I knew what happened if I put myself out there: nothing good. So if I didn't share my deepest thoughts with my best friend, how would I share them with this room full of people I knew, yet didn't?

"We'll take turns sharing something, and if anyone else has that thing in common, they will stand next to the person sharing. Xiomara, why don't you start?"

Xiomara, a few kids down the circle from me, spoke. "The one thing you don't know about me is my neighbor is Aashi Kapoor."

Zara gasped but then immediately tried to play it cool when Air looked at her. But I knew she was thrilled. Aashi Kapoor was a Bollywood actress who had crossed over. She was now a platinum-selling singer here, despite never having sung for the songs she lip-synched to in India.

"That's great, Xiomara," Ms. Lin said. "But is there something deeper there? What does a singer being your neighbor mean to you?"

Xiomara paused, pulling at her fingers.

Ms. Lin nodded. "There are no wrong answers to emotions. Are you proud of that fact? Do you wish you could meet her? Do you wish you could sing like her—"

"I sing better than her," Xiomara said, her curls bouncing defiantly. "I do. But any time I've auditioned, they say I don't have the right look. But Aashi Kapoor does? Her 'look' is just staring into the camera while wind machines blow her hair."

"The industry is hard, Xiomara. I get that. But your voice is important, so don't give up. Use that hurt and apply it to your centaur character. Maybe it's a singing centaur?"

Xiomara nodded, some of the angry red leaving her face. "A singtaur."

"Excellent improvisation! Now, let's all keep going, clockwise."

That meant I'd be up in five turns. What was one thing people didn't know about me?

"The one thing you don't know about me is my mom's getting married this weekend," Davuth, a tall boy next to Xiomara, said. "And I kind of hate the guy she's marrying, so my vampire is going to be full of resentment."

Winnie, the school's star basketball player, rushed across the circle to stand next to him, making cheesy heart hands.

"I'm so sorry, Davuth," Ms. Lin said. "And Winnie. Sometimes actors can find something really helpful in pain. And sometimes it's hard to deal with. You know you can talk to me or the school counselor anytime. Both of you."

Davuth nodded. Winnie wiped her teary eyes and gave Ms. Lin a hug before heading back to her spot. I cringed, embarrassed for Winnie. Everyone must have thought she was such a baby. But I had to get over my mortification fast and rack my brain for what I was going to say when it was my turn. What was deep down, so far down that no one knew it?

My parents fight all the time.

No. I was not going to say that out loud here.

Kiersten, the short girl with wavy red hair next to Davuth, was next. "The one thing you don't know about me is I love the turmeric chai Froyo in Brentwood."

A handful of kids walked next to Kiersten. I tried to be kind and resisted the urge to give Zara a look over the Desi ingredients like turmeric, chai, and holy basil that were suddenly as popular as yoga in Los Angeles. Oh, wait, yoga was also a Desi thing.

"And if you want me to dig deeper," Kiersten added, "all I

can say is, my dad makes cereal for dinner every weekend and it really stinks when I see everyone else eating cool stuff on social media. So, my tooth fairy collects teeth because she's sick of everyone eating good food without her."

Ms. Lin nodded. "Fascinating. Air?"

Air cleared her throat. "The one thing you don't know about me is I like the stock market."

"Okay," Ms. Lin began, but Air wasn't done.

"No, like, I really like it. Like, I wish I could have taken mock market, but my parents wouldn't let me."

Awkward. That was the elective that took place at the same time as drama. I watched Ms. Lin's smile get a little smaller, but Air didn't notice and Air wasn't stopping.

"I love figuring out what the abbreviations stand for. I love that you can use math and make money with it, so my unicorn wants to be something other than what her parents like."

"Very good," Ms. Lin said, smiling, acting like her feelings weren't hurt at all. "Zara?"

I was next, and I still didn't know what I was going to say.

"I haven't ever told anyone this before. Well, other than Sonali because we tell each other everything. But the one thing you don't know about me is . . . I want to be a movie star," Zara announced, looking at Air like she was hoping she could help make it happen.

Air gave her a tiny supportive smile, but from the way her eyes were shifting to the sides, Air almost seemed uncomfortable with the Hollywood talk.

Several kids left their spots in the circle and stood next to Zara.

"Maybe your mom can put us all in the next movie she directs," Landon said to Air, who just twisted her lips to the side like she was biting the insides of her cheeks.

"Landon!" Zara admonished. "That's not cool. Sorry, Air," Zara said, as if she didn't desperately want Air's parents to help her become a movie star too.

Air shrugged, and I felt a little bad for her, like everyone was always talking about her famous parents and she was always stuck in their shadow.

"Anyway," Zara said, changing the subject protectively, "everyone expects my mermaid to be a typical mermaid, but she wants to stand out from the crowd."

"Good," Ms. Lin said. Then she turned to me. "Sonali?"

My insides felt shaky. What was I going to say that was from "deep within"? *My parents snap at each other all the time when they're not giving each other the silent treatment? My brother looks like he is going to cry any time they get into an argument over nothing? My jaw gets really tight whenever my parents bicker, and it's like I'm the parent trying to break up an argument between kids and I hate it?*

No. None of this was okay to say out loud. I had learned that the hard way years ago. We didn't talk about divorce in our family. I only knew a few Indian American kids with divorced parents, and even though many family friends were supportive and helpful during the split, I remember some aunties and uncles gossiping about it any chance they got. I wasn't going to say this out loud, and I wasn't going to bond over this with other kids in class.

"The one thing you don't know about me is I . . ." I looked at Zara. She nodded at me, like she was a parent encouraging her terrified little kid to jump off a diving board at swimming class. "I . . ." I tried to stop the words that were trying to escape my throat. The words that might become true if I said them out loud.

"You've got this," Ms. Lin said gently.

No, I didn't. "I love Bollywood," I mumbled, stifling my secrets.

Zara, Landon, and a few more kids moved toward me.

Ms. Lin opened her mouth, and I knew I had to say something that involved more feelings before she made me accidentally start crying like Winnie.

"And I don't like it when people make fun of it." I looked at Landon for good measure.

He shrugged. "I said I liked it, didn't I?"

Ms. Lin shook her head. "You did, but you also were mocking it, and we respect everyone's backgrounds and cultures here."

Landon nodded, his forehead beading with nervous sweat. "Sorry." He looked my way. "Sorry to you, too. I really do like it," he mumbled as I gave him a forgiving look.

"Thank you, Landon." Ms. Lin gave me a smile. "Sonali, you're passionate about Bollywood. Maybe that will help you figure out what your werewolf is passionate about."

"Not sharing," I muttered to Zara with a nervous chuckle, thinking about the last time I really put myself out there to share something and what a disaster that had been.

I had spent the first week of winter break in first grade determined to stop my parents from arguing. They fought differently back then, loudly arguing their case, all the time. I had gone to the craft closet in our guest room and pulled out a pack of small poster boards, glitter glue, and colored pencils. I went to the dusty bookcase in the den, full of my parents' childhood books, and grabbed a bunch of Mom's old nonfiction books full of facts. I researched and wrote and drew, putting to use all the skills my parents had taught me on the weekends, when I wasn't in school but they made me study anyway. After days my project was done, and just in time, because we were having a big party at our house with Dada, Avni Foi, and all my extended SoCal family.

After Parvati ben finished dancing in the impromptu post-dinner talent show, it was my turn to show off. I grabbed my poster boards and began my presentation titled, "Why Parents Shouldn't Fight." I went over a glittery drawing of what happens to your brain when you get mad, and spent a lot of time on a sketch of my parents fighting while crayon-me held little Ronak with sad looks on our faces. When I was done, I turned to my parents, expecting them to have been totally convinced by my art and ready to change their ways. But, instead, they both looked appalled and started arguing under their breath with each other. The rest of my family just stared at me in shock until Dada began to laugh his gravelly, contagious belly laugh.

He clapped his hands, chuckling and saying it was so cute and sweet and not just parents but all the siblings in the room should stop fighting as well. He laughed at me and soon my aunts and uncles and cousins were all laughing too. Embarrassed, I threw the poster boards down and ran upstairs.

Dad had run up after me. But instead of consoling me, he yelled at me for three long minutes. I stared at the clock as he told me how I had humiliated him and made everyone think bad things about him and Mom. Mom finally came up and apologized for making me think I had to try to teach them how to behave and said she was proud of me for sharing. Dad immediately snapped at me that what I did wasn't a good thing. It was showing everyone our bad side and it wasn't okay. He was always strict about not lying, but I guess in his mind it wasn't lying to just not show the full version of yourself to the outside world. I was sure everyone downstairs heard his yelling lecture, because when he made me go back down to join the party, they all were giving me looks of pity. From that moment on I decided I'd be strong, never sharing my feelings since all it led to was uncomfortable stares, being made fun of, upset parents, and nothing changing anyway.

"What's that?" Ms. Lin asked. "'Not sharing'?"

I felt my face grow hot. I needed to stay on Ms. Lin's good side to get a good grade. "Sorry," I said quickly, probably looking as flustered as Landon had when he apologized to me.

Ms. Lin raised an eyebrow. "You're going to have a lot of trouble in this class if you can't share." Ms. Lin turned to face the rest of the circle. "That goes for all of you. Remember to get those metaphorical shovels out, class. Dig deep."

As Ms. Lin moved to the kid next to me, I swallowed hard, pushing those words that almost got out back down. I wasn't interested in digging them out. I wanted to keep them buried forever.

CHAPTER 4

The following Saturday I walked over the skeletons of a bunch of extinct animals that had been buried probably as deep as my words. I was at one of my favorite places in town, the La Brea Tar Pits, with Mom, Ronak, Baljeet Uncle, and one of my favorite people, Avni Foi.

My aunt worked there and it was her job to dig up bones and catalog them. She clearly didn't mind the farty smell of the active tar pits surrounding the museum, or she wouldn't be able to handle digging through the stinky, fossiliferous dirt to find the bones.

"It's amazing," she said, practically skipping around a pit. "These tar pits are just a few inches deep. But sometimes little things can add up to a lot."

We walked toward the sprawling, bubbling tar pit at the front of the museum. It was fenced off to keep people from falling in.

Baljeet Uncle eyed the growing traffic on the road ahead. “What time did you want to head over to Hugo’s?”

Mom shrugged. “Kirit’s still at work. He’s not picking up.”

“No worries,” Avni Foi said. “I’ll just finish our tour and then we can try my brother again.” The smell of the natural asphalt from the pits made my head hurt a little, but Avni Foi was unbothered as she pointed to a spot next to the towering statue of a mastodon stuck in the pit. “Right there is where the squirrel fell into the pit,” she said, mentioning the squirrel from the radio.

Ronak’s smile quickly vanished. “Is she okay? My friends saw a picture of her covered in tar.”

“Uh,” Baljeet Uncle, who clearly wasn’t used to being around kids, looked nervous.

Avni Foi patted Ronak’s head. “She’s totally fine. A wildlife rescue center took her.”

“Oh, phew.” Ronak sighed, turning back to the tar pit as Baljeet Uncle breathed easier.

Avni Foi turned to me and Mom and mouthed, “Actually, she died.”

I nodded. I felt bad for the squirrel, but Ronak would have felt really bad. Like, sobbing, snot-dripping bad. No one needed to see that, so even though Avni Foi was protecting him, she was also protecting us and our clothes by telling him the squirrel survived.

"Anyway," Avni Foi said, "I'm dying to know what songs you're dancing to at our sangeet!"

My back suddenly felt heavy. I had almost forgotten that I would have to dance in front of the five hundred people Avni Foi and Baljeet Uncle were expecting at their sangeet.

"I'll bet I know one of the songs you're doing," Baljeet Uncle added, grabbing Avni Foi's hand as he loudly sang the song Zara had mentioned in the car last week about a Punjabi man who fell in love with a Gujarati woman.

Avni Foi laughed and sang along with Baljeet Uncle. My ears grew hot as my aunt shook her hips and spun around Baljeet Uncle. My hands got sweaty as Baljeet Uncle thumped his heart with his hand. I knew our culture was all about singing and dancing, but why were my friends and family members putting on so many spontaneous public performances this week? This was like the poster-board presentation all over again, except this time I was the audience.

Utterly mortified by the spectacle, I looked at the tourists and locals taking pictures, expecting to see smirks. But they started clapping. And then some people whistled and cheered when Ronak joined the dance.

I looked at Mom, knowing she would be as aghast at the lovebirds as I was, but she was smiling and clapping too. Despite her expression, her eyes brimmed with sadness, and I could tell her mind was elsewhere.

The peaceful sound of an Indian flute began to play over the family sing-along. Mom pulled the source of the song, her cell phone, out of her purse. Her mouth formed a tight line as she swiped to take the call.

"Where are you?" she asked, and I immediately could tell she was talking to my dad.

Mom took a few steps away from my aunt and soon-to-be uncle, who were now holding hands and looking at the gassy tar pit like it was a beautiful neon-pink and -purple sunset over Venice Beach.

"You're stuck at work? But she's your sister. We're celebrating your sister's promotion," she said irately, chewing on her chapped lips.

My jaw tightened. My lips were scrunching up like I was angry for no reason as I heard Dad's frustrated voice on the other end but couldn't make out the words.

Mom listened, rolling her eyes. "Well, get unstuck. You should be here too." She swiped her finger over her phone and dropped it back into the depths of her purse.

"Should we just meet him at Hugo's?" I asked, my embarrassment and resentment dissolving a little at the thought of the creamy, steaming bowl of mac and cheese I would devour there.

But Mom didn't hear me. She was just staring straight ahead at the mastodon statue and muttering under her breath, "You're stuck? I'm the one who's stuck. I'm the one who's stuck. . . ."

I didn't know what she was talking about, but I didn't like the sound of it. It made me feel uneasy and trapped, like I couldn't get out of what was to come. I stopped the concerned frown that was threatening to wrinkle up my forehead and forced my face back to neutral. The last thing I needed was Ronak asking me what was wrong and trying to talk it all out right now. He was too young to remember what had happened when I'd tried to convince my parents to stop fighting. So he never understood that there was no point in talking about upsetting things. It didn't make it go away. It was always there, surrounding you like a few inches of gummy tar, and if you talked about it, constantly reminding yourself about the bad stuff in your life, it just made it worse until you were sinking deeper and deeper into the abyss.

So with my face as nonchalant as it could be, I watched Mom mumble to herself while shaking her head and blinking away tears. And even though the mastodon statue was actually stuck in the tar and my mom was the one saying she was stuck on repeat, I couldn't help but feel like I was the one who couldn't move and was about to sink into a pit of toxic goo.

CHAPTER 5

I was feeling better after dinner. I had eaten a huge bowl of mac and cheese at the restaurant, and Mom even let me split a tamarind lemonade with Ronak while she told us stories about the tamarind tree in her neighbor's yard, which she and her siblings would climb to get to its sour fruit. And Dad was finally with us. Too bad it was after we had already gotten home.

He started to argue with Mom about missing the dinner with his sister that Mom had made time for. I braced myself for a long, drawn-out argument. But for the first time ever, instead of arguing back, Mom just looked blankly at Dad. And then Dad suddenly stopped too, shaking his head, shoulders slumped.

I was used to their usual annoyed silence with each other. But this was different. They never grew silent in the middle of an argument. It was like there was nothing worth fighting for anymore. It weirded me out. I wanted to shake the discomfort I was feeling. I wanted to stop witnessing any more of their odd expressions and bizarre midfight peace. So I cut across our backyard and headed for Zara's, because their kitchen light was on.

That was a sign that the Khans were home. I dropped in unannounced at their house all the time, and Zara did the same at my house. We were like family. The only difference was, there were just a few times at Zara's that I heard her parents argue. But my parents argued all the time when Zara was over, over the littlest things, like who forgot to put a chip clip on a bag of now-stale spelt pretzels. And my ears would burn just like they did when people stared at Avni Foi and Baljeet Uncle's tar pits dance. But Zara was a good friend who always changed the subject or talked loudly to me to drown out my parents' arguments.

I passed the patio swing near the back border of our yard and made my way through Imran Uncle's garden. I walked around the orange, grapefruit, and avocado trees, under whose shade we had played on a slip and slide when we were younger and weren't in a drought. I ducked past the buzzing bees and wasps by his colorful flowers, the ones we always avoided when we were splitting twin grape Popsicles. I got to the back door, which the bougainvillea branches were nestling around, just as the sun started to set, and knocked on the frame to the screen door.

Mumtaz Auntie, Zara's mom, slid the door open. "Come on in, beta!"

I stepped inside and took my shoes off on the mat.

"Air and Zara are in the den. They must be waiting for you," Auntie said as she poured herself a hot cup of cha at the counter.

"Thanks," I said, not letting my face show my surprise at the fact that Air was at Zara's as I followed the slate tiles down the hall and turned the corner to the den.

Zara and Air were sitting on the teal chaise laughing at a show on TeeVee, the streaming service I had just convinced my parents to get for us after hearing Zara talk about it so much.

"Hey." Air smiled at me as I entered the room.

"Oh, hey," Zara said, and smiled, pausing the show. But it wasn't her usual smile. It felt like she was forcing her face to do it, the way I'd had to force myself to fake smile through a Bollywood dance performance. "I didn't know you were coming."

That was not the welcome I was expecting. "I just got back from Hugo's."

"Yum." Zara smiled. "Well, have a seat. We're watching *Lockers*."

Air scooched over on the chaise as Zara pressed play. But

with Air where I usually sat, next to Zara, there wasn't enough room for me. So I sat with my butt half on and half off the seat, using my shaking thighs to keep me steady.

"I love this show," Air said, as the kid on TV skateboarded through the school halls.

"Her dad's the casting director," Zara added.

Air's cheeks turned pink. "Despite that."

I raised an eyebrow. Did Air not get along with her parents?

"Can you stay for dinner?" Zara asked Air.

Air shook her head. "My parents just texted. They're picking me up. But I'll see you both at the field trip Monday."

"I could stay," I said, hoping to delay my return to my parents a little longer.

"But you just ate," Zara said, with a confused frown.

My toes clenched the carpet. I didn't want to be around my parents right now. Why didn't Zara get it? Why did she need everything spelled out for her? And why was she treating me like a party crasher? I waited for Zara to apologize like she always did when she spoke before thinking. But there was no apology.

Instead, the doorbell rang, and Zara jumped off the chaise. The seat cushion wobbled from the sudden movement, and I slid to the ground. Zara didn't notice though. She was racing for the door before her mom could get there.

"You okay?" Air asked, offering me her hand.

I looked up at Air's eyes, full of pity for me. Before I flashed back to those looks of pity at my party presentation years ago, I nodded, taking her help to get off the ground. "I think she wants to get to your parents before her parents say something embarrassing."

"Ah," Air said as we headed out into the hall.

Unfortunately, Zara was too late. Imran Uncle was already chatting up Air's parents.

"Ever seen a Lollywood movie?" Zara's dad asked Air's mom, who was dressed in a lemon-yellow blouse, capri pants, and lime-green sneakers, her lips a dark purple thanks to her striking lipstick, which my own mom rarely wore. "That's what we called the Pakistani film industry, because movies were made in Lahore. You should watch. We make much better movies than Hollywood."

"Dad!" Zara said, her hand to her forehead.

"You know she walks around the house practicing lines from movies and TV shows all the time," Mumtaz Auntie added. "Maybe she could take your card and—"

"Mom!" Zara cried, before turning to Air with a huge cringe. "I'm so sorry."

I was grateful Air's look of pity was now being directed at Zara instead of me, especially after Zara had just acted like I was some unwelcome guest intruding on her time with Air.

"Tell you what, if I ever do a Bollywood movie and Danny casts it," Air's mom leaned into her husband. "Zara's the first person we'll call to be in it. Deal?"

"Mom!" It was now Air's turn to look appalled. She whispered to us, "Because you can only be in a Bollywood movie. Ugh. So stereotypical."

Air's mom gave her an innocent look. "What did I say?"

"Nothing," Air replied as her dad took her hand and began to twirl her out the door.

"We've got Bollywood and Lollywood on our mind now, Imran!" he sang as he waved bye to Zara and her parents.

"We'd love to have you girls over next time!" Air's mom said, laughing at her husband's song as she linked arms with him and headed outside.

Zara turned to me with a squeal, acting like the old Zara had never left. "Can you believe an Oscar winner was in my house? And next time I might get to hang out at her house?"

I frowned. I was pretty sure Mrs. O'Neil had said she would love to have *both* of us over.

Zara didn't notice though. She just grabbed my hand and pulled me to the den and plopped onto the chaise. "Come on. Sit down so we can finish this episode. Air said Jacob is so funny in it," she added, pointing to the skateboarding kid on screen.

Just like that, Zara was treating me like her only best friend. It was as if her personality had changed back to the old one, as quickly as Bollywood stars changed clothes in different scenes of the song they were lip-synching to. Or as inexplicably as when someone roller-skated to defeat bad guys, or was suddenly transported from India to Switzerland in the middle of a song, or even when a pigeon saved the day. Zara and I called it "filmi magic." "Filmi" was the Hinglish word describing anything that had to do with Hindi movies, and filmi magic was something that was totally unreal and unbelievable but that somehow worked when in a Hindi movie.

I looked down at the seat cushion, still indented on the side where I had tried my best to balance earlier. I wanted Zara to know how annoyed I was. I wanted her to know how embarrassed I felt when I fell, or how awful it felt to be treated like a third wheel. But I knew that would lead to an argument. And

I had witnessed so many of them at home, I was tired of them. Besides, why would I want to put myself out there and tell her what I was thinking just so Zara could laugh in my face like Dada had, implying my feelings had no merit? So I just straightened out my frown and took a seat next to Zara, back in my old spot.

As she pressed play and giggled at Jacob's antics, I let out a puff of air. "That's funny."

"Told you it was good." Zara smiled. "Really good."

I smiled back at her. Sometimes it was just easier to pretend everything was good.

CHAPTER 6

The next day, as Mom searched the kitchen for the fancy dishes we never used, Ronak and I sifted through the family room armoire to find the perfect movie for our Bollywood movie night. I held up a VHS tape, but Ronak shook his head.

"I don't want to have to spend half the movie hearing Dad tell us how it's a copy of some super-old American movie he liked.

"But it's serious. And it doesn't have any fighting in it, so no fast-forwarding."

"It does have fighting," Ronak replied, looking down at his feet. "Just not the dishoom-dishoom kind."

I sighed. I guess a movie about divorce wasn't the best choice for our family. "Okay, new idea." I grabbed a movie off the middle shelf. "Just a bunch of wedding scenes and one million songs. And you can fast-forward the sad parts. Deal?"

The sound of a dish breaking interrupted us. I looked at Ronak and we rushed to Mom in the kitchen.

She was standing by the stove in front of the shattered pieces of what used to be a floral porcelain plate. I guess she finally did find the fancy dishes.

"Watch out," Mom said, bending in front of the white cabinets to sweep up the mess.

"What happened?" I asked, my toes recoiling at the thought of getting poked.

"I wanted us to have a nice family dinner and I . . ." Mom threw the pieces in the trash. ". . . I couldn't reach the nice plates. Your dad always gets them down for me."

"Where is he?" I asked, drumming my fingers on the white-and-gray quartz countertop on the island. "Isn't he back from Urth yet?"

Ronak gave me a look like I shouldn't have asked that question, but I was hungry and wanted my vegetarian chili from Urth Caffé.

"He's late," Mom replied, pushing the trash drawer in a little too forcefully so it slammed. "He can't even show up on time to this," she mumbled, accidentally brushing by the pictures on the fridge, making the one of me in a blue and green chaniyo choli in my room hang crooked.

"To what?" I asked.

But Ronak spoke over me, trying to be extra helpful. "Do you want us to set the table with the regular dishes?" he asked.

Mom nodded as she wiped the floor down with a wet paper towel to get any little bits of glass that were left. "Sure, dikra," she replied, using the Gujarati word for "son" that she sometimes called Ronak when he was being even kinder than he already usually was.

Ronak started putting bowls and glasses on our table. I grabbed the plates and silverware. And Aai was vacuuming the floor when the garage door opened and Dad walked in with the bag of our carryout dinner.

"Hey, Rony-Pony and my little Soni!" Dad said in an extra-loud voice, like Dada, like he thought if he said something really loud and sunnily, it would suddenly make all of us super happy.

"Hi. I'm starving," I said, opening the bag. I could play this game, pretending everything was a-okay like Dad was. After all, he's the one who taught me how to do it.

Mom walked by us with the vacuum. She turned back and looked at Dad. "Hi," she said.

Dad came to a stop, his hunched-over shoulders looking even more saddled than normal, and nodded. "Hi."

I raised an eyebrow at Ronak. "Hi"? I couldn't remember the last time my parents said hi to each other instead of pretending the other didn't exist.

First the weird silence in the middle of their fight the other day. Now this. I went to grab the copper water vessel by the sink, careful to step around the spot Mom had just cleaned. I didn't care if everything looked fine to her. Something was off, and I couldn't help but feel like a sharp poke was in my near future.

CHAPTER 7

I dipped my sourdough bread into my chili, watching as its tough crust began to soften from the warmth of the soup. Mom was making small talk about work, and Dad was eating his pasta, looking up every now and then to give me and Ronak a smile.

It was all unnerving, so I just kept dunking my bread, waiting until it was so soggy, it was about to disintegrate before quickly popping it into my mouth.

Mom finished up her story and poured the last few drops of water out of the little copper water vessel from India. It was engraved with her name in Gujarati, and I used to love tracing the letters that made up her name, "Falguni Shah," when I was little.

"Do you want more water, Ronak?" Mom asked.

Ronak shook his head. "No thanks."

"Sonali?"

I shook my head.

Mom looked at Dad and cleared her throat. "Water?"

I began to spoon globs of the hot chili into my mouth. Mom never asked Dad if he wanted anything at dinner. She just focused on me and Ronak.

Dad, whose forehead looked shiny, wiped his mouth with his napkin. "Uh, no. I'm fine." His eyes darted around awkwardly. "Thanks."

How could I maintain my mask of normalcy when they were being so . . . abnormal? I put my spoon down. "Okay, what is going on?"

"Sonali ben . . . ," Ronak started, but I kept going.

"Why are you both acting so weird? Like nervous and awkward and . . . bizarre?"

Mom looked at Dad and then back at me. She let out a long sigh, like she had been bottling something up forever and was finally able to let it go. "We wanted to tell you both something." Dad cleared his throat as Mom continued. "See, we . . . we love this family and we care about each other. But all this fighting . . . it's not good for anyone."

I swallowed hard. Wasn't this what I had done an entire presentation about five years ago?

"It's toxic, really," Mom added. "And we don't want you to think it's okay."

This was why they had stopped fighting that day. They *were* giving up. I suddenly felt a little nervous and light-headed, but before I could focus on myself, I saw Ronak begin to sniffle.

"It's okay," Dad said, patting Ronak's shoulder. "Remember what Dada used to say whenever that car rewinder would break? Sometimes it just takes a little adjusting. That's all we're doing here. A little adjusting. Everything's going to be okay."

"Are you going to have to get all the dishes reengraved with your old last name?" Ronak asked softly.

"What?" Mom asked, her forehead wrinkled with concern. "No, sweetie pie. Everything isn't going to change like that. This is just a small step. We're going to separate."

"It's not a divorce," Dad quickly added.

"We just want to see if things are better with us apart," Mom continued. "We're going to take turns in the house, one week at a time, so you don't have any disruption. It's called 'nesting.'"

Hot nausea crept up my throat at the thought of my parents

in two different homes. I swallowed hard. "Where are you going to stay when it's not your week?" I blurted, thinking that was the strangest question I could have asked when my parents had just announced they're separating.

"We got an apartment in West LA," Mom replied, her voice cracking a little.

"I'm going there after work tomorrow," Dad said, nodding over and over again like he was still convincing himself this was a good idea.

My shoulders stooped like dumbbells were balanced on them, and I felt like Dad's posture twin. This all felt sudden and out of nowhere, even though a small part of me had to have been expecting it.

"And we'll still do our Sunday night Bollywood movie night together," Mom added, getting up quickly to give Ronak a hug, as tears dripped from his chin into his pesto sandwich.

"But we'll have to go out to eat less often and try to save up, because running two households is going to be expensive," Dad said.

I frowned but quickly recovered, scraping at the bits of chili left on my bowl. If this was the last time I was going to get Urth chili, I was going to savor every last drop. I felt myself getting angry and annoyed at my parents. It was like once again my parents' decisions and behavior were affecting me and Ronak the most, but they didn't even realize it.

"Let them process this before you start talking about money," Mom said softly to Dad.

I quickly brought my face back to my resting indifference face before Mom tried to analyze my emotions.

Dad gave her a stony look and turned back to us. "Everything is going to be okay."

But based on Ronak's trembling lip, he didn't believe that. Mom hugged Ronak tightly. "Let it all out. It's okay to feel sad. But I promise you, this is for the best. I want you to be happy and see us happy."

Mom reached across the table and squeezed my hand. "You okay, Sonali?"

"Always." I nodded, wishing Ronak would stop crying. It made me sad, and I was already feeling . . . well, I didn't know what I was feeling. I was feeling off. I knew Mom and Dad shouldn't be together. But I also felt strange about them separating. And upset that no one asked us what we would think about it when our lives were being totally changed. But also relieved no one consulted us on this decision. "I'm okay. Really. This isn't a shocker for me. I'm not young like Ronak," I added, regretting putting him down at a time like this. But I had to make my parents think I was fine or else it would be "emotions this" and "feelings that," and if I had to discuss it all, my mask could crumble and I could dissolve into a puddle of tears. "Why don't we start the movie, Ronak?" I asked, getting up to clear the dishes, hoping the distraction would help him.

"That's a good idea," Dad said, heading to the bathroom to rinse his mouth. "It will be a good reminder to you that we're still a family and we still have our traditions."

"He should get a chance to talk about what he's feeling," Mom called after Dad, the annoyance in her tone snapping out. "Not just watch a movie and bottle it all up inside."

But I was already on my way to the family room. I struggled to pull the videotape out of its tight paper case and shoved it into the VCR, rougher than I normally would have. I pushed hard at a remote button through Dada's thick plastic wrap to fast-forward the commercials and called out into the kitchen.

"It's starting!" But no one responded. "Come on. I have a math quiz to study for still." I fumbled over my words, realizing that was yet another odd thing to say given the circumstances. I turned back to the kitchen and shouted again. "And a field trip tomorrow!" Another weird thing, but, hey, I was desperate to get things back to normal. "Lots of walking so I need to get to sleep on time," I added, flustered.

Ronak finally entered the room, his cheeks tear-stained, as my parents had a muffled conversation in the kitchen. "My stomach hurts. I think I'm going to throw up."

I rushed to his side, pushing my own feelings down to focus on him. "Think about how sad you feel when they fight. Now you won't hear it." I put my arm around him, trying to convince myself along with him. "Besides, it will actually be nice to have only one parent to deal with each week, right? Now only one of them will get annoyed when you clog the toilet instead of both."

Ronak didn't smile at my bad joke. "I want to deal with both of them at once. I want us to be together always. Don't you feel anything? Don't you feel sad or scared or mad or just upset?"

"I feel different, for sure," I told my brother, before I got accused of being a robot again. I felt nervous, like it was going to be a big change. I felt unsure, like I wasn't sure I could handle Mom's helplessness without Dad there. Or I wouldn't be able to deal with Dad bugging me about school without Mom there. But I had been dealing with our parents for years, way before Ronak was old enough to remember stuff. I was sad and scared and angry all the time early on when they argued. That's why I'd made a presentation about it. But when nothing changes, when you continue to hear it every day, you can go through life being upset all the time, or you can just go on.

"I don't think you feel anything, but I do." Ronak cried harder, running out of the room.

I heard my parents rush after him upstairs, and just sank into the sofa as the movie played. I puffed my cheeks out and exhaled, letting my face fall into its regular, unaffected expression. But despite the catchy song and Madhuri's mesmerizing expressions, it felt weird watching a movie celebrating marriage when my parents had just announced theirs was probably over. So I turned off the TV and walked away, leaving the screen blank.

CHAPTER 8

I sat at my desk in my room, tapping my pencil on a stack of old notebooks on the corner, staring at a bunch of math problems, trying to study for my quiz the next day. But I couldn't focus because I could hear my parents through the thin wall between my bedroom and Ronak's. They were telling him everything was going to be okay. That it hurt now, but soon it would feel better. Soon there would be peace and calm and happiness like he deserved.

In between all the "soon this" and "soon that," I also heard them interrupt each other and bicker over word choices. In other words, this had *soon* turned into any other evening at our house.

I stuffed the math problems back into my backpack and looked at the movie posters from Dada's store, filled with scenes of filmi magic. Too bad a pigeon couldn't magically come save the day in real life. I was sure Ronak would've appreciated being spared the drama of our parents separating, even if it came from a bird.

I scanned the posters and nodded a quick "good night" to the ones of Aamir Khan on the wall behind my desk. I straightened out Dada's old BE KIND, PLEASE REWIND sticker from the video store that leaned against the back of my desk. And then I snuggled into bed, pulling my paisley cotton sheet from our last trip to Ahmedabad up over my shoulders.

I didn't need filmi magic to save me. I could save myself just like I always had. I was strong. I was brave. I wasn't going to shed a tear or puke over my parents separating. The separation was a good thing. I felt my face flush. *Isn't it?*

I felt a lump in my throat as I turned to my side. Why was I getting upset? My parents did not belong together. I used to think that every night in first grade when the fighting started, and I would sit on my bed and try not to hear it, covering my eyes like I could disappear into another reality if I did that, like a sudden midsong scenery change.

My insides were jittery, like they were about to break out in song and dance. I took more breaths, hearing my parents tell

Ronak about all the wonderful things that would happen "soon."

I closed my eyes and told myself that they were right. They had to be. Isn't this sort of what I wanted when I asked them to stop fighting in front of a huge party as a little kid? I wouldn't be alone with my feelings anymore if they were separated. I wouldn't even have those feelings anymore. Soon, my parents would be peaceful. And Ronak would be too, no longer getting emotional over everything.

Because feeling nothing was better than feeling sad or angry or crushed, and sooner or later, he was going to figure out it was just better that way.

CHAPTER 9

I woke up Monday morning with my sheet coiled around my body, like I had been tossing and turning all night. I guess my parents' announcement had messed with my head more than I would like to admit. Nothing would ever be the same again. But was that a bad thing? I took a breath, pushing those feelings down with the oxygen coming in. Maybe Ronak wasn't the only one who could've used some filmi magic to make things better.

I rubbed my eyes and headed through the dim room for my bathroom. I brushed my teeth and threw on the clothes I had set on the counter the day before: jeans and a bright-pink shirt that Zara had gotten me for my birthday. On the back it said, BOLLYWOOD HEROINE. Actresses were called "heroines" in classic Bollywood, and as dated as the phrase sounded now, Zara and I found it funny and it reminded us of the movies we couldn't get enough of.

I ran back to my bedroom window, sliding the curtain open for the day, wondering if Ronak was still upset. I squinted as the light filtered into my bedroom, shining down on my old posters of Aamir, Shah Rukh Khan, Sridevi, Madhuri, Juhi, and me.

Me?

I rubbed my eyes harder. Why was there a massive poster of *me* on the wall? I looked around the room. Correction, why were there *three* massive posters of me on the walls? There was one of me in the middle of eating an ice-cream cone, one of me midlaugh as I swung a badminton racquet, and one of me flying forward on roller skates. The same kind of over-the-top posters some old Hindi movie characters had as their room décor, like it was totally okay to have life-size images of yourself on your walls.

Was this a prank? Was Ronak behind this? He was never very good at pranking people, though, always giving it away so he wouldn't hurt anyone's feelings.

"Ronak!" I shouted, rushing out of my room and booming down the stairs to the kitchen, still slightly perplexed.

"Ronak!" I yelled again, trying not to sound so angry since the poor kid was clearly upset still. "Was that your idea of a joke?"

Ronak, eyes puffy from the night of crying, was at the table, hunched over a bowl of oatmeal. He looked up at me, surprised. "What are you talking about?" he asked, as Mom frantically pushed his water bottle into his lunch bag's pouch as if it were just a normal day and she hadn't made a world-altering announcement the night before.

"Make sure your dad knows I already took care of the water bottle, okay?" Mom asked as I leaned on the gray stool at the kitchen island.

"You stuck giant pictures of me up on my wall," I said to Ronak. "Giant pictures I definitely did not ever take. Did you . . . did you learn Photoshop in school or something?"

"Sonali," Mom said, putting her hand on my back and suddenly stopping her frantic rush, her sympathetic gaze falling on me, like she was about to talk about feelings. "Why are you yelling at your brother about your posters? Do you want to talk about yesterday? I have meetings in the afternoon, but I can go in late if you need me to."

"I'm fine. This isn't about that. It's my room," I said, brushing her arm away to grab a bowl of breakfast.

Ronak frowned. "Mom slept in my room with me. I didn't sneak out and pull a midnight prank. And you've always had those giant posters up on your wall."

"The huge posters of me posing cutely? I've always had those up?" I snapped.

"Sonali, don't stress Ronak out, please. He's had a really rough night," Mom said. "And you know very well that you've had those posters of yourself up for years." She pointed to the picture of me on the fridge. I was in my navy-blue and olive-green chaniyo choli at my desk in my room, finishing up a math assignment before a party. And in the background were the posters of me playing badminton and me with the ice cream.

I began to cough, almost choking on my oatmeal as I neared the fridge. What the heck was going on? I definitely did not have those posters up on my walls before this morning. I for sure did not pose with an ice-cream cone like it was the most adorable thing in the world. That was something people did in old Hindi movies. Not real life. Clearly, Ronak was getting really good at Photoshop *and* pranking people.

"Oh, and I signed you up for that extra-credit talk for math on the portal," Mom added.

"What?" I asked, totally perplexed. Not only did Mom think the posters had always been there, but now she was talking about school? "I don't want to hear some kid genius talk for hours about how amazing math is," I sputtered, trying to sort out all my feelings while staring intensely at the fridge picture that just couldn't be true. Was she in on the prank too? I ran my finger over the picture, trying to make sense of things.

"Your dad wanted you to sign up to help your grade," Mom replied. "Besides, it's during my week with you, I think. It will be a fun thing to do together," she continued, putting on her lab coat with the embroidered DR. FALGUNI SHAH on it.

Her week with us. It felt weird hearing that, like a strange new reality was about to set in. Ronak eyed the embroidered name on Mom's lab coat. I knew he was wondering if she would eventually be changing "Shah" back to "Bhavsar" if the separation did end up in a divorce.

"I want to talk more when I get home from work, okay? I just want to make sure you're both comfortable with"—Mom's eyes darted around the kitchen—"everything."

Dad thundered down the stairs with his briefcase in one hand and a spinner suitcase in the other. My stomach rippled as I realized it was his overnight bag for the week he would be spending in the apartment after driving us to school.

As if on cue, the suspenseful Hindi version of *dun dun dunn* began to play out of nowhere, accompanied by some rapid beats courtesy of tablas, a kind of Indian drum.

I dropped my spoon. Mom and Ronak were right in front of me and were clearly not playing a song from Mom's phone or the kitchen laptop. Nor were they at all startled by the sudden instrumental song. But the music was coming from right next to me. Or *from* me. "Is your phone playing music, Dad?" I asked, with a mouthful of oatmeal. "Is the Alexa on?"

Ronak raised an eyebrow at me. "Are you freaking out about your background music now?"

I swallowed before I began to choke again. "'Background music'? Like in a movie? What are you talking about?" I yelped as the music got louder. I ran to the sink to put my bowl in, and the music followed me. I took a few steps back to the island, but it was still there, everywhere I went. Like it really was background music. "What is this?" I panicked. "Why's the music following me around?"

Dad zipped up his briefcase. "Sonali, you know that's your soundtrack. Why are you getting so emotional? Is this about yesterday?" he added, throwing a look at Mom. "I told you this would happen," he said quietly.

"*My soundtrack*?" I squeaked. Why was everyone acting like this was normal?

Mom sighed, grabbing her bag. "Everyone has one from the

moment they're born, so why are you pretending this is all new to you? Are you trying to reverse-prank Ronak for something he hasn't even done?"

"Do you hear yourself right now?" I said shakily, trying to understand why nothing made sense. "Obviously this isn't a prank, but Ronak is clearly up to something. Or you all are. Or . . . I don't know. . . ."

Mom looked at me with concern. "Are you really okay, or did last night's news shake you up more than you're letting on?"

If this wasn't a prank, who or what was responsible for these changes? First the ridiculous posters of me, now this. Was my life turning into a Hindi movie?

I sat down weakly on the stool. "I don't . . . understand. I don't remember it ever being like this. . . ." I trailed off, dreading to think about what else was Bollywood in this inexplicable world I'd somehow woken up in. Was I going to bust out into a song and dance around trees next?

Mom crouched by my side and brushed my hair out of my eyes with her hand. "I knew you weren't really okay."

Suddenly the sound of a chorus of lamenting women singing "*ahhh*" in a variety of notes played from me, like the theme for motherly love in Hindi movies.

I tried to breathe normally, but my heart felt like it was thumping in my throat. How was this possible? Was I dreaming? No. I was clearly awake. Had I woken up in some alternate reality? I felt sweaty and scared, but I didn't want to talk about it anymore to my parents or Ronak, who clearly had been brainwashed into thinking everything was fine.

I took a shivering sip of water and tried to act like everything really was fine. I needed to get out of here. I needed to talk to Zara. She'd know what to do. I smiled at Mom, trying to get my resting blank face back, even though it was kind of impossible given the circumstances. "I'm okay," I said hesitantly.

Mom's gaze fluttered over my face, like she was trying to see if I was telling the truth or not. "You sure?"

Dad rolled his eyes. "Everyone isn't always talking in metaphors or attaching deep meaning to things."

"You can't stand anyone exploring their feelings even for a second, right? God forbid Sonali actually talks about things for once or—"

"I know we all have soundtracks!" I said quickly, my jaw tightening at the tone my parents were using. I didn't want to deal with more fighting. And Ronak definitely couldn't handle it after the night of crying he'd just had. "I was just . . . acting. Like in drama class. Yeah. It was a homework assignment," I lied, breaking Dad's no-lying rule. But this was clearly an emergency situation.

"See? She said she's okay, so she's okay."

A sweep of violins played from me. I jumped, startled, but quickly played it off to avoid another argument between my parents. "Yup," I said, smiling even though I kind of wanted to cry. "I'm beyond okay. You know me. Totally chill. Always fine."

Mom nodded. "Okay. Good," she said, like she was trying to convince herself I really was all right. "I'll see you after school." She grabbed her keys. "Love you both," she said to me and Ronak as she walked past Dad and his suitcase without making eye contact.

The sad Mom motif music played as she rushed out the door for the hospital.

A flood of emotions rose in me. The weird, forlorn feeling at seeing Dad's roller bag. The lump-in-my-throat sensation from everything that had happened yesterday and how it would affect the rest of my life. The horrified confusion of having a soundtrack and my family thinking it was normal. It was a convoluted, chaotic mix of emotions fitting for this "kahani mein twist," as they said in filmi speak, when there was an unexpected turn in the story.

"All set for your math quiz?" Dad asked, grabbing his keys

off the hook in our cabinet. "You'll need to focus even on the field trip."

I nodded, acting like everything was fine. Although with the sudden addition of a soundtrack in my life, I really wasn't all set for anything, especially not a math quiz, which seemed like it didn't even register on the life-crisis scale of parental separation to world-turning-Bollywood.

"Good. Ready for school?" Dad asked, again unfazed by the existence of background scores.

I tried to shake that sinking feeling. To come up for air. But what if school had gone Bollywood too? What if everyone had their own background music during the field trip? Would I be the only one who remembered how things had been yesterday?

I felt seasick from the million questions swimming through my mind, but like I was so good at doing, I suppressed the wobbly feeling and grabbed my bag and shoes. As my background score played suspenseful music, I headed out the door desperate for Zara's help, totally not ready for school or anything else that was to come.

CHAPTER 10

"I need to talk to you about that," I whispered frantically over Ronak to Zara as she got in the car, pointing to nothing.

The background song became a twinkling of peaceful sitar music as she buckled up.

Zara looked at me and shrugged. "That?"

"The music," I whispered, my voice catching in my throat.

"The soundtrack . . . ," Zara corrected, like it was something we had known about forever . . . since the day we were born, like Mom had said.

No, this wasn't happening. I slumped in my seat. I leaned over Ronak again as Dad changed radio stations. I had to get answers. I had to make Zara remember how things used to be.

"So we all have the same soundtrack?" I whispered. "You hear mine? I hear yours? And this is all normal to you?"

"What is wrong with you?" Zara asked as Dad drove down the eucalyptus-tree-lined streets in our neighborhood to avoid the morning rush. "We have our own soundtracks and we hear each other's only if they combine when we're together for harmony or melody, or disharmony sometimes if it's a scary moment . . . or a weird one. Like this," Zara added, eyeing me.

I clenched my seat belt. Her reaction made no sense. In fact, nothing made sense. This was illogical. Like a pigeon fighting bad guys. My stomach dropped.

This is like filmi magic.

Had all those years of watching all those Hindi movies done something to me? I felt a trickle of sweat go down my neck. "Listen. I need you to believe me. I think filmi magic somehow became real. This isn't how things were. Yesterday, we had no soundtracks."

Zara snorted. "Okay."

"I'm serious. We didn't. This is straight out of a movie."

"This isn't filmi," Zara replied. "We aren't singing and dancing on mountaintops. We don't have super-fancy cars. We just have background music. Like normal."

"Normal," I said, and my voice quivered. "My family thinks this is all normal."

"Because it is," Ronak said. "And you said you knew it was normal too. You said you were acting weird for your drama class homework."

"Well, I lied," I whispered. "I'm telling you, life was different yesterday!" I hissed without Dad hearing.

Zara moved a little back from me. "Then why are you the only one who remembers things differently? What happened yesterday that was so earth shattering, it created soundtracks and made all of us but you think this is how it's always been?"

"I don't know." My heart sank. Why wasn't Zara just believing me without a persuasive essay, like a good friend should?

Ronak opened his mouth, to say something about my parents' announcement probably.

"Nothing happened," I said sharply, silencing him with a piercing look.

"Then what was that look about?" Zara asked.

I glared at Ronak. There was no need to blab about our issues to Zara. Dad wouldn't have wanted that. Besides, our parents' separation announcement hadn't caused this weirdness. Ronak had heard that too, but *he* wasn't remembering things the way they used to be.

"Why are you being so secretive, Sonali? And why do your eyes look so puffy, Ro?" Zara asked, distracted.

"It's—"

"Allergies," I said, speaking over my brother, begging him not to explain our parents' nesting idea to Zara with the slightest nudge, which I hoped he could feel but Zara couldn't notice.

Zara paused, like she wasn't sure she believed me. "Oh."

The car turned, and I felt myself pulling back away from Zara.

"Okay." Zara glanced ahead, peering around the front passenger seat at Dad's carry-on, which rattled against the door from the turn.

"Look, I'm telling you this isn't how things were," I said as the synthesizer on my background music grew louder. "I need you to believe me," I added, trying to be heard over the soundtrack. The soundtrack that was clearly throwing me off my usual stoic game.

Dad glanced back at me, and Zara wrinkled her nose. "Why are you shouting?"

"So you can hear me over my background music."

Zara sighed. "Is this, like, a really bad attempt at a joke? I can't hear your music unless our soundtracks combine. You don't have to shout."

"How would I know that? This is all new to me, remember?"

Zara shook her head like she was giving up, eyes still locked on Dad's bag. "I don't remember, actually. I don't know why you're acting this way. I can't tell if you're messing with me or if you're telling the truth."

I cracked the window, trying to get some fresh air, as the tabla beat on my soundtrack grew faster.

"Yeah, which one is it?" Ronak asked. "Do you believe us that we've always had soundtracks, or do you really think something magical made things feel different for only you?"

"You, who never feels anything," Zara added with a laugh, which felt more like a dig than a joke.

I frowned. I was definitely feeling anger right now, so Zara was wrong. I wanted to tell her this was all new. I wanted to tell her my room had ridiculous posters of me up on the walls that hadn't been there before. But it all felt useless, like I was giving a presentation to someone who didn't want to hear what I was saying. Been there, done that.

"Everything is fine," I said, almost like I was trying to convince myself.

Dad pulled to a stop at school, and the music took on an ominous tone. I gave Ronak a little hug and, like my parents had already done a million times last night, whispered that everything was going to be okay, even though there was no way that was true in this world where nothing was making sense anymore.

I reached for my backpack, almost wishing someone would realize I wasn't as fine as I liked to pretend I was. "Bye, Dad," I said, as Zara and I headed out.

He put his hand back my way and I gave him mine. The background score reached a crescendo, and that strange gurgling feeling filled my gut. Tomorrow would be the first day in forever that Mom drove us to school instead of Dad. I wanted to squeeze Dad's hand back, but Zara nudged me a little with her backpack and I let go instead, exiting the car.

"Bye, Ro," Zara said. "Hope you feel better. And have fun on your trip, Kirit Uncle!"

"Uh, thanks, beta," Dad replied, confused, as he headed down the street, his car getting smaller as it moved farther away from us.

I watched as Dad became the distant memory he was going to be this week, and hoped Ronak was keeping it together.

"What are you waiting for?" Zara asked. "Forget the soundtrack stuff you keep going on about. This is your lucky day. You should be happy there's no drama thanks to the field trip."

I gave Zara a smile that was the total opposite of the jumble of sadness, fear, and sheer panic surging through me, as a new violin tune began to play. Our soundtracks must have combined. The music was almost in harmony, with the exception of a few notes that were just . . . a little off. "I'm happy. I just don't show it well," I said, hiding everything I was really feeling.

"Don't I know it," Zara replied, looking annoyed with me as she pulled me inside school.

CHAPTER 11

With the unusually warm morning sun beating down on my face, I walked with my homeroom class back to the parking lot. I had watched everyone in class for the ten minutes we had to sit there for attendance and announcements. If they had background music, they weren't acting bothered by it.

I, on the other hand, flinched every time my score added a new instrument or changed its tune. My background music was overall pretty slow and melancholy. But it was still terrifying, because, you know, I wasn't a character in a movie.

I climbed onto the shiny white bus our school rented for field trips and headed to the back left, where Zara and I always sat. I passed Ms. Lin, who was sitting at the front with our math teacher, Mrs. Kulkarni, and other parent chaperones.

I wondered if someone as sensitive as Ms. Lin would have known we didn't have our own background scores yesterday. But before I could find a way to ask her without everyone jumping down my throat to insist this is how things have always been, Mrs. Kulkarni spotted me.

"Glad to see you signed up for extra credit, Sonali," Mrs. Kulkarni said, sliding her sunglasses up on top of her wavy black hair.

I resisted the urge to tell Mrs. Kulkarni I hadn't signed up for it, my parents had. I needed to stay on her good side before the quiz later today, since it would probably be even harder than normal to concentrate with random music playing from me. So I just politely smiled and made my way to the back.

Zara was already on the left in the aisle seat. Air was next to her, staring at her phone. I wondered if Zara had told Air what I had said about background music this morning. I wondered if their music had combined in harmony. I wondered why I was even caring what their soundtrack sounded like together when I should have been focusing only on the startling fact that background scores were even a thing now.

Maybe there was a way I could figure out if anyone else thought real-life soundtracks were weird without everyone thinking I was weird for finding them weird. Or maybe I'd have to get used to just how *weird* the world now was.

"I knew it," Air said, scanning the screen. "Garcia Studios' stock went way up after they announced that new film deal. I told Mom it would."

Zara waved at me and removed her legs from the bench across the aisle, where Xiomara was sitting. "Sit down fast before someone else takes your seat."

I did as I was told, taking the aisle seat. I traced a worn-out patch on my jeans. Zara knew I liked to sit by the window on these bumpy rides so I didn't get motion sickness. And having the bus wobble on top of whatever the musical accompaniment did was sure to make me hurl. "Can I switch with you?" I asked Air, as the rest of sixth grade settled into their spots, probably to the beat of their soundtracks.

Zara shrugged. "Why?"

"You know I feel sick if I'm not near the open window."

"Sure," Air said, still staring at her phone.

"I'll switch with you," Xiomara said, walking around my feet and standing right in front of me. "It'll be easier."

My soundtrack was full of playful strumming from me clearly not getting what I wanted. I smiled, but I was annoyed I was now even farther away from Zara, who was deep in conversation with Air about *Lockers* as the bus turned down the street.

I had bigger issues to figure out. "Hey, are your soundtracks really loud on the bus?" I asked Zara and Air, trying to make it sound like I really believed background music was our norm. "And what are they playing?" I added for good measure. "Anything good?"

"Sonali!" Zara admonished. "You know it's rude to ask questions about other people's soundtracks."

"For real," Xiomara muttered, shaking her head at me like I had just asked everyone what their passwords were.

I slumped in my seat. My plan didn't work. Or it did and all I found out was no one on the bus thought any of this soundtrack talk was abnormal. Now what was I going to do?

"Holy caps lock!" Air exclaimed loudly.

"What?" I asked, hopeful Air was about to tell me she remembered how life used to be.

"Jacob says that on *Lockers*," Air explained. "Remember? Anyway, I forgot to tell you both." She lowered her voice. "My dad just hired a new actress on *Lockers*."

"What?" Zara asked, practically flying out of her seat as the bus went over a bump on Sepulveda Boulevard. "Who? A transfer student? Someone to fight with Callie?"

"Not a kid. A woman. She's going to play Jacob's dad's new girlfriend."

Zara gasped so loud, I could hear it over the rumble of the bus's engine. "Jacob's parents are getting a divorce?"

Air nodded. "Spoiler alert."

"Ooh, that is so scandalous," Zara squealed.

I squeezed my belly as the beat of a dhol started in low on my soundtrack. Was this how people were going to be talking about my parents once they found out about them separ-nesting? Before I could think about it anymore, the brakes squeaked and the bus came to a stop.

Ms. Lin stood up. "All right, everyone off the bus calmly and quietly. Our guide is waiting."

We filed out. I was two people away from Zara, thanks to Air and Xiomara. I didn't know why I felt so anxious to be next to her, especially when she didn't believe me when I told her soundtracks weren't normal, but I did. Everything was strange and I needed some normalcy. Besides, I had dealt with enough separation for one day.

The tour guide, a short man with brown skin and a curly goatee adjusted his large sun hat, casting a shadow over his sunglasses. "Hi, folks. Thanks for joining us for this tour of the nature surrounding us and how we impact the world, causing climate-emergency-sparked wildfires, and are, in turn, impacted by it. I hope you have your hiking shoes ready."

I had to stop panicking. I had to focus. I had to stop drawing attention to myself with questions about soundtracks, and get through the day. Then I could get home and brainstorm and research and find an answer to stop the background music from playing and make things go back to how they were before. I stood taller, determined to stop freaking out. I stepped around Xiomara and got between Air and Zara as the guide continued.

"Follow me, up this path. This is Rattlesnake Way. So stay on the path. And if you see a rattlesnake, remain calm and let a grown-up know. Do not antagonize the snake. Got it?"

We nodded. Feeling clammy and a little scared at the mention of snakes, on top of already being clammy and a little scared by the magical changes in my life, I turned to Zara. I hoped she would get what my look meant and I wouldn't have to spell out my fears in front of everyone. But she just looked at me blankly.

"You know I'm afraid of snakes," I whispered to her. *And I'm afraid I'm the only person on the planet who remembers how things were yesterday,* I added in my head.

"You're going to be fine," Zara whispered with a sigh.

I listened to our combined background music, which still had a few notes that just weren't in sync with the rest. What was that sigh for? Was she forgiving me for daring to question her about this peculiar new world on the car ride this morning? If anything, I was the one who should have been annoyed with her. Why couldn't she see I wasn't just afraid of snakes?

I swept my hair out of my eyes as the Indian flute joined my soundtrack. I had to pull it together. I reminded myself yet again that in the grand scheme of things that could go wrong in my life, new posters and nonstop music wasn't the worst thing ever. At least we weren't all breaking out in song-and-dance numbers. This was manageable. I'd be able to take the posters down when I got home. And that dusty pile of Dada's old Hindi film encyclopedias had to have some answers. I just had to put that mask on and relax, and in a few hours I'd have a solution.

But it was hard to relax when the soundtrack emitting from me was a constant reminder of everything wrong in my life. As we passed a bunch of holes in the ground that looked like they could have been the perfect size for a snake to burrow in, I began to think of all the random Bollywood scenes about fear. Sometimes there was even a sexist song with a heroine looking helpless as she danced around whatever it was that scared her, in perfect unison with her background dancers.

"So do Jacob's parents ever get back together?" Zara quietly asked Air, with me sandwiched between them.

Air shrugged, and I wondered if Mom and Dad were ever going to get back together. I felt sad and as helpless as a heroine as I jumped over a hole. My back felt heavy, and the tabla beat in my soundtrack was reverberating in my heels.

I reached for a nearby tree branch for support, gasping for air. No one else was being affected by their soundtracks. Why was mine making my feet itch to dance?

"Some people just aren't meant to be together," Air added.

Like my parents, I thought, feeling strangely devastated. I swallowed down the feeling. *Thump. Thump. Jump. Jump.* I dodged and skipped, and the rhythm inside me seemed to get stronger. *Thump-a-thump-jump. Jumpa-jump-thump.*

"What?" I mouthed to myself. Could background tracks become full-fledged foreground songs?

Before I could consider the questions any longer, my hips started to sway. This wasn't possible. Zara told me there was nothing else filmi about this world. My toes started to tap. I clenched them, but they unfurled. It was like my feet were moving on their own, thanks to some magical internal force, swaying to the rhythm my body was creating. I pushed my heels hard into the ground to stop them, almost causing Air to trip on me, but after a second they were back to tapping and jumping.

I felt a surge of terrified tears flood my eyes, but I blinked quickly to fight them off. I could still control my blinks, but why couldn't I stop myself from dancing? I needed help. I turned toward Zara, but she was unaware of what I was doing and kept talking about her show.

"These are definitely two people who shouldn't be married," Zara said. "I just hope Jacob doesn't get too sad about it. He's the funniest guy on the show. I know some kids totally change when their parents get divorced."

Jump jump. Thump jump thump. My hand shot up to my forehead as I twirled to the right of Zara and spun to the left, using fancy footwork to jump over and around the holes in the ground. "Ooi ma!" I exclaimed, biting my lip like a scared, helpless Bollywood heroine. I guess it was fitting since it said that on the back of my shirt.

I gasped and shut my mouth, tightening my hand over my lips, trying to seal them shut. How did those embarrassing words escape? What was my brain thinking? And who else had heard?

I turned to see Zara's eyes on me. But instead of staring me down like my family after my party foul, she just put her hands to her cheeks very dramatically like a background dancer, giving support to my exclamation. Like she was part of whatever it was I was about to do.

Why was Zara joining in instead of putting a stop to it? My hands flew down to my sides, moving like they were gracefully turning lightbulbs, Hindi-movie-dance-style.

"*Bachao, bachao,*" I sang, loud and clear, wiggling my hips as I asked for someone to rescue me in Hindi.

I froze. What had I just done? How did those words come out of my mouth? Had I just sung in front of my entire class? I tried to breathe normally, but I was hyperventilating, desperate for air, sweat dripping down my head. What was this strange rhythm pumping through my veins like a pulsating tempo? My eyes widened as I turned to Zara again for help, but she had her arms around Air and Landon and was just swaying back and forth.

I squeezed my hands together, willing them to stay put and stop the show, but it was like I was a puppet and someone else was in charge. And that someone else wanted my hands on my hips and my mouth singing. "*Bachao, bachao, what is happening to me? I'm singing in Hindi like a Bollywood movie. Mujhe bachao,*" I sang again, as I bit my lip and bugged my eyes out like Sridevi dancing on screen.

From midway through the sea of kids in front of me, Mrs. Kulkarni pointed back to me while scanning the group for help. "Ms. Lin!" she called out, looking not at all shocked by my singing. "Is this for your class?"

At the front of the crowd, Ms. Lin turned back to me. "Everything okay, Sonali?"

Not really. I was singing and dancing in front of my class like I was in a movie. This was mortifying, humiliating, embarrassing, and every other word you could find in a thesaurus next to them. I pulled my hands down as hard as I could to put a stop to the performance, but they wouldn't budge. My face flushed and my whole body felt hot as I continued to dance, and then a breeze suddenly spiraled around me. It wrapped me up as I shook my hips, making my hair look windblown, like I was a Bollywood actress in a song.

Xiomara pointed to me while leaning over to Davuth. "Okay. I see it now. I see why that wind machine makes Aashi Kapoor look good."

I twirled around Xiomara and Davuth, who started clapping

to the beat behind me too, like I was the star and they were my background dancers.

I threw my head back and sang again. *"Look up what I'm saying on your phones as a group. My life is turning into a big load of poop."*

Poop? Was I really singing about poop? I guess there was precedent in an old Hindi song about a guy having to pee, but still, this was mortifying. And from the way my mouth was opening up wide, the verse wasn't finished yet.

"It's stuck inside and I want to yelp. Up here there's no cell reception. So I'll give you the translation. . . ." I sang, moving from toe to heel, the wind still blowing only my hair back, while everyone else's stayed perfectly in place. "*'Bachao' is a cry for help*!" I sang even higher, catching my reflection in our stunned tour guide's sunglasses.

I was glowing. Not like I was proud. I was actually glowing as if I were being filmed in soft focus by a Bollywood cinematographer. My eyes were twinkling. My lips were shimmering. I was radiating as I hopped around, batting eyelashes that suddenly felt like hairy caterpillars had crept onto my eyelids, obstructing half my vision. I did need help, but I definitely didn't want to sing my request. My eyes were stinging like I was about to cry when Ms. Lin neared.

"Sonali, let's save our school musical numbers for an appropriate time, like when you're older, in an intercollege dance-off."

I shook my head, confused. Intercollege dance-offs were from Hindi movies about kids in college. Why was she acting like this was all normal?

But instead of listening to Ms. Lin, I just kept dancing because I couldn't stop. Zara and Air clapped behind me. I wished they would stop clapping and actually help make everything better. I put my hands on Zara's shoulders and moved from side to side like I was telling her a secret in the most annoying way possible.

"Help me. Things are hiding. I'd rather be slipping and sliding. But I don't have a choice," I sang, throwing my arms into the air as I twirled around Zara. I wanted to sing to them that I needed help stopping the song instead of whatever the lyrics were making me ask for help for, but none of the words I wanted to say was coming out.

The wind circled me, making my hair look like it was doing the wave at a baseball game. *"My parents made the call. No more restaurant food at all. No one listens to my inner voice."* I drew out that last word as I backed away from the group and strayed off the path, spinning, almost colliding into a tree right next to a burrow.

"Watch out!" Air pulled me back onto the trail.

"Sonali, we all love a good song-and-dance number," Ms. Lin

said. "I did one myself this morning with the neighbors when I was heading to school. But this isn't the place. We have to be safe and respectful on a field trip."

I wanted to respond with words expressing how weird it was that her neighbors had also gone Bollywood. But, instead, I threw my hands on my cheeks and whimpered pathetically, overacting. "*Do you see what's under the tree, hidden in that hole? Can't you hear the voice inside me? It's what makes me whole. Maybe it's better left buried. Maybe better left unsaid. Unspoken, unknown, concealed forever. Let the feelings stay dead*!" I sang as the exaggerated sounds of a synthesizer began to play in the background, ramping up the drama like it did in a movie. I was like a one-kid Bollywood show, a multihyphenate actress-director-choreographer-lyricist-singer all in one.

What was I even singing? "Let the feelings stay dead?" I suppose it was pretty on brand for me and it rhymed. But I had to put a stop to this before I sang about something else. Something Dad wouldn't want the whole school knowing about. I gritted my teeth and groaned loudly as I forced my hand to fight back the invisible force making it swirl around. I pushed it forward, my biceps aching until I got my hand over my mouth.

In an instant my feet stopped hopping around the holes, and

my windblown hair fell back flat into place. As the foreground music suddenly returned to the background, I saw all the shocked, openmouthed expressions around me, just like when my family stared at me after my presentation years ago.

"I don't think we've ever seen you do a solo. That wasn't bad," Xiomara said. "Even though there wasn't really any sort of ending."

My cheeks grew hot. I looked to Zara for help, but she just stood there with a totally stunned frown. I needed to get out of there. I needed help. Before I started singing for it, I turned and ran down the path, away from my classmates, away from the burrows, away from the talk of fictional Jacob and his divorcing TV parents.

I could run all I wanted, but I wasn't sure I could outrun the filmi magic.

CHAPTER 12

I passed the bus driver, who was waving her cell phone outside the bus for reception, and clambered up the stairs. I ran to the back left of the bus and plopped down in my window seat, inhaling deeply as the fresh air came in. I glanced at my reflection in the tinted bus window. The glow was still there.

"What . . . is . . . happening?!" I managed to get out. How was any of this real? Why had I sung a made-up Bollywood song while the wind swept only my hair and no one else's? And even worse, why was everyone acting like this was just how things were? I felt sweaty and my whole body was shaking in panic.

I heard footsteps up the stairs, and some of the tension eased from my shoulders as Zara rushed down the aisle toward me. "What was that back there?" she shrieked.

I clenched my hands together to try to stop the quivering, trying to breathe normally. Zara looked stunned. Maybe I could still convince her that something strange and Bollywood-like was happening in the world, and we could solve this together.

"I don't know." I trembled. "I don't know what happened. It was like . . . like some Bollywood ghost took over my body or something. What? How?" I squealed, fighting back the strange urge to cry.

"I know. You're always a background dancer, if that. I can't believe you finally had the courage to do a solo," Zara said, eyeing me like she had no idea who I was.

"You're saying this has happened before? We have background music and we sing and dance now and it's totally normal for Ms. Lin to sing with her neighbors as she heads to work?"

Zara shrugged. "I mean, it's not normal during class or a field trip, unless you want to hang out with the principal. You normally just move out of the way if someone is singing. Now. Things were different when we were younger, of course."

"No way," I said, feeling faint. "You just told me this morning we don't sing and dance like Bollywood. That was, like, one hour ago. Don't tell me you forgot. And what do you mean things were different when we were younger?"

"What?" Zara let out a small laugh. "I didn't say that. And you used to sing and dance all the time. Remember when we would split those grape Popsicles that were stuck to each other?" Zara began to hum. "And we'd sing that song, '*Grape Popsicles, what a pair. Break them, break them, and let's share. Cuz we are two and it's only fair.*' And then the purple flowers would fall from the branches, showering us in slow motion."

I looked at Zara blankly. Not only had she forgotten what she had said just this morning, now she was totally fabricating memories? "That never happened," I replied. "We shared those Popsicles, but that song . . . ? This is like some alternate reality. Like every time the filmi magic introduces something new, something you said would never happen in this world, everyone just acts like it's normal. People sing and dance in movies, not in real life."

"They sing and dance in movies because movies are realistic. I mean, I just sang a song about the succulents in my yard on my way to your house this morning." Zara ran her hand over the seat backs as she neared me. "You're upset because I don't remember things any differently, yet you can't understand why I might be frustrated because you can't remember things the way they actually are. It's like I asked you this morning, if your version is true, what happened that was so major, it could have caused all this change?"

I opened my mouth to answer, but then quickly shut it. Nothing unusual had happened. Sure, my parents had decided to separate, but was that really such a big difference from them not getting along? Besides, there was no way I could say anything about the separation to Zara. "I don't know," I said softly.

"Then what about the lyrics?" Zara asked, taking the seat across from mine.

Our soundtracks must have merged, because more and more notes began to sound off-key. "What about them?"

"'Can't you hear the voice inside me'?"

"I have no idea what that means. I swear." I looked down at my sweaty hands. Did I really not know what that meant?

"Your lyrics are your emotions. They're what you really feel."

"They're just lyrics," I said, not wanting to get into it. "There's an old Hindi song comparing someone's eyes to strawberries. Do those lyrics make sense to you? No. So why search for some deep metaphor in what I'm saying?" I asked, sounding like Dad this morning.

"Is there something you're keeping inside that no one knows about, like you sang?" Zara asked gingerly. "Is there something you want to tell me?"

How could lyrics be my real feelings? No one knew my real feelings, because I usually kept them to myself.

Zara's forehead scrunched up at my silence. "I'm your best friend. Just tell me."

"This isn't about you. Honest," I said, wondering if maybe I wasn't *really* being honest. "Sometimes Hindi movie lyrics are just made-up words. We used to laugh about them all the time, remember?"

"Of course I remember that," Zara replied. "I could list them all right here. You laughed so hard you cried when I reenacted 'Love-eria,'" she added.

Apparently, she did have some memories of us that were true. We had watched that song where Shah Rukh and Juhi sing about how they don't have a cold or a cough or malaria, they had love-eria, like a love sickness that rhymed with "malaria."

"Well, this is like love-eria," I said.

"In that it doesn't exist?"

I frowned at the sharp off-key notes that played from us. "In that it's a magical condition that's causing me to bust out in Bollywood moves and have a soundtrack and giant posters of myself on my walls."

"Well, if it's true, you're going to have to figure out what caused it. And I'm probably not going to be much help if I don't know the whole story."

"You do know it. You're *part* of my story," I replied, frustrated. I clearly understood what Zara was getting at, but I had no desire to talk about my parents and they hadn't caused this anyway.

Zara chewed her lip, softening. "Okay, then, I don't know, did you find some old artifact from India and get cursed or something?"

I stared at Zara. "That sounds like some racist old Indiana Jones movie."

Zara shrugged. "Well, I'm running out of ideas here, and nothing makes sense. Magic isn't real, and everyone else remembers things the way I do."

I opened my mouth, wondering for a split second what would happen if I told Zara about the big changes in my life. That I felt like she was replacing me with Air. Or that my parents were nesting. Or that it was making me feel . . . something. I almost laughed, thinking how proud Mom would be of me processing my feelings. How upset Dad would be that our good friends knew something this personal about us. "Nothing caused this, Zara. Unless VHS tapes are ancient artifacts, I haven't even been in contact with anything super old."

More footsteps suddenly clunked up the stairs. It was Ms. Lin. "You feeling okay, Sonali?"

I shook my head, blinking back some tears that were threatening to spill.

She took a seat next to Zara. "Sometimes when we're so overcome with emotion, it all just pours out of us like an unstoppable waterfall. I can tell from what your classmates are saying that you usually don't participate in musical numbers. I'm glad you felt safe enough to put one on. It's good to let it all out. To share what we're feeling," she added, with a knowing look.

Zara stared at her feet, not even making eye contact with me. She wasn't helping me, and I needed to get out of there to find out how to stop the magic. "I want my parents," I mumbled. "I want to *call* my parents," I said, correcting myself. "I'm sick and need to go home."

Ms. Lin nodded, taking her cell phone out as she felt my forehead with the back of her hand.

Since I wasn't supposed to see Dad until the next Bollywood movie night, I typed in Mom's work number instead. "Can you come get me?" I asked when Mom answered.

Mom sighed. "Oh, Sonali. I'm so sorry. Is everything that's

happening with me and Dad too much for you? I knew I should have stayed home this morning."

"What?" I snapped, before remembering Ms. Lin was standing right there so I should act as polite as I do at school. "No. I just . . . I don't feel good."

"Dad is in Anaheim with clients, and I've got patients and meetings until three thirty. But Avni Foi is off on Mondays, so I'll give her a call. You just rest at home, and I'll be back in a couple of hours, okay?"

A couple of hours. Who knew how many more Bollywood song-and-dance numbers I would be busting out in that time.

CHAPTER 13

I sat in the back of Avni Foi's car, windows down, as she took a break from asking how I was feeling to tell me all about how she knew Baljeet Uncle was the one for her when their soundtracks played the most beautiful sitar duet.

I knew it was impolite to ask about people's background music in this strange universe I was now in so I didn't say much other than, "Oh." Besides, I was busy brainstorming anything that could have started the filmi magic and anything that could stop it.

"I talked to Parvati," Avni Foi said, as she turned onto Veteran Avenue. "She is going to pull me and Baljeet onto the dance floor at the very end to join in."

I nodded, briefly thinking about the math quiz I'd have to print at home later. I started to feel carsick, and focused instead on the gravestones at the veterans' memorial before Avni Foi turned in to our neighborhood. We'd be home in a minute, and I could get the books on Hindi cinema and find some answers.

"I thought you all could grab your parents then too, so we could do this big freestyle family dance, all of us cousins and siblings together."

I felt queasy as I crumpled the loop on the top of my backpack and the soundtrack played mischievous notes. Would Mom even be at the wedding if she was separated from Dad? Of course she would. She loved Avni Foi like a sister. She was there when my aunt needed her most, helping her at the hospital when Foi was sick. I was almost sure Mom wouldn't miss the wedding. But I was also pretty sure she wouldn't want to be pulled onto the dance floor with Dad like we were in some movie about happy families that danced together in extravagant clothes.

"I don't know what my mom will feel about that," I said. "About dancing, I mean. I don't think she can dance."

Avni Foi gasped. "What? Haven't you seen that old video of your mom's kathak dance in college? I think that's when your dad first fell in love."

The queasiness in my gut grew stronger, and I groaned.

"Oh, Sonali . . ." Avni Foi glanced at me through the rearview mirror. "You poor thing. Let's get you to bed."

Avni Foi parked in our driveway and opened the door for me. She felt my forehead. "Still no fever, luckily. You want to go up and I'll make you some hot kadhi? I'll even put extra sugar in it like you like. That should help you feel better."

I nodded, heading to the family room for a pit stop as Avni Foi went to the kitchen. I blew several layers of dust off the coffee-table books on the history of Hindi cinema that Dada had left me, and ran up with the heavy load.

I could hear the clang of stainless-steel dishes in the kitchen as I rushed into my room. The swinging of my bedroom door caused a gust of air that made the bottoms of my movie posters ripple up. I stood by my navy-blue beanbag, ignored the horrific poster of me giggling on roller skates, and ran my finger over one of Manisha Koirala and Anil Kapoor, flattening it back down. It had a little tear on the bottom corner from when Dada had pulled it off the wall of his store with a *shhhhhk,* the tape slowly releasing, when he was closing the place down for good.

I remembered how little Dada said that day. He always wanted us to be happy. He wanted to know he had given us a happy life by immigrating here. He was always joking and laughing, sometimes even laughing at me, like when I made my presentation, but usually just to make us smile. That's why it was so hard to see him that sad when the store was closing. But he didn't talk about it. He just looked out the window, staring at nothing in particular, while he moved his ladder around the room, and the *shhhk shhhk shhhk* noise got quicker and quicker as he pulled the last bit of Bollywood off the walls of Indian Video.

I was desperate for someone to pull the Bollywood off me. *Shhhk.* Make me stop singing. *Shhhk.* Make me stop dancing. *Shhhk.* Cancel the background music. But I didn't know how to stop it yet. My parents and Ronak thought it was all normal. And Zara, the one person I thought I could count on for help, didn't believe me either, so who would? This was just like when I tried to talk to my parents in first grade about how upsetting their fighting was. It didn't work. And eventually I stopped trying. Stopped telling them about any feelings.

Dad had jokingly asked Dada, the day he closed the store down for good, if he had laryngitis, since he was barely making a sound. I seemed to have the opposite problem. I couldn't stop singing. And dancing, too.

I put the books down on my desk and took a seat, skimming the images as they went from black-and-white to faded color until I got to the dazzling colors of my favorite era of Bollywood. The book was pretty, but it had no answers. I moved on to the next book, on the music of Hindi cinema. It was about singers, music directors, and all the thought lyricists used to put into their songs. There was even a short chapter on background music, but nothing that talked about what to do if background music happened in real life.

I scooched my chair back. This was hopeless.

I scanned the room. Maybe it wasn't. Maybe if I could stop the thing that started all this magic, I could stop the magic. I ran to the poster of me smiling at my ice-cream cone like it was a long-lost relative. I got on my tippy toes, grabbed the top corner, and pulled it down, waiting to hear a satisfying ripping sound.

But there was no *shhhk* sound. The poster hadn't budged. It must have been like what happened when I finally stopped myself from singing on the field trip. It would take a bunch of tries to fight off this magic. I grabbed the sides of the poster and yanked at it, my shoulders aching from the resistance.

The poster stayed put.

I grabbed a pair of scissors off my desk. But I couldn't get even a tiny crack of space between the poster and the wall for the scissors to slide between.

"Stop the filmi magic!" I clawed at the poster as my music turned melodramatic. But it didn't even get scratched.

Instead, as twinkling bells played from my soundtrack, a colossal sweep of bright, sunny yellow began to swipe ever so slowly over my light-gray walls, like someone invisible was painting them with a gigantic brush right before my eyes. Like a sign of what was to come.

"Avni Foi!" I shouted, dropping the scissors. I backed up to my door and opened it with my shaking hands. "Avni Foi, come up here, quick!" I called out again, finally hearing Avni Foi thunder up the stairs.

"What is it? What's going on?" she asked, in a panic.

I pointed at my room, my whole body now trembling. "This," I squeaked.

"Your room?" she asked, perplexed as the last wall was slowly coated highlighter yellow. "What, you made the bed?" she laughed, not even noticing the live paint job being done by an unseen force.

"My room has yellow walls."

"It's always had yellow walls," Avni Foi replied, raising a concerned eyebrow at me.

"What are you talking about? It just happened. I saw it

happen! You saw it happen!" I ran to the ice-cream-cone poster. "And this? Have I always had an enormous picture of myself posing cutely with ice cream on my wall?"

Avni Foi shrugged. "As long as I can remember."

It was just like with Zara and the musical numbers. First, she said we don't do them. Then as soon as one happened, she acted like it had been happening since the beginning of time. Like dinosaurs had sung their way to extinction.

"My life is turning into a Hindi movie . . . ," I mumbled as I took a step back from Avni Foi and almost tripped on my beanbag.

"You need some food and some rest," Avni Foi replied, cracking the door open so the smell of gram flour, buttermilk, cinnamon, and clove in the kadhi filled the room. She smiled, heading downstairs. "Come on. I've got just the cure for you."

But as I headed down, all I could think was that Avni Foi was wrong. There was no cure for what I had. I didn't have love-eria. I didn't have laryngitis. I had Bollywooditis. And the filmi magic causing it was growing more powerful by the minute.

CHAPTER 14

My stomach tilted. I ran as fast as I could, sweating, a queasy burn heading up my throat. I heard the garage door open just as I made it around the corner to the bathroom, slammed the door, and threw up.

Avni Foi knocked at the bathroom door. "You okay? Can I get you something?"

"I'm . . . fine," I lied, breaking Dad's strict never-lie rule yet again. But it was easier than saying, *Yeah, I could use something. Can you find a wizard or someone powerful enough to stop this filmi magic from existing?*

"Okay. I'll give you some space. Just call me if you need me," Avni Foi said.

I washed up, wiping my eyes before the tears could come out, and opened the door.

Ronak was right in front of it, back from school. "Are you okay, Sonali ben? We heard you . . . you know . . . narf."

I sighed, a damru, a handheld, two-faced Indian drum, now thumping on my soundtrack. "Yeah. I'm fine. I . . . what color is my room?" I asked quickly.

Ronak shrugged. "Like a super-bright, banana-peel yellow."

Of course Ronak thought my room looking like a dated Bollywood bedroom set was normal. He was under the spell of the filmi magic just like Avni Foi and everyone else.

Mom started to walk toward us, her lab coat still on from work, and Ronak's voice dropped to a whisper so Avni Foi wouldn't hear. "Are you feeling bad about them?"

I shook my head irately. Feel bad about them? I didn't feel bad about them, and I didn't feel bad *for* them, either. They're the ones who had gotten themselves into this mess. "I feel bad because I hurled. And I might do it again," I said sharply.

"Oh." Ronak turned pale and backed away, into the kitchen.

"Do you really feel like you're going to be sick again, Sonali?" Mom asked.

That depended on just how far the filmi magic was going

to take things. "What color is my room?" I asked, even though I already knew what she was going to say.

"Yellow."

I shuddered as Mom felt my forehead just like Ms. Lin and Avni Foi had already done. I tried to act like my usual self, but it was hard. "It's like I'm living in some messed-up new reality."

"I know. It's tough. And I'm glad you're finally letting it out." She gave me a big hug, and I could feel her heartbeat against my ear.

Even though Mom had no idea I was really upset about this Bollywood curse, something about her soothing heartbeat made my stomach start to settle. Mom's theme began to play on my soundtrack, and I actually started to calm down. The magic wasn't going to get the best of me. I just had to focus. So far the magic had affected my room, my family, and my teachers and classmates. If I could put a stop to it, I could prevent it from changing the whole world.

Mom brushed my hair back behind my ears. "The school said you disrupted a field trip with a solo? That doesn't sound like you at all. Although I do miss the days when you would sing and dance, carefree, around trees, about your thermal underwear. . . ."

Maybe it was a good thing I didn't have any of these false

memories of what life was allegedly like back in the day in this reality. "I don't think I ever sang about thermal underwear."

"Sure you did." She sang softly, "*Don't you dare, shrink my thermal underwear.*" Mom smiled. "You were only five, but it was a pretty catchy tune."

"Can I use the computer?" I interrupted.

"Right now?"

"What if you upchuck on the keyboard?" Ronak asked from the kitchen island.

"I already sent your math quiz to the printer, if that's what you're worried about," Mom said.

I shook my head. "It's not the quiz. I need to research something for school." It wasn't a lie. I needed to stop my school from turning into the gaudy set of an old movie.

"You want to do homework when you're this sick?" Avni Foi asked. "You're really all over the place today, Sonali. You need to rest."

"I don't need to rest. I need answers!" I said, louder than I intended. I looked at my stunned aunt. "Sorry."

She nodded, forgiving me.

I turned to Mom. "I'm sorry, Mom," I said, desperately. "I shouldn't have sung on the field trip. I won't do it again." I hoped.

But there was only one way to really make sure that was the case: stopping the filmi magic.

"No. *I'm* sorry," Mom said, crouching down to get below my eye level, because she had once read it was the best way to connect with a child. "Is this all happening because Dad and I upset you too much yesterday?" Mom combed my hair with her fingers. "You always act so brave, and you never show what you're feeling. Sometimes we forget things affect you, too. I don't want you to feel like this is, what did you call it? 'A messed-up new reality.'"

I shook my head, becoming irritated all over again. Did she want Avni Foi to hear? Dad wouldn't have wanted that, and I didn't feel like explaining to Avni Foi that her brother and sister-in-law were separ-nesting when she was about to get married. But instead of snapping at my mom and making her worry more about me, I just put my face back to neutral and gave her a small smile. "This doesn't have anything to do with that. I was talking about something else."

Mom nodded like she believed me, but her eyes were getting shinier by the minute. "You know, it's also brave to share what you're feeling."

"I . . ." I paused, trying to figure out how to convince my mom that my room hadn't always looked like that. That soundtracks weren't normal. That breaking out into musical numbers wasn't the best way to communicate your innermost thoughts. Avni Foi was staring at me with the same perplexed look she had when I gave my first-grade TED Talk. And I quickly remembered how useless it was to talk anything out with my family. "I didn't have my kadhi," I said softly, giving up.

"That's okay," Mom replied, standing up, her dark-brown eyes looking at me like orbs of love as her thinning eyelashes fluttered. "I just made you some limbu nu sharbat. Why don't you sit down and sip on it? It may help with the nausea."

I nodded and took a seat at the kitchen table, across from Avni Foi. The kitchen was its normal white and gray self. It hadn't had a Bollywood makeover. Mom was still dealing with her perpetually dry lips and wasn't coated in makeup. So she hadn't had one either. Maybe it wasn't too late. I just had to feel better, to get over the Bollywooditis, and this nightmare would be over.

I took a deep breath. I could smell the sulfuric aroma of the Indian lemonade Mom had made, with black salt mixed into the sugary lemon-water mixture. I stirred the drink with the spoon Mom had left inside the tall glass, watching as the black specks spiraled in a mini tornado in the drink. I took a tiny sip. As the tangy, savory, sweet mixture hit my tongue, my lips twisted, and I started to feel a little less hot and queasy.

Ronak was hovering over his backpack, excitedly handing Mom the quizzes and tests that he had aced, when the front door opened and Dad walked in. My soundtrack switched to the Bollywood *dun dun dunn*, again, symbolizing my surprise, I guess.

Ronak shoved his work into Mom's hands and ran down the hall to jump into Dad's arms like he hadn't just seen him in the morning, and the music suddenly changed to an uplifting synthesizer melody.

I watched Mom frown as Dad greeted us with his usual:

"Hi, Rony-Pony and my little Soni!" Dad slipped off his shoes and ruffled Ronak's hair while they walked into the kitchen.

I wouldn't admit it the way Ronak did, making a scene, but I was really glad to see Dad too. Even though I knew what his answer would be to my room-color question, my stomach suddenly felt steady with him in the house, like something normal was finally happening today.

Dad inhaled deeply in the kitchen. "I smell kadhi. Glad to see you're eating a home-cooked meal instead of eating out."

I crossly gritted my teeth at the mention of Dad's new rule to save money, thanks to the second home he and Mom decided to get for this little experiment of theirs.

"What are you doing here?" Mom asked softly, the look of concern she had for me now totally gone.

Dad shrugged. "You texted that Sonali was sick. I left Anaheim a little early and beat the traffic to get here." Dad pulled a chair next to me. "Are you feeling better?"

"But that's not how this works," Mom said, eyeing Avni Foi.

My back suddenly felt like it had a boulder tied to it. Was she trying to let Avni Foi know what was going on? Why couldn't she just whisper and be subtle like Dad?

Avni Foi raised an eyebrow at Dad, like she was asking him what Mom meant.

The tabla beat filled my soundtrack.

"If you didn't want me to come, why'd you even tell me what was going on?" Dad said softly to Mom, but I could still hear it, and it made me feel angry and fed up with their little fights.

I acted as calm as I could so Avni Foi wouldn't suspect anything, when my right hand pulled the spoon out of the glass, clenching the handle tightly.

"I should go," Avni Foi said, scooching her chair back and avoiding eye contact with my parents. "I need to beat traffic too."

I tried to release my grip. I had to stop this from happening again. I pried at my fingers with my left hand, but they wouldn't budge. And then it started. I began to clang the spoon against the glass to the tabla beat. *Dha dhin dhin dha. Clang clang clang clang . . .*

My family turned to me, some of them midargument, as the sound of the spoon hitting the glass began to echo melodiously.

I scooted forward in the chair and dropped my face so I was eye level with the glass, like the close-ups I had seen in so many Hindi movies at the start of a song that used dishes for percussion. And then the breeze started. Just around me, and no one else, flickering my hair.

"*Sour and twisted, when mixed together,*" I sang loudly, my chin tilted upward in a classic Bollywood defiant pose.

Avni Foi held her keys frozen by her face as she watched my humiliating performance. "Is this for the wedding? Is this a flash mob?"

Yeah. A one-person flash mob. My left hand squeezed the glass, still on the table, and the magic moved my face to either side of it, causing the specks of salt to once again separate from the lemonade.

"Sonali ben?" Ronak asked. "Are you doing a solo?"

"*Sour and twisted, when mixed together,*" I repeated, skipping backward with the drink in my hand. I twirled around Mom and Dad, pointing with my finger. I tried to put my finger down, to make a fist, to stop twirling, but it was like the magic had been weight lifting between the field trip and now, and I couldn't get it to stop. I just kept singing. "*You're sour and twisted, no birds of a feather.*"

"Sonali," Mom said sharply.

What were these horrible words coming out of my mouth? It was like the opposite of my "Can't we all get along?" presentation. It was a public scolding of my parents and their marriage, kind of like when Dad yelled at me and everyone heard. "*So don't flock together. It's better to sever.*" I danced with my left foot hitting the ground and my right foot arched so just the toes did, in a typical Bollywood step. Then I took a big swig of the lemonade and caught my reflection in the glass. My eyes were red.

Some Bollywood stars had red eyes for crying scenes because they needed eye drops to make them cry on cue.

"*Cuz it will never be sweet again. If it ever was, I can't remember when.*" I pointed to my first-grade picture, which hung in the hallway behind me, along with all our other school pictures.

"Stop this, Sonali," Dad said quietly.

I wished I could stop, but I didn't even know where this

magic was coming from. Dada's books had proven useless. I had to get to the Internet. I groaned, grabbing my pointing hand with the other, trying to pull it down. It was like a fight against a super-strong rubber band though. Every time it budged a little, my arm snapped right back where the filmi magic wanted it to be. Like the magic was already stronger than it had been during the field trip.

"I can't stop," I sang, almost in tears. It was scary to have some internal force in control of what I was doing. *"Just like you can't stop. Can't stop fighting. Or comments that are biting."* I flicked the glass by my left hip and created an arc with my hand as I moved the glass. *"It's too late. Separate. Separate. There's too much hate."* No. What was I singing?

Avni Foi kept glancing at me and then my parents. My dad's face was turning redder than when he yelled at me all those years ago for spilling the beans about how he and Mom fought. I was embarrassing them all over again. I was spilling their secrets. I switched hands to do the same arc motion from my right hip. *"Separate. Separate. There's too much hate."*

I spun faster and faster like the specks of black salt spiraling in my glass, using my hands to push my parents apart without touching them as the music inside me reached a crescendo. *"Separate. Separate. There's just way too much hate!"*

As I spun, I saw tears trickle down Mom's face. It was now her turn to run to the bathroom around the corner as her sad maternal theme played in the soundtrack, and the notes from my performance faded away.

I wished the impact of what I had just done would fade away too, but that wasn't very likely.

"Mom!" Ronak cried, walking after Mom as the bathroom door shut.

I dramatically ended my spin by collapsing on the ground like an exhausted kathak dancer in a classical Bollywood dance, lemonade sputtering onto my clothes and the floor as the wind stopped spiraling around me. How would I ever be able to stop the magic from taking over if I could no longer stop myself from singing and dancing? If I had no idea when it would start or stop or what it was planning to do next? I felt my cheeks burn with frustration.

Avni Foi grabbed some rags and dropped to my side. "I'll clean it up, Kirit bhai. Go check on—"

Dad knelt next to me. "I'll take care of this. You can go. Before the traffic gets bad."

"Oh." Avni Foi nodded. "Okay," she said, rising to her feet. "Hope you feel better soon," my aunt added, as she bit her lip uncomfortably and walked out the door.

"I knew this was a mistake," Dad muttered. "I told her this isn't how we do things, showing everyone our bad sides. Does she want the whole community gossiping about us?" he asked, his voice rising. "And look at what it's doing to you. Now you're doing a solo? You gave those foolish things up years ago. This is just like all that modern nonsense your mother was talking about when Avni Foi was sick. Forget it, Soni. Don't worry. I'll move back in, okay?"

I shook my head, my face burning. "This doesn't have to do with the two of you," I muttered. It was true, wasn't it? They weren't there when I sang at the field trip. "I'm sick." I motioned to the bathroom hall across from us. "Besides, she got this mad when you dropped by. Do you think she'll be thrilled if you move back in before it's your week?"

"Don't go," Ronak said softly, walking toward us.

"He has to, Ronak," I said, touching the sticky lemonade stains on my BOLLYWOOD HEROINE shirt. I looked up at Dad. "You have to." My voice dropped to a whisper. "Or you'll get Ronak's hopes up for no reason."

Dad stared at me, like he was searching for something to say. But then his shoulders slumped and he nodded, almost like he was listening to the words from my song.

"I'll clean this mess up," I said, grabbing the rags, wishing my messy life—full of confused, fighting parents and an unstoppable, proliferating, magical force that made me sing and dance like I was in a Hindi movie—could be cleaned up as easily as some lemonade on the floor.

CHAPTER 15

With Dad and Avni Foi both gone, I quickly filled in my quiz, grabbed the top notebook from the stack on my desk corner, and began to write down possible reasons for the magic to have started. Had my parents' separation really caused it? Was this all their fault? I looked at the word "separation" on the lined paper. Something about seeing it in writing disturbed me, so I quickly scratched it out. Besides, it was silly to think that introduced filmi magic into my life. People got separated all the time. That couldn't have been the cause. But then what was?

I chewed on the insides of my cheeks. It was hard to concentrate on finding a solution when my room was still bright yellow, my face was still all over the walls, and everything still looked glossy like a movie. Plus, my soundtrack was still playing an up-tempo synthesizer tune for some thinking music.

Was this just the start of what the magic could do? Like when you first got a cold, it could start with just a runny nose but then turn into a stuffed-up, snotty disaster?

I grabbed the little wooden elephant statue Dada had gotten for me when we had gone to a handicraft fair in Ahmedabad together last summer. I ran my fingers over the carved paisley design on its back. I remembered Dada singing the songs from an old film about an elephant as he held my hand with his soft, wrinkled hand. That was when he first told me he was sick. I had started to cry, but Dada said he wanted me to always remember him with laughter, not tears. I told him I could try to stop crying now, but there's no way I was keeping my promise when he was gone. Dada had gently pressed the elephant into my hand and told me I'd adjust, and soon the painful memories would be replaced with happy ones.

Feeling a lump in my throat, I squeezed the little elephant. The design pressed into my palm, and when I released my grip, I saw little dents in my skin. I stared at them as the pink marks in my flesh began to disappear, and my skin went back to how it was. It had adjusted, just like Dada had said.

Maybe I'd somehow adjust to this new life too. Maybe things would get better. Maybe I'd figure out how to stop the magic.

I set the elephant down, squinting at the glare from the sun in the gap between my curtains. When I sat up to shut the curtains tighter, I spotted Zara in her yard doing homework at the patio table.

Had she forgotten about what had happened to me? My yard was right there in front of her, in case she needed a reminder of my existence. Shouldn't she be checking on me?

"Sonali?" Mom called softly from down the hall.

I hopped into bed. I didn't know how to apologize for making Mom feel so bad. I didn't know how to even start to explain what had happened to me and how I had no control over the words I was singing. Besides, she wouldn't believe me if Zara didn't.

Mom knocked lightly at the door and slowly opened it. "Are you sleeping?" she asked.

I squinted as the setting sunshine from the hallway windows poured into my room.

"No," I said, sitting up.

"Do you feel any better?" Mom asked, touching my forehead again.

"I don't feel like throwing up anymore," I replied, looking down at my hands. I didn't really know how to make eye contact with Mom after what I had sung.

Mom nodded, absentmindedly running her fingers up and down the cell phone in her left hand as her theme played on my soundtrack. She looked around my room, taking in more of the vintage posters of old movies from Dada's store. There was a tattered poster with Sridevi in a sari. There was the faded poster with Karisma Kapoor and Madhuri standing next to Shah Rukh Khan, all of them sweating in their spandex like they had just had a dance-off. And right next to it was the yellowing poster of Aamir Khan jumping in his school uniform, his school tie flying, middance.

I watched her taking it all in, while pretending I was straightening wrinkles out of my now bright-yellow cotton sheet any time I felt her eyes near me. I wanted to tell her I was sorry, but I just couldn't find the words. I was sorry for making her cry, but I was also annoyed and angry at her for some reason.

"Do you want to talk more about what happened? Or what's happening . . . with me and Dad?"

I rubbed my eyes to avoid her gaze.

"I'm really proud of you for doing a solo today. I miss hearing you sing," Mom said. "But those words you were singing. 'Separate. Separate. There's too much hate. . . .'"

I squeezed my hands together. I didn't know why I'd sung those words. Maybe because they rhymed? Was the filmi magic trying to cause drama, since Hindi movies could be so melodramatic? Or was it saying something I wanted to say but didn't know how to say? Of course not. I wasn't in control when the magic was at work.

"I wasn't thinking," I said, apologetically. "I don't know why I started singing. I think this sickness is making me . . . sick," I said. Clearly, I didn't have a way with words when the Bollywooditis wasn't making me sing poetic, rhyming lyrics.

"It sounds like you were sick of the way things were," Mom said. "Like maybe you think what we decided was a good idea?"

I frowned. "You decided it. Not Dad."

Mom began to blink back some tears.

"I'm sorry," I quickly said. "It was just a song. It didn't mean anything. Honest. I've just had a bad day."

Mom patted my shoulder. "I hope I get to hear you sing more. It reminded me of the good old days."

"When I sang about grape Popsicles and thermal underwear," I muttered.

Mom laughed. "They were silly, nonsensical songs, but they were an expression of who you were. That's important. Expressing yourself." She gave me a knowing look.

I was done expressing myself. I wanted answers on how to put a stop to all of this. "May I please use your phone?" I asked.

Mom handed it to me. "Who do you want to call?"

"I need to look something up for school, remember?"

Mom nodded permission, and I opened her web browser. I had to find a subtle way to ask the questions I needed to ask without Mom worrying about not only her separation but also why I wanted to stop the magic she apparently loved. I typed, "How to stop magic," into the phone. All that came up were a bunch of magician sites and sites on plants I'd need to cook to cleanse myself of a curse. I wasn't allowed to be online by myself. No way would my parents be fine with cooking plants on a stove unsupervised, either. Besides, this wasn't regular magic. This was illogical filmi magic. No way something as simple as plants would stop it.

I gave it another shot, typing, "Randomly singing Bollywood songs."

But all that popped up were magazine articles with videos of flash mobs, instructions on how to organize one, and suggestions for the best catchy songs to do them to.

I tried again, typing, "How to stop singing and dancing." A ton of websites popped up. But they all said the same thing: "Why would you want to stop?" The magic was stirring up again.

A frustrated anger flushed over me as I typed the question again, all in caps: "HOW DO I STOP SINGING AND DANCING?"

"There's only one way" was the response. Below it were images featuring Madhuri cry-singing, her black sari fluttering in the wind; Sridevi doing a wordless, powerful Taandav dance; Aamir lip-synching a comforting song to his on-screen son about his separation; Shah Rukh lip-synching intensely about love; and scene after scene of all the old hit movies.

"This is useless," I muttered, closing the search. I was sick of the magic messing with me.

"Couldn't find what you needed?" Mom asked.

I handed her the phone, trying to mask any signs of my frustration that might lead to Mom worrying about me. "It wasn't there."

"Do you want to talk more about what you're going through?" Mom asked.

I sighed. There was no way Mom, or Dad, for that matter, would believe me. They didn't believe me when I said we didn't have soundtracks. They were under a powerful spell. Besides, they had enough on their plate. I wasn't going to add to it by telling them about magic and making them worry about me. "I'm fine," I said, looking up at Mom. "Really."

Mom gave me a concerned smile. I hoped she'd finally gotten the hint that I didn't want to talk about anything. "I'm always here if you want to talk about what you're going through."

I nodded.

"If . . . ," Mom started, ". . . if you're really feeling better, can you help me?"

I sat up in bed as Mom's forehead scrunched up a little. "The toilet . . . Ronak clogged it, and I don't know what to do."

I quickly got to my feet. I was right. My mom couldn't even handle fixing a toilet. How would she ever be able to handle knowing about filmi magic and how things were before? "Is it overflowing?" I asked.

Mom shook her head. I rushed down the slippery wooden hallway floor to the toilet Ronak broke a couple of times a month.

Mom was right by my side. "I turned the water off before it could. I don't know what to do next though."

I scrunched my nose. I was feeling like crap and now my mom was making me deal with literal crap. "You're not helpless," I said, thinking I was the one who was actually helpless until I could figure out what was causing this magic. Mom had it easy in comparison. "You can do so much stuff at work that doesn't scare you," I continued. "You deal with blood and sick people. But you can't figure out how to take care of this."

Mom's eyes narrowed. "Your dad isn't here."

"Yeah. I know. You just told us at dinner yesterday all about how he won't be here for a week, remember?" I said softly. I sank a little in my spot. I hated when I said mean things to Mom. It was like I had this anger hidden somewhere inside me, and I didn't know why it even existed in the first place. But every so often, when I was trying my hardest to act like I was fine, it would burst out.

Instead of getting mad at me, though, Mom shook her head, her lip trembling like she might cry. "I'll figure this out. Maybe I can find something on the Internet?" She took her cell phone out again.

I sighed. Although I hated putting myself in Mom's shoes, I guess I would feel a little nervous and scared if I was suddenly alone in a house full of things that could go wrong that I'd never dealt with before.

"I'll get the snake from the garage," I said, walking down the stairs. It wasn't a real snake. It was this long plastic pole with a turn to its shape at the bottom. I had seen Dad put this contraption into the toilet, while giving me the play-by-play like it was the Super Bowl, enough times to know what needed to be done. He was adamant I learned so I wouldn't be as "helpless as Mom," as he liked to say, taking a dig at her even when she wasn't the reason the toilet was clogged, Ronak was. A part of me was almost glad he wasn't here to fix the toilet. It was gross work, but I kind of preferred it to hearing him call my mom helpless when she did most of the work at home and he was the one who forgot Ronak's water bottle all the time. I bit my lip, realizing I had just done the same thing to my mom a minute earlier when I put her down for acting helpless when she wasn't.

When I got back upstairs, Mom was just standing there, looking at the toilet like it was the foulest thing she'd ever seen, despite all the bloody surgeries she had done on patients.

"You put the snake in the bowl and turn this handle here. That pushes the clog down," I said gently, trying to make up for how harsh I had been earlier.

I handed the snake to Mom, who churned the handle. A loud scratch replied, and the background music played a jarring horn sound.

I quickly guided Mom's hands. "Dad says that sound is not good. You don't want to scratch the toilet. So if you hear that, sometimes it just takes a little adjusting," I said, using Dada's favorite phrase.

I watched Mom groan as she repositioned the snake and tried again. She looked hesitantly at me and pointed to the water valve below the toilet.

I nodded, watching as Mom turned the water back on and flushed.

"Looks like it's still there. Try it again."

Mom wiped her forehead with the back of her hand and put the snake in the toilet again, getting back to work.

I watched her struggle for a few seconds, scratching the toilet before she repositioned the device and the sound finally went away.

It looked like we both had some adjusting to do.

CHAPTER 16

Early the next morning my room still looked like it was out of an old movie, and the soundtrack was still there. My brainstorming, the old books, and the internet had proven useless. I had no answers for how to stop this. But maybe I could outsmart it.

I dug through a box of old clothes and pulled out a denim jacket. It would look normal in this breezy February weather, even though it was stiff and outdated. But what the filmi magic didn't know was, because it was so old, I had grown since I last put it on. That meant I couldn't raise my arms that high when I was wearing it. I hoped that without that motion, I would be able to stop my body from breaking out in Bollywood dances today. And without impromptu musical numbers, I hoped I could stop spewing hurtful lyrics I had no control over and prevent the Bollywooditis from ruining my life.

I headed downstairs in the tight jacket, bracing myself for some new gaudy décor after my lemonade song. But the kitchen looked normal. I breathed a little easier and poured my cereal, barely able to lift my arm to grab the almond milk out of the fridge. I scarfed down my breakfast quickly, then grabbed my backpack and headed to the patio before Mom and Ronak came down and I would probably have to deal with some new Bollywood catastrophe.

I grabbed a badminton racket and a stray birdie Ronak had left in the lawn. I was bouncing the birdie up and down with the racket, trying to figure out who I could turn to for help, who would believe me, who could make this all stop, when Zara ran up from her backyard. She handed me a bouquet of wilted branches and thorny weeds.

"Um, thanks?"

Zara shrugged. "I thought you could use a pick-me-up. But you know my dad would not be cool if I plucked his flowers, which I'm pretty sure he loves almost as much as his own children."

"They're very nice." I smiled sarcastically at my droopy

bouquet. It was clear Zara didn't realize how serious this was. A bouquet wasn't going to solve my problem. It didn't even really make me feel better.

"They helped my parents with the weeding too. Win-win," Zara continued, but her smile still looked a little uncomfortable. And her eyes, watching me with doubt, felt/seemed like they belonged to a different face. It was like those books we used to play with, where you could mix and match animal eyes, noses, and mouths by turning the sectioned pages.

I didn't like how weird things were between us suddenly. I needed to fix that, and I desperately needed Zara's help to figure out how to stop the magic, since I kept hitting dead ends. I needed her to listen to me. I took a breath. "I went through all these books and looked online for ways to stop the magic."

"And?" Zara asked, as we headed to the garage on the side of the house.

I shook my head. "Nothing. The Internet just said the only way to stop singing and dancing was to . . . sing and dance." I shrugged. "It was just a bunch of pictures from old Hindi movies."

"I guess that means you're going to be singing your secrets out to the world again."

I frowned. "Those aren't secrets. Those are lyrics."

"Well, they're a lot deeper than you've ever been with me," Zara said softly.

I stiffened as Zara continued.

"Anyway, it's fine."

"Actually, nothing is fine. My room magically turned yellow last night. And I didn't even tell you about the gigantic posters of myself all over my walls, because at first I thought Ronak was playing a joke on me, but they don't come off. They're part of the magic." I stopped, noticing how Zara was staring at me. "Let me guess, this is how it has always been? Nothing out of the ordinary? Totally normal?" I asked, my shoulders drooping like Dad's as we walked toward the driveway.

Zara shrugged. "You're not acting normal, but your room? Yes. It's been yellow forever and you put those posters up a couple of years ago. This isn't magic. This is normal life."

"I'm telling you this is not normal. I did another solo last night about lemonade and . . ." I trailed off.

"And what?"

I shook my head, not wanting to let Zara know the lemonade somehow became a metaphor for my parents splitting up. "Nothing. Remember when I told you it's like love-eria? It's Bollywooditis. An inflammation of Bollywood," I said, remembering what "-itis" meant from the random homemade tests Dad would write in notebooks for me over summer vacation. "Every time it strikes," I said, punching in the garage code to put the racket and birdie away, "Bollywood spreads to the real world."

I stepped back as the garage door opened. There, in place of Mom's white car, was a flashy, freshly washed red sports car with a giant spoiler on the back.

"What . . . ," I barely managed to get out as the weed bouquet slipped out of my hand. I pointed at the car. "What is that?"

Zara shrugged. "Your car?"

"That? That car that looks like it cost a million dollars?"

"Yeah," Zara said, nonchalantly walking by me to enter the garage.

"That car that looks like what old movies show Desi people in America driving, like we're all billionaires?" I squeaked. "That car that's exactly what you said we didn't drive yesterday morning?"

Zara opened the car door. Only it didn't open sideways like a regular car. It went straight up like the kind of car Shah Rukh would step into in an old movie.

"Look, I want to help you. But you're being super weird," Zara said. "This has always been your car. Your mom has one and your dad has one. I really want to believe you that this isn't how things were before. . . ."

"But you don't," I said, opening the other car door and ducking to not get hit in the face.

"Because I don't remember it ever being different from this," she said, pointing to the car. "Maybe I'm affected by the magic, or the curse, or whatever you think this is. I don't know. But if this is really happening, you have to figure out why. What started it?"

"Filmi magic. Remember?" I said, getting into the car. I took a deep breath. The car didn't smell new. It was like it really had been around for a while. More filmi magic. I reminded myself that at least I wasn't singing and dancing, and having a fancy sports car wasn't really a problem, if you thought about it.

"But why now? What changed?" Zara asked, taking her seat.

"You keep asking me that, but I don't know," I replied, frustrated and struggling to shut the strange door.

"So it wasn't about anyone in particular?" Zara asked, now looking at me.

"Who would it be about?" I asked softly.

"I don't know. Me? Air?" Zara said, running her fingers around the illuminated cup holder in front of her.

I buckled my seatbelt and shook my head, a little annoyed at the accusation, annoyed that Zara was prying into things I wasn't ready to share.

The garage door to the house suddenly opened, and my mom and Ronak rushed out, not at all shocked by our new ride.

"Sorry we're late," Mom, in her wrinkled lab coat, said as she easily opened Zara's door and she and Ronak buckled up. "The bulb went out in my closet, and I couldn't find the paperwork I needed to bring into the office today."

"Where's Uncle?" Zara asked, as Mom started the engine and I struggled to figure out how to crack open the window.

"Oh, he's . . . We're nest—"

I caught my mom's eyes in the rearview mirror and begged her not to tell Zara anything, shaking my head ever so slightly, causing the tiny dangling beads on my gold earrings from India to tremble. What was it going to take to get Mom to understand Dad wouldn't want people talking about their situation? Did she not remember how upset and embarrassed he got all those years ago? Besides, I was dealing with enough questions from Zara about my Bollywooditis. I didn't want to have to field questions about my parents' marriage, too.

"I'm going to take you girls this week," Mom said, smiling. "We're alternating."

"Cool," Zara replied.

Mom fumbled around the papers in the front seat. "What is the name of that place?" she mumbled to herself as she backed out, half paying attention to the steering wheel.

"Mom!" I yelped as the strange car swerved slightly down the driveway with a squeal.

"Whoops. Sorry," she said, eyes on the road as she pulled onto the street. "Your dad always buys the specialty lightbulbs for that weird closet light. I was trying to find the name of that store that sells them in Santa Monica. I'll just text him."

I dug my shoes into the car mat. Text him? Did Mom not get what a separation meant? I flicked some lint off my pants. I was being hard on Mom again when she was trying her best to deal with her new life, just like I was.

Zara didn't seem to pick up on anything being off in their marriage though. "So, Ro, when do you start practicing your dance for the sangeet?" Zara asked.

"Tonight, actually," Ronak replied, as Mom turned onto Wilshire.

"I hope the group dance doesn't turn into another solo with your family's new singing sensation over here." Zara laughed.

I was annoyed, but I laughed too. And then I immediately got mad at myself for laughing and encouraging Zara to keep taking little jabs like this instead of helping me.

"Maybe you'll figure out what's causing everything, since you seem to be a lot more truthful when you're doing a musical number," Zara whispered over Ronak to me.

"What's that supposed to mean?" I leaned toward Ronak as Mom took the turn into school. She came to a stop, and I hit the red button on my buckle forcefully.

"Nothing," Zara said, just like I had. She said bye to Mom and Ronak and got out while a bunch of flat notes played on our soundtrack. This time though, it wasn't just her eyes that seemed like they belonged to someone else. Her whole face felt off. Like I wasn't talking to my best friend anymore but someone I barely knew.

CHAPTER 17

The elementary-school-era jean jacket had worked. Despite the constant soundtrack playing for me and probably all my classmates, I didn't sing a single note during English. I didn't break out into dance in computer lab. My eyes didn't turn red from imaginary eye drops during math. And there was no invisible wind machine tickling my scalp during history.

I finally knew how to control it, and maybe even stop it from redecorating my whole house. Although the soundtrack was still there and my room was still tacky, I had gone a whole twenty-four hours without singing and dancing. Things were looking brighter, even if it meant wearing ill-fitting clothes for the rest of my life. If I had figured out how to stop the song-and-dance numbers, I was certain I'd soon be able to put a stop to the car and room makeovers and silence the soundtracks once and for all.

So, I had a big, triumphant smile on my face that evening as I stood on a porch in Santa Monica with Mom and Ronak, and rang the bell for dance practice. My aunt, Beejal Foi, answered the door. She was my dad's older cousin, but in our culture, cousins are like your siblings, so your parents' cousins are your aunts and uncles.

"Hi, kids!" Beejal Foi said, ushering us in with hugs. I watched as she gave Mom an extra-long hug, and blinked quickly, like she was trying not to cry. "You're going to get through this," she whispered, but it was loud enough for me and Ronak to hear.

Ronak raised his eyebrow at me, and I knew he was wondering the same thing I was. Did Mom tell Beejal Foi about the separation, even though Dad wouldn't have wanted anyone outside of the four of us in our nuclear family to know?

"They're in the backyard," Beejal Foi said as we took our shoes off. She led us down the hall and pointed to the sliding-glass door in the family room. "Go ahead. Your mom and I will catch up in here with some cha."

We headed to my cousins in the grassy yard.

"Yay! You're here!" Parvati exclaimed, giving me and Ronak longer-than-usual hugs, just like her mom had done to my mom.

Parvati whispered into my ear. "Don't worry. The others don't know about the separation, and I won't tell them."

I cringed a little from her hot breath tickling my ear, but mostly from the fact that she knew about my parents, even though Dad didn't want anyone else to know and start gossiping about us. I guess *I* didn't want people to know either, just like I didn't like seeing the word in a notebook. It made it seem real.

Parvati gave me a long look with her hazel eyes, like we were sharing some deep moment. I hated how she was acting, like she was my mom or aunt right now instead of my cousin.

Before I could focus more on it though, Parshva bhai, Parvati's older brother, who was also in high school, gave us high fives. Sheel and Neel, the twelve-year-old identical twin sons of my dad's other cousin, smiled, showing off their maize and blue braces. And Tejal and Shilpa, my other cousins from Santa Monica, who were also in middle school, ran up to give me hugs.

"Parvati ben picked out the best songs," Tejal squealed, pulling me out farther into the grass, next to the portable speakers Parvati's sparkly green phone was nestled in.

Parvati ben was good at everything. I remember Dad seeing my face when he told us Parvati ben had gotten into the gifted school even after skipping two grades. He told me I looked like a green-eyed monster. When I reminded him my eyes were dark brown, he reminded me a green-eyed monster was a saying for what jealousy looked like. I wasn't jealous though. I was more feeling bad that I was struggling to answer my sixth-grade math questions, which Parvati could have probably done in third grade. And annoyed that despite all the summer notebook tests, I still didn't seem to make Dad proud the way Parvati ben's grades did. But I didn't know how to explain those complex feelings to him, to express myself properly. All I could do was snap back, "I'm not jealous!"

Parvati ben bounced from toe to toe and stretched her calves. "So we're going to do a five-song medley, and in the end, we'll pull all our parents to the dance floor, and Avni Masi and Baljeet Uncle, too, for a big, freestyle family dance."

I shivered a little, trying to hug my arms, except I couldn't, thanks to my jean jacket.

"First is the song my mom and Avni Masi used to dance to all the time when they were kids. "Masi" meant your mom's sister, so even though Avni was a "Foi" kind of aunt for me, aka our dad's sister, she was the "Masi" kind for Parvati and Parshva because she was like their mom's sister.

I nodded as Parvati ben played a sample of the tune, thinking about how Zara and I had danced to it too once, during a sleepover at her house, thanks to its catchy beat. Actually, Zara had danced to it, and I sort of clapped and smiled awkwardly until she pulled me to the "dance floor" just like in the movie. I quickly put an end to my performance that night though by bringing up the point that it was kind of funny that Shah Rukh was singing about beautiful dark eyes to an actress who had hazel eyes, like Parvati ben.

Parvati ben began arranging us into position as if we were in one of the meta Hindi movies about characters in the entertainment industry rehearsing for stage shows or films. In the center were Neel and Tejal, and Shilpa and Sheel. Ronak and I were to their left, and Parvati ben and Parshva bhai were on the other end.

"Five, six, seven, eight," Parvati ben counted, moving to the left and right for the opening music as we followed her steps to the beat. She showed us the first two minutes of the dance before heading to the speakers. "Okay, now to the music." She hit play and the song began.

I hunched to the left and right, barely able to make the right moves thanks to the jacket. I followed Ronak and my cousins, wiggling my hips, shaking my head, jumping, twirling, and tapping. As

I shook my shoulders and pumped my fist, I suddenly saw my mom, Beejal Foi, and her husband, Arvind Fuva, standing on the deck watching us, steaming cups of tea in hand.

I forced a smile at my aunt and uncle and forced my eyes down to my feet as I felt my ears burn from their stares. Was everyone looking only at me? This was like when I had come down after Dad yelled at me at that party all those years ago. Maybe they felt bad for me, with my parents separating. Maybe they were worried about me. But that didn't make the intensity of their looks any better.

When the music finally stopped, Arvind Fuva clumsily raised his teacup. "Excellent job, kids!" he cheered.

"Arvind! Are you seriously raising your teacup to them? You're going to spill it!" Beejal Foi laughed.

Arvind Fuva paused, his mouth dropping. "Um, aren't you the one who . . ." He smiled.

Beejal Foi laughed. "Okay, yeah. True."

What were they talking about? Did they have some sort of ESP connection where they could read each other's minds? And why was I finding it so annoying?

"I grabbed the water pitcher, and as I was refilling it, it somehow got caught on my sweater and I went to set it free and . . ."

Beejal Foi squeezed Arvind Fuva's shoulder, laughing so hard, she was almost crying.

"She was drenched. Like Hindi-movie-rain-song drenched," Arvind Fuva continued, finishing Beejal Foi's sentence for her. "And then . . . it gets better . . ." Now Arvind Fuva began giggling so hard, he began to cry a little.

". . . it went up my nose."

Ronak and my cousins began to giggle at the story, but all I could do was stare at my aunt and uncle, leaning on each other as they chuckled through the story, finishing each other's sentences like they had some deep connection my parents never had. A frown crossed my face.

"Did we mention this was all in front of the president of the PTA, who just happens to be a certain Emmy winner's husband?" Arvind Fuva added, and then Mom couldn't help but join in the laughter too.

"You are so ridiculous," Parvati ben said with a grin.

I dug my fingers into the stiff denim cuff of my other sleeve as some resentful tanpura notes played on my soundtrack. She thought that was ridiculous? Ronak would have given anything to see our parents laughing and joking with each other. I ran my finger around the old metal button on the cuff. It was cold.

Kind of the same way I was feeling toward my selfish, insensitive cousin.

I stopped myself before I frowned. Why was I feeling so angry? It felt like a bubble of crabbiness was starting to grow bigger and bigger and rise to the surface. Was this the Bollywooditis? Or was this the real me, and the magic was tearing away at the mask I always put on?

"And you're interrupting our practice," Parvati whined, finishing up her thought.

"All right, all right. We'll go," Beejal Foi said, linking her arm with Arvind Fuva's.

"I might actually head to that lightbulb store for a bit," Mom added. "That is, if I can find parking."

"There's street parking," Beejal Foi responded, opening the sliding door.

"I can't parallel park," Mom said, shrugging sheepishly like a kid.

"What?" my aunt said.

"Remember? My high school driver's ed teacher just had me pull over on an empty street and checked off the box saying I could parallel park," Mom replied, turning a little pink. "You know what, I'll just have Kirit get the bulbs."

I watched as Beejal Foi and Arvind Fuva exchanged a glance next to my mom.

I didn't like that look. It was full of pity for my parents and us, full of worry for how my mom would survive by herself. I felt annoyed and protective of my mom as my soundtrack grew loud with trumpets.

"Are you sure you want to do that? With everything going on?" Beejal Foi asked Mom, motioning with her head for Mom to follow her inside.

Now my ears were burning, and I was sure my face was even pinker than Mom's. So much for that mask.

The glass door slid shut, and I couldn't hear the grown-ups' conversation anymore. My back felt like an overloaded backpack was strapped to it, and try as I might to lift it, I couldn't.

Parvati ben dropped to her knees and threw her chin up to the sky dramatically, like she was lamenting a huge loss in a Hindi movie. "My parents are sooo embarrassing!"

I dug my shoe into the ground, and faked a smile. Parvati ben was embarrassed by her parents? At least she had both her parents in her house to be embarrassed of. A drumbeat raged from my soundtrack, and before I knew it, my head flew down to my toes, my hair flapping behind as a synthesizer sounded loudly.

No. Not again. I clenched my blazer tightly, willing it to put a stop to this nonsense, hoping it could actually outsmart the magic. But when I looked back up, my long black hair flipped back cinematically. And it was drenched, like Beejal Foi had spilled that pitcher of water on me instead of herself. Glistening droplets splattered everywhere.

I felt my insides sink. Despite my jacket being so tight I could barely move, the unseen force that I thought I had outwitted made my hands shoot up into the sky. My pointer fingers touched my thumbs. I tried to pull them apart, but they were like super-strong magnets, and I couldn't get them to budge. And then my hands began fluttering. Like Parvati's but way more dramatic. A suspenseful guitar strumming seemed to come out of my hands as I shook them, eyes glaring at Parvati.

But she suddenly looked different. Her face had Bollywood heroine-level makeup. Her lips were glossy pink, her eyelashes were long and thick, and she was suddenly drenched in what looked like perspiration except instead of looking gross it was radiant. It was a lot more Hindi-movie-ish than when my classmates swayed back and forth at the field trip.

Before I could process it any more, my legs did a hop and

a skip. "*Green-eyed monster,*" I spat out in a deep voice, different from the normally high-pitched, romantic Bollywood songs.

I glanced sideways at my cousins and Ronak. They seemed . . . sweaty. Like a makeup artist had sprayed them with water on their collars and cheekbones. They swayed and clapped to the beat, like good background dancers.

I suddenly began to do an aggressive gallop around Parvati, my right hand pointing straight at her as the left hand still fluttered with the taunting guitar strumming.

"*Green-eyed monster,*" I sang hostilely at Parvati, glaring at her hazel eyes. "*Dha-dha-dha. Tirakita,*" I said loudly, using the words for the various beats as my feet stamped the ground and my head shook from side to side.

Parvati paused and then nodded, copying my steps.

I was getting angrier with each step. Like dancing it out wasn't going to solve anything. It wouldn't change the fact that I was angry because Parvati was embarrassed by her parents when Ronak would've given anything to have parents who got along. And maybe I would have too. And unlike before, when Dad accused me of being jealous, this time I actually *was* jealous of Parvati ben's life.

"*Na-na, na-na, naaaa*," I said to the rhythm, shaking my head no as my hands pumped the air despite the tight jacket, and my elbows jutted to the sides.

Parvati effortlessly mimicked my moves, like we were in an epic aerobics-style dance-off from one of the movies whose poster was on my wall.

My blazer tugged painfully at my armpits as I held my head and whipped my hair back and forth. "*Dha-dha. Tirakita dhoom*!" I exclaimed, my feet in a frenzy as I shouted, crossing and jumping and twisting and turning, my elbows flapping in what can only be described as a Bollywood version of the Chicken Dance.

Parvati missed a few steps and was suddenly unable to keep up. I spun around her, my hands fluttering faster and faster as the guitar strumming grew louder and louder, until I finally collapsed in my cousin's arms.

Parvati, her shimmering makeup still on her face, helped me back to my feet as everyone cheered around me. "Wow, Sonali. We haven't seen you do a solo in forever!" She whispered her annoying hot breath into my ear again. "But who is the green-eyed monster you were singing about? You were pointing to me but . . ." She twisted her lips into a sympathetic little bundle. "Were you talking about yourself? You know, because my parents were being super gross and in love you and yours—"

"What?" I felt sweaty all over, even though we had stopped dancing, and I took a step back from my overachieving, overbearing, overly concerned cousin. Had Parvati ben been learning about emotions from Mom or something? "No. That wasn't it at all," I said, trying to shut down the line of questioning. "It just felt like a good time for a dance-off, that's all," I said, not wanting to talk about this in front of the rest of my family. My dancing, shimmery-sweat-covered, Bollywood-movie family.

"Do you want to incorporate the new moves into our dance?" Parvati asked, like we did unchoreographed yet in-sync performances all the time.

The filmi magic had done its thing. It hadn't been outmaneuvered. It was getting more powerful. I shook my head fast. "No, it's fine. I was actually going to suggest I go in the back for this first dance."

It was now Parvati's turn to shake her head. "No way. Everyone needs to see what a great dancer you've become. You're staying put right in the front with all of us."

Parshva nudged me with his elbow. "You know there's no stopping Parvati from getting her way." He gave me a tired smile.

I nodded, tugging hard at the useless jean jacket that had

done nothing to prevent my Bollywooditis from striking. I tossed the jacket to the side, watching it fall limply into the grass, dark pink imprints visible all over my arms from the tight sleeves. I rubbed them with my hands, but they still hurt.

It was useless.

Forget Parvati ben. The real thing that couldn't be stopped was this awful, inescapable Bollywooditis.

CHAPTER 18

"You're just giving up?" Zara asked as she walked me to the computer lab Friday afternoon. She almost sounded happy I was giving up trying to stop the magic. "I guess now I'll always know what you're thinking, thanks to your Bollywoodrhea," Zara said, winking.

"It's Bollywooditis," I corrected her. This wasn't Bollywood diarrhea. More like verbal diarrhea. "It isn't what I'm really thinking, and *shh*. I don't want everyone hearing about it."

"Why not?" Zara asked. "If everyone knows about it, more people can help."

My ears felt hot as I thought about how Dad didn't want anyone to know about the separation. Could more people be there to help if they knew, rather than to gossip about us? I shook my head as we entered the classroom full of the familiar sounds of keys clicking away.

"Nothing is causing it," I replied, as we passed Mr. Raven, the computer teacher, at his desk. "It's just happening." I cringed at how out-of-tune our soundtrack was.

"That doesn't really make sense," Zara said, her face turning into a huge grin as she quickly brushed by me and my problems to run to Air.

"Thanks for letting me borrow these," she said, handing Air a set of metallic markers. "You're right. My brush lettering looked awesome with them."

"You could've just kept these," Air replied as I squeezed past Zara to take my seat in between Air and Davuth to her left.

Zara smiled. "Aw, you're the best, but my parents already ordered them for me. I'll see you at lunch?"

Air nodded and Zara waved to us as she rushed out of the classroom, and my soundtrack returned to just my music. I didn't have lunch at the same time as Air and Zara, but I didn't think it would have mattered for finding a way to stop the magic, because Zara was clearly not going to be much help. She had other things on her mind, like her new best friend.

The bell rang, and Mr. Raven looked up from his desk. "All

right, folks. Today we are going to create a Word doc to organize your research for your PowerPoint presentations, and then next week we will begin making the slideshow." Mr. Raven brought an image of his computer screen up on the smart board. "Open up Saephe and get to work."

I clicked on the *safe* search engine that we all had to use in school. I had to try one last time to find a way to outsmart the magic so it couldn't give me a snarky response to my search. So I typed in the vague question, "When will this nightmare end?"

"There's no turning back after the grand finale," replied the website headings, along with a picture of Dada's BE KIND, PLEASE REWIND sticker with a giant red *X* on it. A grand finale? What did that mean? In old Hindi movies, the big moment was usually when there was a long action sequence, or a fight, or a huge musical number. Before I could figure out what the grand finale was in this new, filmi magic reality of mine, or why the sticker was crossed out, a huge swipe of peacock blue paint washed over the walls in a broad stroke, sweeping across them until they were brilliant blue instead of white.

"Holy caps lock," I gasped, almost falling out of my seat in surprise. This paint job seemed to be happening almost twice as fast as when the yellow color swept across my bedroom walls. I quickly looked over at Air, but she was looking up at the walls and then back to her computer like she was thinking about her work and not at all noticing that the wall color had just changed before her eyes.

Was that the grand finale? It didn't seem big enough. I braced for the magic's next response as I hurriedly typed, "Bollywoodi-tis." Maybe someone else in the world called it that too, someone who remembered how things were before this curse. Maybe this was how to get some answers without the magic realizing what I was doing.

But instead of some cryptic phrase for me to figure out, the screen was just frozen. And then the drab-looking computers in the lab suddenly flashed to a brilliant rainbow of colors. Davuth was on a bright-pink computer. Air's was neon green. Mine was a translucent, shiny purple. And nobody even blinked. Could I really get used to being the only one aware of how out of the ordinary all of this was?

Dun dunn dunnn, went my soundtrack.

"Look at your computers," I said, my voice trembling, as I turned back and forth between Davuth and Air.

"I am," Davuth scowled. "And I'm trying to work."

"Look at the colors," I tried again, but Davuth just turned

back to his computer and Air was giving me a concerned look, like I was the weird one here. I raised my hand. "Mr. Raven! The computers! Everything changed!" I sputtered.

Mr. Raven headed over to my computer. "Ah, I see it now."

"You do?" I asked, my voice squeaking. Finally, there was someone else who was aware of just how strange all of this was, and just in time. Based on how quickly the computers changed colors, the magic was getting way too strong.

"Yeah. Looks like you got a typo there in 'Bollywood,'" Mr. Raven replied.

I groaned. Of course no one else got it. I hit backspace, hoping maybe deleting my question would make the Bollywooditis less angry so it didn't change the whole school to look like it was a gaudy college set in an old Hindi movie. But Air had already noticed what I had written, based on her raised eyebrow, the eyebrow she didn't bother raising when our classroom got a live makeover.

"Thanks," I said, forcing a smile as Mr. Raven walked away to hover over someone else's screen.

"What are you researching?" I whispered to Air before she could ask what "Bollywooditis" meant and the magic turned another classroom into a movie classroom.

"The stock market," she said softly. "I'm going to make a portfolio based on the research and put it all into my PowerPoint."

I nodded, not quite understanding what she was saying, and watched as she typed "clean energy stocks" into Saephe.

Nobody was fazed by the room remodel. Nobody even blinked. I was all alone, the only person aware of what was going on. I started to feel sweaty and scared, but I took a breath and gritted my teeth. I was used to feeling all alone. But I needed to know what exactly I was dealing with if I was going to be getting used to it. I needed answers, even if this ticked off the magic. So with Air busy with her stocks and Davuth scanning articles on presidential pets, I quickly typed, "What do lyrics mean?" into Saephe and hit the magnifying glass icon next to it. I prepared for the next makeover to happen, but the computer just flashed to a results page.

"They mean you," the response said in dozens of website headings.

I shook my head. That made no sense. I tried again, typing, "How do you stop Bollywooditis?"

The next screen on my purple computer just said, "The answer you're looking for can be found within."

I tried to catch my breath. Now the magic was taunting me?

I wanted to cry. I wanted to scream for help. I felt my eyes burn with tears, like the emotions were now just beneath the surface instead of pushed deep down where I had left them. This was all the magic's fault.

"Neat subject," Mr. Raven said, startling me again. He pointed to Davuth. "You too." He glanced at Air's screen. "Wow. Looks like you're learning a lot in mock market."

Air shook her head. "My mom made me take drama instead. Said it would be a good way to appreciate how hard her job is."

"Oh," Mr. Raven brushed his hair back awkwardly. "Well, you're doing a great job learning on your own." He smiled and quickly moved to the next kid over.

I looked at Air. She was typing pretty furiously now, like she was taking all her annoyance out on the keys.

"Sorry your mom didn't let you take mock market," I whispered. "If it helps, I'm only taking drama because Zara begged me to. I don't like it either."

Air gave me a little smile as she copied and pasted some of her research onto her Word document, probably trying to figure out why I did a whole field trip performance if I didn't like drama. "My mom just doesn't get that not everyone wants to do something in the film industry. My grandpa was a makeup artist back in the day. My brother is at UCLA, studying to be an editor. I feel like I'm all alone and no one gets it."

I chewed the insides of my cheeks. I definitely knew what that was like.

"And mock market is a sixth-grade class," Air continued, "so I can't take it later. I missed my chance all because of her."

Air's eyes were glistening now, and I suddenly realized all the uncomfortable looks she gave me when I first showed up at drama class maybe weren't directed at me. They might have been meant for drama class.

"That stinks," I said, eyeing her bright-green computer. I might have been a little wrong about just accepting stuff. Air shouldn't give up her dreams. "Maybe you can show her this PowerPoint, and she can see how much you love this stuff?"

I didn't know why I said that. I knew what had happened when I had shown my family my nondigital poster-board presentation back in the day: a disaster. But was there a chance it could work for Air and her family?

"This is like all my inner thoughts and what I really feel . . ." Air trailed off as I thought about what a bad idea it was that I'd suggested to her. But Air shrugged. "Yeah, maybe." She made a table in Word and began filling it with weird letter combinations.

"Thanks," she added, looking at me with a small smile.

Air's eyes weren't shiny anymore, and her fingers weren't beating the keyboard like they had been earlier. Maybe I had helped her feel better. Maybe she wouldn't have to just get used to things being a certain way. Even if I'd never feel better myself, I felt a little happy that Air wasn't so upset anymore. But with my world turned upside down and the magic growing so strong that it was keeping answers from me and taunting me, a huge part of me did wish the solution to my problem was as easy as showing someone a PowerPoint presentation.

CHAPTER 19

I'd spent the rest of the weekend trying to solve this magical mystery, writing clues down in my notebook: 1) The world would become permanently Bollywood after some grand finale. 2) The only way to stop singing and dancing was apparently to watch a whole bunch of old Hindi movies. But I already did that to no avail. I tried to focus instead on what the magic meant when it said the answer to stopping everything came from within. Like it was saying what Zara had accused me of: the lyrics were my innermost thoughts. That wasn't true. Was it?

I set my pen down a little too forcefully and it rolled behind the stack of notebooks. I moved them, and the corner of a small faded-green notebook that Dada had bought me in India jutted out.

After Dada died, I had started making some doodles in that notebook with the old Camel pencil set Dada had saved from when Dad and Avni Foi were little in India. I liked how the pencil lead wrote so differently from my pencils in school. It was darker and scratchier on the paper. But somehow one of my drawings turned into me absentmindedly writing "I'm sad" over and over again. Like those innermost thoughts the filmi magic was alluding to.

I pushed the notebook back into place and headed down for dinner. I'd have to keep thinking if I was going to find a way to stop the magic.

I took a seat next to Ronak and Mom at the kitchen table, picking at my black-eyed peas, and taking an extra helping of kaarela nu shaak to stomach it. That's how much I hated black-eyed peas. I'd rather eat the grossest, bitterest vegetable in the world than eat black-eyed peas. I mean, kaarela's English name was "bitter melon." Did that sound appetizing? But compared to Mom's black-eyed peas, kaarela was as good as a slice of pizza.

Dad walked in, late as usual, a plastic bag and a paper bag in his hand.

Mom looked over at him with a curt smile. Actually, I wouldn't even call it a smile. It was more like when you were rolling Play-doh into a straight worm and a part of it wobbled ever so slightly up in a corner, not because it wanted to, but because of how forcefully you were rolling it.

"There are three rotlis left for you," she said.

Dad set the bags down on the counter behind the table. The paper bag said "Badmaash," the name of a restaurant here. "Thanks. I actually ate. Those clients from overseas came into town, and I had to take them out. I just brought the extra chutney home in case you could use it in something."

My cheeks grew hot and my stomach rumbled as an orchestral hit played on the background music.

It wasn't fair that Dad got to eat at Badmaash. It wasn't fair that instead of bringing us some food from there, he just brought home chutney. And it wasn't fair that Dad got to make all these rules about food and then break them when we were forced to save money and not eat what we liked because of his and Mom's decisions. I felt a bunch of emotions rising to the surface like reflux burning up my throat. I wanted to shout about it. But I didn't want to deal with the aftermath of Mom asking me to talk or Dad lecturing me for talking back or being disrespectful. So I just bit down hard on my black-eyed peas and stared angrily at the homemade food on my plate as a splash of plum color, even deeper than the hue Air's mom wore on her lips, suddenly flashed across our top white cabinets.

I started to choke, coughing as I pointed at the kitchen. The bottom cabinets suddenly turned a fire-hydrant red, but my family just looked around the kitchen, like they couldn't tell what I was pointing to.

I gasped. It was happening because I was upset. This is what the filmi magic meant when it said the answer comes from within me. Any time I looked for a clue about Bollywooditis or buried most of my thoughts or feelings, the magic would grow more intense. It didn't bother taking its time to paint colors on this like it had before. It was almost instantaneous. I swallowed my bite. "Let me guess. This is how things have always been?" I squealed.

"Things weren't always like this," Mom said softly, not talking about our kitchen, based on how hard she was avoiding looking at Dad. "If there's something you want to talk about, you know we're always here for you," she added, pouring herself some more water from the copper water vessel.

Yeah. We were really open in this family. I scoffed, shaking my head.

"Sonali ben," Ronak said softly, shaking his head ever so slightly so I wouldn't start another argument. He hastily turned to Mom before I could even roll my eyes in annoyance. "May I please have some more chola? It's really good."

Mom smiled as she scooped a big spoonful of black-eyed peas onto his plate.

I watched some of the beans spill over onto the place mat, thinking about how Zara had accused me of spilling secrets in my solos. As Ronak picked up the black-eyed peas, it dawned on me. The magic was striking when I was feeling intense feelings, and Bollywood was all about intense feelings. So I had to calm down and stop thinking about how much everything was bothering me, like Dad did. I had to make that mask even tighter than it already was. Make sure it never fell off. That was the key to stopping the Bollywooditis.

"Sorry, Sonali," Dad said, looking a little guilty at his paper carryout bag. "It was for my job. Work paid for it. But, yes, we do have to watch our expenditures." Dad opened the plastic bag and pulled out several boxes of the weird lightbulbs Mom had asked for.

"A plastic bag?" Mom asked, frowning. "The reusable ones are in the back of your car."

"You want to do it next time?" Dad snapped.

Mom rolled her eyes and stared out the sliding-glass door

at the world outside. Dad huffily headed out of our gaudy new kitchen to change his dress shirt and pants. Ronak looked down sadly as he ate his gross black-eyed peas. I just stood up as calmly and unbothered as I could, despite my annoyance and anger and sadness at my parents fighting over a plastic bag, and reached across the table to get myself more kaarela.

Apparently, it wasn't the most bitter thing in the world. Not even in the room.

CHAPTER 20

I woke up the next morning with a strumming sitar on my soundtrack and Mom not in the house. I felt weird, like a piece of me was missing. Waking up without Mom in the house hadn't ever happened before. Mom was always there for breakfast, even if Dad was out of town for a weekend. She worked fewer hours at the hospital to make sure she would be there with us for a little bit in the mornings.

The soundtrack switched to Mom's theme for most of the day, but I fought hard against any feelings it evoked. I pretended everything was fine all day at school, and since I didn't break out in a musical number, it actually was a little fine. Because I might have finally figured out how to stop the singing and dancing, unless this was another fake-out like with the jean jacket.

Being back at home felt weird again though, without Mom around. Ronak seemed sad but kept himself busy with a book. And as the rain came down like a faucet on full blast, I went over to Zara's to hang out in her kitchen and use her hundreds of colorful markers to practice our brush lettering.

"So has my house had a Bollywood makeover or is it normal?" Zara asked.

"Normal," I replied, ready to give up on my paper full of letters that didn't turn out right.

Zara sifted through some markers. "I really want to believe you."

"Yeah. You keep saying that," I said, biting the inside of my cheek hard. "Would you believe it if Air told you it was happening to her?"

"What's that supposed to mean?" Zara asked, reaching for a metallic gray marker, probably from the set Air had introduced her to, to write her full name out: Zara Zareena Khan.

It means she is all you care about lately. It means you're replacing me. I felt a tiny bubble of jealousy and fear coming up to the surface and popped it before it could lead to a solo. "Nothing," I replied, forcing peace onto my face. "Besides, I figured out how to control it."

Zara looked up at me. "You did?"

"Yeah. I wanted to test my theory out before telling you today. The filmi magic acts up any time I'm feeling something. So the answer is to just not feel anything."

"To just act like everything is fine and never tell the truth about how you're feeling?"

I nodded.

Zara shuddered. "That's like as 'robot' as you can get."

"Yeah. And that's the solution to all my problems."

Zara sighed, writing her full name in neon blue, over and over. "All I know is, if I did what you're doing, there's no way I'd get the part at auditions next week."

"For what?" I asked, putting the cap on my marker.

"For the eighth-grade play."

"But you're not an eighth grader."

Zara put her finger to her lips. "I know. But one of the actors got a real movie role and can't do the play anymore, so Ms. Lin has to hold auditions. And with all the kids who like to act from eighth-grade drama already in the play, she's opening up auditions to the rest of the grades if they have acting experience. I think a lifetime of watching Hindi movies counts as experience, don't you? Or is this a touchy subject for you?"

I ran my finger over the other markers in front of me. Why couldn't Zara get how serious this filmi magic was? Just because I didn't always experience things Zara told me about didn't mean I couldn't feel sad when it was something bad that happened to her, or happy when it was something good. Why didn't Zara get that this wasn't something I wanted to joke about? I quickly remembered these intense emotions were the exact thing that triggered the magic, and smiled like everything was okay. "I hope she lets you audition," I said, as the Bollywooditis wind swept around my hair. Was I about to sing again despite stopping my emotions?

"Thanks," Zara replied, thinking nothing of the magical indoor wind.

But I could barely hear her. Zara's parents were watching satellite TV in the family room to the side of us, and they had just switched to the Indian news channel with really loud volume. The anchor and his panelists were shouting over each other, as the caption below them read, INDO-PAK TENSIONS RISE.

Mumtaz Auntie shook her head. "This is so one-sided. Why are you watching their news?"

"Mumtaz," Imran Uncle gave a wide-eyed head turn in our direction, reminding Mumtaz Auntie that Zara and I were in the kitchen.

"You girls hungry?" Mumtaz Auntie asked, turning toward us.

"No thanks, Mumtaz Auntie," I replied loudly, concentrating on making an orange-colored orange on my paper and ignoring the wind.

Zara shook her head. Her parents turned back to the TV, and the shouting grew noisier than the pouring rain outside.

I stopped writing and turned to the TV, a lump forming in my throat, which I quickly swallowed away. Every few years India and Pakistan would have some sort of issue with each other. And it made me feel tense because I was Indian American and my best friend was Pakistani American, and our parents were good friends but would act a little strange with each other when their motherlands were on the verge of war, smiling extra wide, like they were trying to remind themselves to talk about anything other than India and Pakistan.

But just decades earlier, our grandparents had all lived in the same land. I remember Zara's grandmother telling me how at her elementary school reunion in Pakistan, her Hindu best friend, Naina, came back. Zara's grandmother hadn't seen her since they helped Naina's family escape the violence of Partition, when some people had hurt one another due to religious tensions between Hindus, Muslims, and Sikhs, and get to India. And Dada couldn't tell me about his Muslim best friends, Iqbal and Sohail, without getting teary. They were like his brothers, just like Zara felt like my sister. But then Partition happened, and Dada said the British succeeded in tearing us apart one last time. Iqbal's family in North India had fled the violence to get to Pakistan. And Iqbal and his family in Ahmedabad needed to go with them, so Dada's and Sohail's parents helped them get out safely. Dada and Sohail never saw Iqbal again.

I turned to Zara, every muscle tightening up. I wanted to push those feelings down, but I was worried and sad and felt awkward. Zara shook her head at me, and I knew she was saying not to worry. As much as Zara liked to talk, I liked that we could also communicate with silent looks every now and then, and totally get what the other person was saying.

"Look outside. It's like sheets of water out there," Zara said, distracting me, helping me go back to keeping my cool. "The perfect weather for a rain dance."

I felt my stomach tighten at the thought that I might break out into a song about India and Pakistan, but Zara hummed one of the many songs where actors danced in the rain, and opened the sliding-glass door with a dreamy, Bollywood-heroine look on her face, and nothing happened to me. I was right. The Bollywooditis took a break when things were calm.

Raindrops hopped on Zara's outstretched palm, and a breeze swished through her hair. And then she quickly shut the door. "Never mind. It's cold."

Zara and I laughed.

"I should probably help my dad with dinner," I said, putting my markers away.

"Where's your mom?"

That lump suddenly felt like it was back, and Mom's theme played on my soundtrack. "Oh, she . . . she'll be back later."

Zara handed me the umbrella we passed back and forth between our houses. "See you at school. And I hope you don't sing any more solos, if that's not what you want to do."

I gave Zara a small smile. I guess she did care a little bit, even if she couldn't quite understand how bad my problem was. "Bye, Zara Zareena Khan."

"It does have a good ring to it, doesn't it?"

"It's perfect."

As the yelling on TV continued, I opened the sliding-glass door and ducked under the umbrella, sheltered from the storm around me. I closed the door and ran through the rain, silencing the shouts of tension.

CHAPTER 21

I fought off every thought about my feelings over the next few days, concentrating instead on homework. It actually worked. There were no new Bollywooditis outbursts. If I could figure out how to turn off my background music and undo the makeovers, I'd actually be free of the magic.

I stood before a produce shelf at Ralphs, trying to brainstorm, as Ronak helped Dad load the cart with vegetables for yet another homecooked dinner. A dinner that tasted nothing like my mom's cooking. I thought about what I had scratched out in my notebook. I seemed to always come back to that. Could my parents really have something to do with the magic? It did all start right after they announced they were separating, didn't it?

My palms grew clammy so I stared hard at the variety of potatoes in front of me, trying to be calm.

"You know what makes some of those potatoes sprout?" Dad asked, turning toward me. "The starch in them turns to sugar and the potato works hard to make that happen. Without hard work, there's no growth." He glanced down at me, one eyebrow raised, expectantly.

I sighed, knowing another Dad talk was coming. "You saw my quiz?"

"Mrs. Kulkarni emailed me and Mom. You have to work harder, Sonali."

"I was sick that day. I will," I said, hoping Dad would stop the lecture. When I shopped with Mom, she would talk my ear off with stories of the vegetable vendors selling produce on wooden carts they wheeled through her childhood neighborhood. Or her garden, full of chiku, bor, and jaamphal trees. They were fun stories. Not lectures about grades like with Dad. Sometimes it felt like I just couldn't relate to him.

"Just be thankful Mrs. Kulkarni is giving you a chance to raise your grade with that extra-credit assignment next week," Dad added. "That girl giving the talk is just two years older than you and already halfway through college."

I wasn't thankful. I was annoyed. I had no interest in hearing someone talk about math for an hour and then spend hours writing about what she had said about math. Instead of telling him how I felt though, I grabbed a handful of purple potatoes. I ran my fingers over the smooth skin and occasional bumps when someone squeezed my hand.

"Sonali!" It was Revati Auntie, my mom's friend, dressed in her scrubs from the hospital.

I felt the tight hold of her hand on mine and, for a second, felt jealous that she had just seen my mom at work, or eaten lunch in the cafeteria with her, or any of the things I couldn't do this week, unless I called her on the phone to chat or FaceTimed while I ate at the house and she ate at the apartment.

The grocery store shelves suddenly become turned neon pink as Revati Auntie pulled me in for a hug and waved Dad and Ronak over. "Ronak! Look how tall you've grown!" Auntie bent down to squeeze his cheeks while still holding on to me. "And how're you, Kirit? I heard Avni's last scan was good?"

Dad looked taken aback. I watched his fingers tap the shopping-cart handle as he nodded ever so slightly.

"Thank God," Revati Auntie said. "That must have been such a scary time for all of you. If you ever want to talk about it, I'm here. I know I was a good listener for Falguni."

Dad shook his head quickly. "I don't want to talk about it," he said a little severely before catching himself. "Thanks, though."

Auntie nodded. "I can't wait to see her at the sangeet. It's going to be so grand! I can't believe Avni was able to book that resort for it. I heard it's reserved years in advance and—"

"Uh, you know, Revati," Dad said, sorting through the bag of okra in his cart, "the rest of our family doesn't know about . . . about Avni." He looked up at her with pleading eyes.

"Oh, you don't have to worry about me," Revati Auntie said loudly. "Falguni told me you didn't want anyone else to know, even though you could've used help from all the friends."

Mom's theme began to play on my soundtrack as I thought about how much she and Dad had argued when my aunt was sick. How much she had insisted they needed help and our friends and relatives would be there for us if we just let them in. I remembered seeing how exhausted Mom was from everything she was doing for us while taking care of Avni Foi and working. I remembered thinking we could use help. But then I also remembered thinking back to how embarrassed Dad was when our family found out he and Mom fought, thanks to my presentation. And how he was all about making everyone think everything was perfect after that, even more so than he already did.

I did it too, thanks to Dad. And now I had to do it to fight back against the magic.

"My lips are sealed." Revati Auntie made a zipper gesture on her lips but then seemed to unzip them without even trying as she finally released my hand. "Falguni just had one patient after I was done. She should be home soon after that extra shift she worked. Poor thing seems so tired. Anyway, see you at Avni's sangeet, if not sooner!"

Ronak and I said bye and the blood began to rush back to my hand and his cheeks after being held in Revati Auntie's vicelike grip. But despite not even being squeezed by Revati Auntie like a zit about to pop, Dad's face was totally pale.

CHAPTER 22

I stood at the kitchen counter, my long hair now in a braid so it wouldn't fall into the food as I shredded cabbage for the shaak Dad was going to make, all the while wondering what Mom was up to at the apartment. I didn't like that Revati Auntie knew some of our family's news and was loudly broadcasting it at the grocery store, but a part of me was happy Mom had someone to talk to while she was away from us.

Ronak was washing the cilantro, getting ready to break it into little pieces to put in our food. I twisted my lips, thinking about how Mom would ask me to do that, but I'd complain about the sharp smell of the kothmir and make Ronak do it instead. Her theme began to play even slower and sadder than it had ever played before on my soundtrack.

Dad was at the stove, next to the tacky combination of dark-purple and bright-red cabinets above and below him. He stirred a bubbling pot of daal that made me think about my pot of emotions, and the nutty aroma of the lentil soup filled the air, mixing with the almost floral scent of the basmati rice that was cooking next to it.

"I can't believe she told Revati." Dad stewed, next to the stewing food. "She knew Bapuji and I didn't want anyone to know," Dad added, talking about Dada. "It was for Avni's own good. Who needs everyone in the community knowing her business? Who wants to hear all these questions about what's going on and have to answer them repeatedly? And why would Revati ask me about Avni so loudly at the grocery store? Do I want to talk about it? No, obviously."

Ronak put the pieces of green kothmir onto a little steel plate next to the daal ladle and the giant face of the stainless-steel rice paddle. "Some people feel better sharing what's going on, Dad. That's just how Mom is."

"And Ronak," I added, conflicted, because I could see both my parents' sides to this, but also a little upset Dad was putting me and Ronak in the middle of an argument yet again, even if Mom wasn't here to argue her side.

"Well, she was wrong to tell Revati. Our business is our business. Nobody else needs to hear about it. Why give them something to gossip about?" Dad turned from the stove. "Is the bathroom light on?"

I peered around the corner, grateful for the distraction so I could calm down and stop these feelings from bubbling up. "Sorry." I put the cabbage down, ran to the bathroom, and used my elbow to shut the lights off.

"Do you know how much electricity costs?"

I shrugged. "Pennies?"

"Pennies add up. And it's not good for the environment, as your mom would say, to waste energy." Dad sighed. "I didn't tell you this earlier, but we had to cancel our subscription to TeeVee."

"What?" I asked, shredding the cabbage faster, watching as it surrendered into tiny, waving white flags on the plate below. "But the new episode of *Lockers* goes up this weekend!"

"We are already paying for cable. I wish we could keep it for your show, Sonali, but you have no idea what this apartment is costing us. Add to that paying two electricity bills, two cable bills, two gas bills, it's just too much. All because your mom had this silly idea."

She wouldn't have had this silly idea if you two could get along, I thought, fuming. Mom's theme was suddenly overtaken by an angry guitar sound, and my hand slipped on the shredder. "Ouch!" I screamed, terrified I'd start singing the old song that started with the most dramatic "ouch," all because I hadn't kept my own dramatics hidden. But thankfully I didn't. I just watched as a string of skin hung from the tip of my thumb.

"Are you okay?" Ronak asked.

I blew on the cut, thinking of how Mom used to blow on any little scrape I had, and how that somehow made the pain go away. What was I doing? I had to push this feeling down and make the pain go away like I always did.

"She will be." Dad reached over me, grabbing the masalano dabbo. He quickly spooned a little turmeric out of the tiny steel spice bowl inside and sprinkled it from above into my cut, to disinfect it and help it heal. "All better?" he asked.

I nodded, watching as some blood mixed with the turmeric, looking like slow-moving lava.

"That looks gross. And like it hurts," Ronak said, turning away from the cut.

"It's fine." I shook my head, suppressing the pain, masking how annoyed I was at Dad, how sad I was without Mom, how confused I was about which parent was right, how upset I was that I was being put in the middle of this debate in the first place.

I exhaled, trying to remember some of the meditations Mom had taught me. Trying to calm down. Then the iPad rang.

"Is it Mom?" I asked, as Ronak ran over to the counter.

He shook his head. "It's Parvati ben." He swiped his finger to answer the call, and Parvati ben's smiling face was on the screen with our other cousins'.

"Everyone came over and we went out to the pier," she said. "And as I was watching the Ferris wheel, I suddenly thought that spinning step at the beginning of the second song could be different from what I showed you last week."

Dad nodded at us as he diced up a tomato and a bit of onion for raitu. "Go ahead."

Ronak picked up the iPad but then stopped. "Are you sure, Dad?"

"He's sure," I said, pulling Ronak and my virtual cousins into the family room, my thumb still throbbing from its shredding. I needed space from Dad to calm down.

Parvati played the opening notes to an old Aamir Khan rain song. On cue, she began spinning to the left side of the room, her arms twisting and twirling to her side as Tejal and Shilpa followed. After a count of four beats, Parshva, Sheel, and Neel spun the other way, to the right side of the room, hopping from one foot to another midspin like they were doing garba.

"*Tip, tip, tip, tip . . . ,*" the singer began, using a Hindi onomatopoeia for the sound of raindrops.

"Cool, huh?" Parvati asked, pausing the music so we could once again hear the sound of the real rain pounding against our windows, which sounded more like *drip, drip, drip* to my ear than *tip, tip, tip.*

Ronak nodded and I smiled, squeezing my thumb, which was still throbbing like a heart was beating inside it.

"Avni Foi said she and your dad used to reenact this song when they were kids, pretending those bright-orange plastic feather dusters Dada had in the store were umbrellas," Parvati said, talking about my grandfather. "Your mom saw an old video of it when she and your dad first met, and it was so funny and embarrassing, Avni Foi was positive your mom was going to run away and never speak to your dad again." Parvati laughed, then her eyes suddenly widened. "Oh. I didn't mean . . ." She looked around awkwardly when an orchestral hit sounded on my soundtrack. "I just meant the video is apparently super embarrassing and you need to find it and watch it," Parvati said, regaining her composure as I fought to regain mine. "Okay, now this time you join in. Ready? Five, six, seven, eight."

Parvati's music started and I spun with Tejal, Shilpa, and Parvati, reminding myself I had been expecting my parents to split up one day. But as I spun faster, I couldn't stop thinking about my mom watching my dad reenact this song on a fuzzy old home video, thinking about Mom actually laughing at something Dad did and thinking it was sweet, thinking about Dad being embarrassed because he cared what she thought, sad, angry, and resentful that I couldn't remember a time when they had feelings like that for each other. I reminded myself to not let the feelings get the best of me, when a blinding flash of lightning lit up the sky outside. It was like that scary shot of booming thunder and lightning that was in all the old Hindi movies before it rained on-screen. Startled, I collided into the long gray sofa, falling into its sagging seat cushions.

"Whoa. You okay?" Parshva bhai asked from the iPad.

I nodded, throwing my hair back out of my face, but water sprinkled out of it, like I had just taken a shower. Or worse, was just about to do a Bollywood rain song. I had messed up. I hadn't controlled my emotions.

"Oh, wow, another solo?" Parvati squealed excitedly.

I looked at Ronak. He snapped to the beat as I dropped to the ground and held my soaked braid, watching raindrops that held rainbow prisms inside twinkle melodiously out of my hair. Raindrops, inside my house. I knew what was going to come next. My head cocked from side to side as I batted my eyes at the raindrops, like they were the most spectacular thing I had ever seen. "*Tip-tip . . . tip-tip . . . ,*" I sang.

I did a thumbs-up with my hurt thumb, and flipped it back and forth so the cut on the tip of my thumb showed. My cousins suddenly began to snap in unison, just like Ronak. And soon they were all swaying their hips at the same time.

I stood up and began side-galloping like I was splashing in the monsoon in India. And every time I dramatically kicked my foot, water sprinkled out of the carpet. Ronak kept snapping, unbothered by the possible flood in our carpet.

"*Here's a tip. Don't let it hurt. Tip-tip . . . tip-tip,*" I sang, swinging my hips.

My cousins and Ronak swung their arms back and forth as more water dripped from my hair to my face. "*Another tip. Put a Band-Aid on. Tip-tip . . . tip-tip.*"

I took my hair out of the braid and shook my drenched head, singing in a higher voice, my eyebrows going fully diagonal like I was constipated, or a Hindi movie heroine singing really emotionally. "*Cover it up, cover it up. Tip-tip . . . tip-tip.*"

Was the magic ridiculing me again? I had tried to cover *it* up, hadn't I? Why rub it in by making me sing about it?

I threw my hands in the air, my clothes getting saturated in rain, which just seemed to appear on me without ever falling from a cloud. And I began to spin, faster and more gracefully than Parvati had shown us. "*Don't show it. Hide it. Let the scab form like a shield. They'll think your family's perfect from afar. Because you covered it up so perfectly . . .*" I jumped in the air for what I hoped was the end. "*. . . there won't be a scar*!" I landed and water splashed next to my feet. "*Tip-tip*!"

Ronak and my cousins began high-fiving like supportive background dancers.

"That was so fun!" Parvati cheered.

No, this was the opposite of fun, I thought. This was the magic telling me it knew my plans and they wouldn't work because any time someone said something about my parents, try as I might to hide the feelings and not act bothered, some of them escaped to my brain and forced me to fixate on them. "This is all my parents' fault," I muttered, trying my best to not let more out.

There was a flash of color behind me, seen in the little rectangular image of us in the corner of the iPad. I turned. The walls instantly turned magenta and large white statues of people straight out of Renaissance paintings bent artistically around fountains sprouted up, one on each wall, as our family room got the Bollywood makeover.

My mouth dropped, even though I should have been used to what the filmi magic could accomplish by now.

"We are going to be so great at the sangeet," Parvati continued on her screen, not even blinking at the changes happening to our house.

My shoulders slumped. Maybe I just had to accept that these musical numbers were going to happen any time I messed up. Maybe if I didn't react every time the magic acted up, it would get bored of trying to ruin my life and go away.

Parvati lowered her voice so only Parshva, standing by the iPad, was close enough to hear. "But, Sonali . . . you know what's better than covering things? Ripping the Band-Aid off. I'm here if you ever need to do that."

Parshva raised his eyebrow. "Why do you always have to be so bossy? She can do what she wants with her Band-Aids."

"It's obviously not about Band-Aids. You know her parents are going through a divorce," Parvati admonished softly, but the microphone still picked it up for Ronak and me to hear.

I brushed my suddenly dry hair out of my eyes and hissed back. "It's not a divorce. It's a separation. And no one is supposed to know about it." I quickly hit the red button, ending the call before I accidentally started screaming and turned my whole family into Bollywood movie stars or something.

"You okay?" Ronak asked.

I nodded. I wasn't going to react. I didn't care that it rained in the house. I didn't care what the magic did next. How bad could it be? Dad wearing bad wigs? Loud jarring sound effects when someone made a joke or dropped something by accident? Flashbacks? Bring it on. I didn't care. And the sooner the magic realized it, the better.

Ronak's brow furrowed. "Sonali ben? Do you want to talk about it?"

I dug my toes into the now-dry carpet.

"No. I don't want to talk about it," I snapped, like I was Dad talking to Revati Auntie. But then I looked at the hurt in Ronak's eyes and reminded myself that he was only trying to help, and I was doing a bad job of acting unbothered if I was yelling at my brother. "But, thanks." I forced a smile, patted his shoulder, and headed back to the kitchen.

The food didn't smell the way Mom's did, but I had accepted it. Just like I had accepted, years ago, that I had no control over my parents. And the way I had accepted the magic. I had accepted it all.

CHAPTER 23

"Set the table, please, kids," Dad said from the pantry. I couldn't see him, but I knew he was digging around through his collection of Indian pickles, which he always had to have with homemade Indian food.

I grabbed four plates from the bright-red island cabinets and was putting them on the place mats from India that Ronak was setting on the table when he gave me a look. He had three place mats for us and Dad. And I had *four* plates.

I quickly put the plate I had gotten for Mom out of habit back in the cabinet, then Dad exited the pantry with a bottle of pickled shredded turmeric rhizome in his hand. That was normal. What wasn't normal was what was on his head. Because there, covering his bald spot, was the worst wig I had ever seen. It looked like a dead skunk, with a very dramatic stripe of white going straight down the middle, and I burst out laughing.

"Very funny, Dad," I said, wiping a tear from my eye.

"I don't think I said anything funny?" Dad replied, putting the pickle jar on a peacock coaster on the table.

He ran his fingers over his hair, if that's what we were calling the fake roadkill on his head, and brought the pot of daal and rice to the table next to the cabbage shaak we had made.

"Oh." I quickly stopped laughing, realizing from the way Dad and Ronak were acting that the thing that looked as fake as the wigs dads and villains wore in old Hindi movies was Dad's new filmi magic hair. The magic always seemed to vomit magic into the real world after I hadn't concealed my feelings. Oh, well. I wasn't going to be bothered.

"I'm starving," I said, quickly changing the subject and serving myself dinner. Dad's cell phone rang, saving me from having to come up with an excuse for what I was laughing about. I could tell from the cold look in Dad's eyes that it was Mom.

"The extra credit is today," Mom said frantically when Dad answered the FaceTime.

"What?" Dad asked. "You said it was during your week. We're about to eat dinner."

"At seven thirty pm?" Mom snapped. "You know Ronak has to be asleep in an hour, right? How's that going to happen? And let me guess, he hasn't even showered yet?"

Ronak took a bite of the cabbage shaak, clenching his spoon so tight, his knuckles were turning white.

"You're not in any position to critique me," Dad huffed, pacing around the tacky kitchen. "You told us the wrong day for the extra credit Sonali needs to get her grade up."

"You could have logged in to the parent portal anytime to see the date. Besides, you can still get there," Mom replied.

I pushed my feelings down. They weren't going to bait me into ruining my mask of calm.

"She's already missed half of it. She'll have missed forty-five minutes of it by the time we get there, and it's just an hour long," Dad replied, glancing at the clock on the oven.

"That won't be enough to write a paper about," I said, shoving spoonfuls of dinner into my mouth as fast as I could in case my parents decided to force me to go anyway. "It's pointless."

"Fixing your grade isn't pointless," Dad said sternly.

"You're the one who said I'd miss most of it," I replied.

"Okay," Mom said, through a burst of static. "I'll email Mrs. Kulkarni and tell her it was Dad's week with the kids and I thought the extra credit was during my week."

"No," Dad said. "Don't tell her that."

"Then what should I say?" Mom asked, as I felt a surge of annoyance creep over me. Why couldn't they accept everything too and just stop bickering all the time?

"That we scheduled something at the same time by accident," I said.

"No," Dad said again, the hair on his wig glistening like plastic doll hair under the kitchen lights. "We can't lie."

"We can't tell the truth," I said, my temper rising. "We can't lie. What exactly can we say about . . . about *this*?" I stood up, shoving my chair back from the table, hard. I winced as my cut stung when the Band-Aid tugged at it, and reminded myself to stay calm.

In a flash Mom got the Bollywood makeover and suddenly had long, thick, flowing locks, thick eyelashes where her thinning ones once were, and glossy lipstick instead of chapped lips.

I didn't flinch though. I had expected something to happen the moment I lost my temper. And I didn't care that I was missing extra credit either. I was actually happy about not having to suffer through Genius Math Girl's talk and having to write a paper. But I didn't want to deal with Dad getting upset about my math grade anymore and did want it to go up to stop the constant math lectures from him. So much for accepting everything and being calm.

"I'm sorry, Sonali," Dad said. "But Mrs. Kulkarni is in the Indian community. What if she tells someone who tells someone who tells Revati, who tells everyone?"

I looked at my thumb, at the end of the Band-Aid that was unraveling. I thought about what Parvati had said about ripping the Band-Aid off. That was great advice from someone who had no idea what any of this was like. Someone whose parents laughed at each other's jokes and finished each other's sentences. Someone who never had to hide anything because she was so perfect.

Rip the Band-Aid off? How? Dad didn't want us telling anyone on the outside. And we couldn't show them what we were feeling on the inside. All we could do was suffer alone.

All alone.

I knew how to do that. I'd been doing that forever. I took my seat again, scooching back to the table as I pulled the loose end of my Band-Aid and put it tightly back into place, hiding my hurt from everyone.

CHAPTER 24

The rest of the week with Dad went by pretty quickly. I couldn't concentrate in school when Ms. Lin asked us to play "yes and," where we had to accept whatever the person said before us and expand on it. When Zara said aliens had landed here in search of peanut butter, all I could think of saying was "yes, and it was interesting." Ms. Lin's lack of a smile showed she wasn't happy with my participation, as did the note she sent my parents on the parent portal. Apparently, I was okay with the acceptance part. Just not with what to do next. That sounded about right.

I expected to get lots more notes home on the portal too, because I could barely put together my memoir project in English, getting stuck on the first page where I had to draw my family tree, because I didn't know if I should draw a nest between the line that was connecting my parents or just erase it altogether.

And I was definitely not listening in math, which gave Mrs. Kulkarni many opportunities to mention the extra credit I missed because we got the dates mixed up, which was the only acceptable half-truth Dad let me use.

Nothing was really going my way, despite my decision to go with the flow when it came to the magic, so I was happy for the weekend to arrive and my mom with it for Bollywood movie night. Tonight we were going to watch my favorite Aamir Khan movie, full of sibling love and dramatic bike races.

With a violin strumming softly in my soundtrack, I ate Dad's potato and peas shaak and his misshapen rotlis, which looked more like continents than the perfect circles Mom made. When she walked in the door, she paused at the sight of my dad like she wasn't expecting to see him, even though she knew he was here. "Hi," she said, after a short breath.

"Hi," he replied.

I wasn't sure I'd be able to sit through any more of their awkward "hi"s. Couldn't they go back to not acknowledging when the other walked in the door like in the good old days? Not that those were good days. But even with my parents' fighting, having them both living here felt . . . normal. It was like their trying to say hi was just drawing attention to how messed up things were around here. Or like false hope. I swallowed the feelings down with my next bite.

Ronak held up two rotlis at the table. "Look, this sort of looks like Pakistan and India." He turned one of the flatbreads. "Or maybe more like South America?"

Dad looked at the Indian American newspaper next to him at the head of the table. The headline said, JETS SCRAMBLED. TROOPS MOVED TO LOC. WHAT NEXT?

The LOC was the Line of Control, the military border between India and Pakistan. We had been to the official border once, not the LOC, with Dada, right before he told me he was sick, to see the Wagah border flag ceremony. That was when Indian and Pakistani border forces on either side of the border lowered the flag and did a dramatic march, each trying to outdo the other with their moves for a packed audience. I remember sitting with the huge Indian crowd by the border gate and staring at the crowd on the Pakistani side as one border guard on the Indian side and one on the Pakistani side did an over-the-top strutting show of their patriotism and love for their respective countries. It was almost like Bollywooditis, except it was intentional.

"They're always causing trouble," my dad muttered, reading the paper.

Mom cleared her throat loudly, trying to get Dad to be quiet without having to talk to him anymore. Maybe she was fed up with the awkward "hi"s too.

Ronak took a bite of both rotlis. "I hate when India and Pakistan fight. It makes me sad."

"Me too, dikra," Mom said as she hugged him. "Things are always better when they get along."

I swallowed my last bite of food and looked at my parents. Almost every time I got upset, it was because of them, wasn't it? Maybe if my parents got along, my Bollywooditis would actually be cured, because these emotions would finally go away.

I rushed to the sink to wash my dishes and put my plan into action. "I'll go find the movie," I said, shuffling past Dad to rinse my mouth and rush to the family room.

"I'm still eating," Ronak called after me, with a mouthful of India and Pakistan.

Ignoring Ronak, I opened the cabinet and reached to the back of the top shelf. That wasn't where the Hindi movie was. I had already put it in the car rewinder. That was where Dad's old family movies were kept after Dada died.

I read Dada's neat handwriting on the labels of each tape, making my way past Dad and Avni Foi's basketball tournaments and Gujarati folk dance performances, until I finally got the tape I was searching for. I popped it in the VCR and fast-forwarded, pressing hard on the plastic-bag-coated remote control until it was cued up.

"Ready?" Mom asked, as she and Ronak finally took their seats on the long gray sofa.

I nodded, sitting by one of the massive statues, where I could have the best view of my parents' faces. Dad walked in and sat by himself on the love seat, a pretty badly named piece of furniture, if you asked me. I pressed play. Instead of the opening of the movie, a fuzzy home video started.

"What is this?" Mom asked, her elbow resting on one of the gaudy statues.

The rain song we were doing in our medley began to play, and my dad, when he was my age, entered the screen, dancing around Dada's video store with an orange feather duster umbrella as four-year-old Avni Foi sprinkled hole punches from a three-hole puncher on him like rain. Rain the tiny feather duster did not protect him from at all.

Mom and Dad let out a laugh at the same time, and I suddenly felt a strange, featherlight feeling of hopefulness.

"Where did you find this?" Dad asked, turning as pink as the walls.

"Is that . . . Dad?" Ronak asked, confused.

Mom nodded, letting out another giggle as the faintest twinkle could be seen in her eyes. "Aamir Khan was his favorite."

I grinned. It was working. My parents were remembering what really were the good old days, before they grew apart and the arguing started.

"I had this plan to go to Mumbai and become a movie star," Dad added, smiling at me and Ronak. "I guess it's a good thing everything doesn't go according to plan, huh?"

Mom suddenly stopped smiling, and cleared her throat, the joy disappearing from her face. "Should we start the movie?"

"Yeah. I want to see when they dance on their desks and throw their tests everywhere in slow motion," Ronak added.

"Maybe Sonali can tell us a little about that," Dad joked as he got up to put the real movie in. "Sounds like she's doing the metaphorical version of that at school."

"There's more to life than just grades," Mom said softly. "There's happiness, too."

"Would you have become a doctor with just happiness?" Dad

asked, annoyed, as he took his seat again and the movie began to play.

I felt my eyes sting a little as I tried to ignore my dad and watch the bike race on-screen.

"No. Right?" he continued, the wig shaking on his head. "She has a big math test in two weeks. It's her chance to raise that grade. In fact, she has to raise all her grades and take all her classes seriously, even drama. Did we get anything other than As when we were kids? Of course not. It was unheard of. Our parents wouldn't allow it. She needs to study hard and get better if she wants to have a career and earn a good living when she gets older."

Mom rolled her eyes. "And never see her kids because she's working all the time, and never know how to express herself because she's been told to put on a brave face and pretend everything is fine all the time, and—"

"I can't hear," Ronak said softly, his eyes looking big, worried, and sad.

Our parents turned to him. "What?" they both said at the same time, finally breaking out of their angry tirades long enough to notice him.

"If you fight, how will we hear the movie?"

I glared hard at my parents and my soundtrack began to thunder. Ronak had just told them how sad he felt when two countries fought. Didn't they remember how he felt when his own parents fought? He made it obvious all the time with his tears. Why couldn't they put their differences aside for once and just get along for his sake? Why couldn't they get along so this magical condition would stop for *my* sake? But based on the way Mom was subtly shaking her head and muttering under her breath, and the way Dad was staring at the screen like a mannequin devoid of any expression, it was obvious that would never happen.

Before I could even try to say "om" in my head to calm down, the sofa Mom and Ronak sat on suddenly turned a dazzling orange, like a warning.

Of course it did. Because thanks to my parents and their selfish fighting, my Bollywooditis would always happen.

CHAPTER 25

I woke up the next morning, staring at the poster of me and the badminton racquet, knowing I really had to give up on finding a way to stop the magic because I couldn't win the fight. With my renewed attitude of surrender, I rushed into drama to find Zara and Air, wearing purple shirts with the *Lockers* logo on them, in deep conversation a few feet from Ms. Lin. I sat next to them, hoping Zara would notice the blue shirt I was wearing with the words BUT SHE'S YOUR BEST FRIEND, YA? But Zara barely even noticed me, let alone what I had on, despite it being a shirt she made me last year at a sleepover. I had made her the same quote on an orange shirt, since it was our favorite line from an old movie, even though one of our shirts said "ya" and the other said "yaar" since we could never agree on what the singers were saying.

"What are you talking about?" I asked with a smile, even though I was thoroughly annoyed I wasn't being included and Zara wasn't even asking me how I was or if I had sung and danced again. I pulled at the corner of a fingernail that was just barely hanging on.

"Last night's episode," Zara said urgently. "Tell us you saw what Rodrigo said to Jacob."

I swallowed hard. "My dad canceled TeeVee."

"What?" Air asked. "Why?"

"Something about saving money," I replied, a little embarrassed to be saying that to someone who clearly had a ton of money.

"You can come to my house and catch up one day. And we'll keep it spoiler-free for you. Earmuffs," Zara said, before leaning in to Air to whisper about the show in her ear.

A little twinge of jealousy gnawed at my insides as I watched Air's eyes widen. I felt myself getting annoyed and upset as Zara continued to whisper and Air nodded enthusiastically. "Yes! That part was so awful!"

I ripped the rest of my nail off and flicked it to the ground.

Just then a flash of bright green threw itself over all the walls, fast and sloppy and instant. This was a swifter, more powerful transformation than ever before, like someone had thrown the exact amount of paint onto the walls in one split second. As usual, nobody gave the makeover a second look, continuing what they were doing like nothing had even happened. I shut my gaping mouth and blinked once. When I opened my eyes, the entire floor had turned from gray to a flashy red-and-black-checkerboard pattern.

Zara smiled at Air. "Right? It was the worst." She turned my way. "Okay, that was the last secret spoiler. Did you see that the prime ministers of India and Pakistan tweeted about everything going on at the LOC this weekend? And because of what they said on Twitter, the whole mess has been sorted out and there's peace again?"

I shook my head, tapping my toes in the red and black squares, trying to quiet the feelings inside me.

"So now we don't have to fight anymore." Zara grinned, and Ms. Lin called for our attention.

I sank in my seat, unable to totally hide my annoyance. I knew I had given up trying to stop the magic, but that didn't mean I wanted to go back to my first-grade emotional ways. But the magic was making me feel everything I had given up feeling. Why couldn't Zara see how horrible she was being to me without me singing about it?

"All right, class. Today we're going to learn how acting is more than just words and expressions," Ms. Lin announced. "A true actor acts with their entire body."

My stomach twisted, like it was being wrung out, like the magic was getting too intense to handle. Like I was going to give this class a performance the likes of which they'd never seen before. This wasn't happening. Actually, it really couldn't happen, right? My Bollywooditis only struck when I got upset because someone said something about my parents, or because my parents fought. No one was talking about them, and they definitely were not in class.

"So today we're going to do a little interpretive dance." Ms. Lin twirled around the fake jacaranda tree, to a green glass jar on a table. "With your monologue midterms just a month away, I want you to really pay attention to today's class and earn those participation points. Because today we're going to pick an emotion and see how that makes our whole body act."

Zara's hand went up. "If we do a really great job, will you consider opening auditions up to sixth graders too?"

"I'll consider considering it," Ms. Lin replied. "Now come on up. You're first."

Zara confidently took her spot by the jar. She reached in and pulled out a scrap of paper. "Shy," she said, tilting her head to read the words without even unfolding the paper all the way.

Zara looked around the stage and grabbed an orange scarf from the pile of props on the side. She threw it over her head like it was an odhni and she was wearing a chaniyo choli. And then she began what was sure to be a legendary performance, full of the typical shy-girl steps old movies were full of. Zara tiptoed around the stage, bit her lip nervously, and danced while tilting the edge of her scarf over her face and back off, on repeat. It wasn't a filmi magic solo, since that was against the rules during class apparently, but it was still full of emotion.

"Amazing work!" Ms. Lin said, standing up to applaud when Zara was done.

Zara blushed. "Thanks." Her eyes twinkled and I knew she was envisioning herself onstage for the eighth-grade performance one day.

"Xiomara, you're next," Ms. Lin said.

As Xiomara took her place, I tried to make eye contact with Zara, to tell her with a look how amazing her interpretive dance was. But instead of looking at me, Zara's eyes were locked on Air's.

"That was so good," Air whispered.

"Thanks!" Zara exclaimed. "If Jacob's really dead, I'll have to try out for *Lockers* and fix everything," she whispered back.

"Um, hi," I said softly, trying to remind Zara I exist.

"Oh, whoops," Zara whispered. "Spoiler alert."

Air gave me an apologetic look. But Zara turned her back to me again. "Do you want to come over Sunday to watch the next episode together?"

Air nodded. "Sure. And Sonali too, right?"

"Of course," Zara said. "Except you have family movie night, right? You can come over another time. Just don't get too far behind or we'll have nothing to talk about," Zara whisper-giggled.

I tried to watch Xiomara act out "irritated" while stomping, but my attention kept going right back to Zara and Air, feeling like the words on my shirt were less of a movie quote and more like something I should just come out and ask Zara about Air: *She's your best friend, ya?*

My shoulders and back felt heavy. The soundtrack grew desperate as more questions popped into my mind for Zara: *Do you like hanging out with her more than me? Are your inside jokes funnier? Do you get along better than us?*

"Sonali?" Ms. Lin called me up, breaking me from my spell.

I walked onstage, reached into the jar, feeling my hand get

hot and humid inside it as I picked out a scrap of paper and read it through the haze of the green glass. I glanced at Zara and Air, deep in whisper-conversation, not even looking my way and forced my feelings down.

The background music started slowly, full of melancholy. It was perfect for the word I had picked: sad.

Before I knew what was happening, the magic made me look into the jar like it contained lost memories of my friendship with Zara. Like every scrap was a sleepover or a movie we had seen together or a twin grape Popsicle we had split apart after an afternoon on her slip and slide. My eyes were shiny and my eyebrows turned diagonal, like Madhuri's when she lip-synched through a sad song on-screen, like in the image from my web search.

"It's getting clear to me," I sang to the see-through jar, my voice quivering as an indoor breeze blew my hair back dramatically and my eyelashes grew thick, blocking half my view.

How could this be happening when no one had mentioned my parents?

Before I could even come up with a reason, the Bollywooditis made me grab the jar and put it on my head like I was gathering water from a well. I walked with graceful, purposeful steps that felt like I was carving into something deep.

Zara's eyes were now locked on me, as I swung the jar. "*Clearer than a jar. Whether I'm near or whether I'm far. I'm not needed.*" Cringe. I was singing about Zara, just like she had wondered all those weeks ago at the field trip. Was she going to be mad? Or would she finally understand what a bad friend she was being?

I twirled around the tree, the wind growing stronger around me. "*I'm not needed. I'm not needed. I'm not needed.*" Purple flowers began to fall from the tree like in Hindi movies, shimmering as they showered me, like the tears dripping down from my dramatically pained eyes. "*I'm a shirt that's been forgotten. I'm a streaming service that's been canceled. Permanently off. I'm being expelled from her life, like I'm just something you cough.*"

The lyrics were revealing all my thoughts to Zara, but I was almost glad. Since she couldn't tell what I was thinking without talking like true best friends anymore, it was obvious Zara needed it spelled out for her, or sung to her, in this case. I reached my arm out as the flowers danced in the air around me.

"*But what she doesn't know is, I need us to be together. We have to make it through this stormy weather. Because everything is coming apart. Nothing's how it was in the start. The only split I can stand is twin grape Popsicles for sharing. Not a friend who's no longer caring. Completely alone despite all the staring."*

I dropped to my knees, stray flowers drizzling on me as I stared up at the ceiling, my voice trembling so much, it was barely audible. "*Clearer than a jar. Whether I'm near or whether I'm far.*" I hugged the jar to my chest. "*It's clearer . . . than . . . a jar.*"

The breeze stopped and a slow clap began, courtesy of Ms. Lin. "Brava!" she shouted.

The rest of the class clapped along, except for Zara, who just stared at me with cold eyes.

CHAPTER 26

I rushed out of class as soon as it was over, feeling sweaty and embarrassed, eager not to see anyone, but Zara was right behind me, a couple of tears falling down her face.

"I gave that performance my all so Ms. Lin would realize my potential and let me try out. And then you go and upstage me with an even bigger number when you're not supposed to do disruptive solos in school? Have you ever seen back-to-back songs in a Hindi movie? No. The only time that happens is in a competition."

"That's not what that was," I said, fuming over what a bad friend Zara was. A gust of magical indoor wind twirled around me, throwing my hair back like a fiery heroine giving a speech in a feminist movie.

"No? Then what was it? There's a time and a place for singing and dancing. Everyone knows that."

"I don't!" I said, louder than I had intended. "I don't know these rules because, like I keep telling you, this is not how the world used to be."

"And like I keep asking you, then what changed it?"

"My parents!" I shouted. I gasped. What had I just done?

"What?" Zara cocked her head, unsure. "What did they do?"

I opened my mouth and almost let it all come gushing out, about the fighting and the nesting and still fighting after nesting. Maybe it would be easier. Like how my lyrics forced Zara to deal with what a horrid friend she was. Dad was always all about being truthful. But how truthful was hiding parts of your life? That wasn't really being honest, was it? Unlike with my Bollywooditis flare-ups, I was in control here, so I shut my mouth and just shook my head. I felt a hot rush of frustration as the hall linoleum began to transform into the checkerboard floor from the drama room.

Zara scoffed, not noticing the transformation. "That's what I thought. You called me a friend who is no longer caring back there."

I kind of wanted to tell her I meant it, but Zara kept going.

"And don't bother saying it because I already know your line: you don't control what you say. But somehow the rest of us do.

Right. Well, you can tell whoever is in charge of those lyrics that I'm not a friend who is no longer caring. I care a lot. But anytime I ask you about stuff, you shut me out or lie or make up excuses or bizarre stories about Bollywoodtosis."

"Bollywooditis," I said softly.

"You keep avoiding what caused it. What does it have to do with your parents? All it looks like to me is that you're trying to mess up my chances at showing Ms. Lin I can act. Or you're trying to impress Air. Or embarrass me in front of her, or—"

"You're not a good friend," I blurted out. I gasped, quickly throwing my hand to my mouth, but it was too late. The wind around my hair suddenly stopped.

"What?"

I knew I wanted to keep my mask on, keep that wall up, but the wall suddenly felt like it was cracking. "You're right. I was singing about you. Because all you care about is Air. And acting. And so what if I have secrets? Not everything is for you to know," I muttered. "But instead of considering that, you think I'd try to break up your friendship with Air? Trust me. I've had enough breakups."

Zara frowned. "What does that mean?"

"Nothing." I looked at my feet as the wind began to pick up again.

Zara shook her head. "Of course." Zara's face was turning pink, and her eyes were getting as shiny as Ronak's. "It's always *nothing*. But here's something for you. You didn't even mention all the times our soundtracks combined and the music sounded awful."

I scowled. That wasn't fair. Zara hadn't mentioned it either. Besides, wasn't it rude to mention what's going on in other people's background music?

"You're so closed off. You hide everything from me because you're jealous of Air." Zara nodded, like she was piecing together a puzzle. "Yeah. You're jealous of our friendship. You're even jealous of the new friends I'll make if Ms. Lin lets me audition. But you won't talk about it. Maybe this really is our interval."

An interval was a dramatic midpoint, when the film would go to freeze-frame and INTERVAL would pop up in huge letters across the screen. If you were in the theater, this was when you could pee or buy popcorn. It was fun for the audience, but for the characters in the movie, it wasn't usually a good place in their lives.

"What does that mean?" I asked. "You want a break from me?"

"It means I want to know what's really bugging you instead of hearing stories about classroom walls being magically painted. I want to know the truth, or else, yeah, we do need a break."

It felt like my feet were sinking. "How can you even think that," I cried, my voice cracking. Why was everyone leaving?

How much more splitting was I supposed to take?

"You want to go through everything alone, but you don't have to. Just tell me what it's about," Zara said tearfully. "Or we don't have a real friendship, and I'll always wonder if I can trust you."

Just then Air neared us and so did Ms. Lin. "Amazing work today, girls." Ms. Lin whispered to me, "And I hope you didn't run out because you felt embarrassed. That was great participation. Keep it up and your grade's going to go right back up, kiddo." Ms. Lin turned to Zara, who still looked angry. "Zara, you girls have convinced me. I'm opening up the auditions to all grades."

Zara beamed, suddenly getting that twinkle back in her eyes.

"I'll tweet the audition details. And you both should try out," Ms. Lin added with a smile as she headed back to the classroom.

Just like that, Zara's smile vanished. I guess this tweet wasn't going to lead to any peace, the way the Indian and Pakistani prime ministers' tweets could. "Congrats. Part of your plan worked. Maybe. How would I know, since you can't tell the truth about anything?" Zara glared.

I fumed inside but bottled all my words up so I wouldn't end up screaming at the top of my lungs in school.

"Good-bye." Suddenly Zara froze, the anger stuck on her face, burning in her eyes.

I tried to say something, but I couldn't move. And it wasn't just because I felt petrified that one little secret was destroying not only my family but my friendship, too. It was because I was as frozen as Zara, as gigantic white letters began to pop up over us. I tried to scream but nothing worked. And then a massive letter *A* unexpectedly rested on the top of my shoulders.

I gritted my teeth and squeezed out from under the *A*. I fell to the ground, exhausted, crawled forward a foot, and stood back up, turning around. The white letters spelled "Interval."

I looked at Zara. The letter *N* was in front of her face. Suddenly my anger dissipated. I didn't want to lose Zara because I had put a wall up between us, almost like Dad had done with Mom. I had to break it down a little, but how could I do that without betraying my dad, who wouldn't want people to know about him and Mom? I ran toward the letter and shoved it as hard as I could, until the *N* fell to the ground and shattered, causing all the other letters to self-destruct with it, and everyone in the halls began to move again.

I turned to Zara with a hopeful look, but I was too late. She grabbed Air's elbow like they were grape Popsicles no one could split apart and walked down the hall, far away from me.

CHAPTER 27

Zara gave me the silent treatment for the rest of the week. She would show up for our drive, brushing by me to get into the bajillion-dollar car, and slam the door shut. She barely even looked my way in drama, our only class together. And instead of getting a break from feeling miserable on the weekend, Dad came over early Sunday for his week and made me practice math problems. It was hard to concentrate on algebra with everything going on with Zara. How could I solve for *X* when I couldn't even solve this weird issue in our friendship?

The afternoon of the math test, I walked across the school atrium, full of indoor fig trees that reached for the skylights above, and headed past the drama room, when I almost collided with Zara. She was exiting with a script in her hand.

I gasped. "You got the part?"

"I'll tell you as much as you tell me: nothing." Zara scowled as she walked past me.

That wasn't true. I told her about Bollywooditis. And I told her she was right about my lyrics accurately reflecting my feelings in my last song and that I agreed with them: she was a bad friend. How much more did she need me to tell her? What would she gain by knowing about Avni Foi's cancer or my parents?

I entered the classroom and plopped down at my desk. She was clearly the fake one in our friendship. Just hanging out with me until someone better came along.

My background music beat fast and furious. I fumed as Mrs. Kulkarni began to pass out the tests. I didn't care that I was about to have a full-blown Bollywooditis song in front of my math class. My classmates' stares weren't like the ones from my poster-board presentation. They were almost encouraging. I wasn't afraid to do another number. I was ticked off and I didn't care who saw it.

Besides, Zara and Air weren't in this class. And neither was Ms. Lin. It would prove to Zara I wasn't trying to come between her and Air or steal her role in the play she was so obsessed about.

The music got faster. The magic made me tap my pencil

rhythmically to the beat. Winnie, chewing her pencil, glared at me and sighed dramatically.

I frowned right back at her, my temper rising as quickly as the thoughts racing through my head. *Oh, Winnie. Do you want to see drama*? She was in luck. Try as I might to hide them, my emotions were intense, and I was about to bring the real, live traveling Bollywood show to the classroom.

Tap-tap-tap. Tap-tap-tap. The Bollywooditis made me smile at the pencil like it was magic as the truly magical indoor wind swirled around my stray hair.

"*You think this is hard*?" I sang to the beat of my pencil as the classroom immediately changed into a glossy version of a classroom in one of the nonrealistic school sets in a nonrealistic movie. The floor turned checkerboard, the walls, bright purple.

Mrs. Kulkarni looked up at me from her desk. "Sonali? Do you have a question?"

"*You think this is hard*?" I sang again. So much for hiding things from Mrs. Kulkarni like Dad wanted. "*You think this test is hard*?" I sang louder, as a breeze swished through the pages of my test and caused them to fly away like feathers in the wind. Another breeze grabbed everyone else's tests, making them float away in a loop before falling to the side of the room like I was in the Aamir Khan movie or any of the countless Hindi movie songs disrupting a classroom.

Everyone gasped, and Mrs. Kulkarni scrambled toward the fallen tests, like a teacher who was being outwitted in a movie.

As my classmates got up to help her, I stood on my desk. "*Life is much harder than algebra.*"

"Sonali!" Mrs. Kulkarni shouted. "Get down from there!"

"*Parents are fighting,*" I sang, my hands forming fists as I did a weird boxing dance to the right as the desk wobbled below. "*Friends are fighting.*" I did the boxing dance to the left.

"*Solve for X and tell me Y. Tell me why this is happening,*" I sang, leaping from desk to desk as the rest of the class began to sway along.

"*Why this is happening,*" my classmates echoed, singing and dancing in unison.

Everyone was singing with me. All seventeen kids were my backup dancers and singers. "*Running two houses is not efficient,*" I sang, grateful my mom wasn't around to hear this and feel hurt, even if it was how I felt. "*Tell that to your coefficient.*"

"Coefficient," the kids echoed, while I nodded along to the lyrics I clearly agreed with.

I skipped onto Winnie's desk and shook my hips while bending my knee in a twist. *"Having two best friends is inefficient. Tell that to your coefficient!"* I sang loudly, hoping Zara could hear it down the hall.

"Get down from there, Sonali. What's gotten into you?" Mrs. Kulkarni asked as the papers began to swirl up around her like a mini cyclone.

"Oh la la," the rest of the class sang over and over again as I began to spin around like the spiraling papers.

"I may not be proficient at expressing why I'm reeling. It's not energy efficient to dwell on all the feeling. But at times it's just too much. It spills out like a question with no answer. Just problem after problem that I can't solve. I've never been good at division. What's fogging up my vision?" I wiped at the random glistening tears spilling down my cheeks.

"So much division. Dividing and dividing and dividing and . . ." I leaped to Mrs. Kulkarni's desk and slid all her papers to the ground.

". . . making a mess. I can't stand this test. And I can't stand that test. You think this is hard?"

I twirled to the ground. "*Life is much harder than al-ge-bra*!" I threw my hands to the air and the breeze suddenly went away, leaving a mess of papers on the floor and burying Mrs. Kulkarni so only her nose and mouth were visible.

"Sonali," Mrs. Kulkarni said sharply, papers blowing off her face. She sat staring, frazzled, at the mess. "To the principal's office. Now."

CHAPTER 28

I sat before Mrs. Espinoza's desk, sandwiched between Mom and Dad, who had both somehow managed to get to Oceanview in record time. The whole building had changed into a brightly decorated Bollywood version of a school as I walked through it to get to the equally gaudy principal's office with bright, eye-catching colors on the walls.

Mrs. Espinoza arranged some papers into a stack on her desk. "Sonali, there's a time and place for a song and dance. Sometimes you're at a basketball game, and it just happens naturally."

My parents nodded like what my principal was saying about singing your heart out at a sporting event was totally right.

"Sometimes you're opening a letter in the mail, and you have to sing about it," Mrs. Espinoza continued. "And of course, when someone's in love. But singing and dancing to avoid a test and disrupt class just cannot be tolerated."

"She won't do it again," Mom said, as Dad just sat there with his arms crossed. "Unless the circumstances are appropriate, of course," she added.

"It is really uncharacteristic of her," Mrs. Espinoza said. "She never struck me as the solo type."

"There's a reason for it," Mom started.

"Falguni," Dad said, suddenly uncrossing his arms.

"It's not a secret," she said sharply, before turning to Mrs. Espinoza. "We're in the middle of a separation. And I think it's having a bigger effect on Sonali than we thought."

The background music reached a crescendo. I was annoyed Mom was telling my principal all of this, but also kind of hopeful that it would make Mrs. Espinoza feel bad and she would go easy on me.

"Does she have someone to talk to?" Mrs. Espinoza asked sympathetically.

"We're always here," Mom replied.

"Someone outside of the home perhaps? The school counselor can—"

"That's okay," I interjected. "I don't want to talk about it. I'm fine. Really. The test was hard and I just . . . I overreacted."

Anxious tears suddenly rushed to my eyes. I'd never felt this emotional at school before. Was Bollywooditis making me melodramatic? "I'm sorry. Do I have detention?"

"You know we don't believe in that at this school, Sonali. But you will have to take accountability for your actions and write Mrs. Kulkarni and your class an apology letter. And you do need to go home today to consider your actions and their effects and think of better reactions the next time a test seems overwhelming."

"I will," I said, standing up as my parents thanked the principal.

We were headed to the door when Mrs. Espinoza called out after me. "Oh, and Sonali?"

I turned.

"There are lots of people here for you, when you are ready to talk about what you're going through, or sing about it, okay?"

I walked out of school with my parents, who were looking equal parts embarrassed and angry, just like when I had given my family room TED Talk. It looked like they were finally in agreement on something, and that was the fact that I was in serious trouble. I wanted to tell them it was hard to concentrate on school when your whole world was changing and no one believed you so you had to bottle it all up and keep everything inside. I wanted to, but as usual, I just kept my mouth shut. What was the point in bringing up something no one would believe anyway?

"You failed the quiz and now this test," Dad said softly, which meant he was extra mad.

Dramatic music suddenly played to our side. A man in a tweed jacket and khakis was dancing on top of his car. *"No paper airplanes. No spitballs,"* he sang. I stared with my mouth open, but Mom and Dad just gave him a polite smile and kept walking as he continued to sing. *"I'm the new substitute teacher in these halls. . ."*

I had never actually witnessed someone else's solo. The magic was getting so powerful, it was a little unnerving.

"And your grade has dropped," Dad continued, his voice sinking to a whisper when Ms. Lin passed us in the parking lot, carrying a box overflowing with masks and wigs. "Ms. Lin wrote us that your participation points are low, other than the one time you did a solo."

I rolled a loose wad of parking lot tar around with my shoe. Didn't Dad think solos were ridiculous? I guess he liked them when they improved your grade.

"She wants to make sure you understand how much of a role participation has on your grade and that you're taking the midterm monologue seriously. Your science test grade was lower than it was last semester too. I can't believe you're just slipping up like this. You've never been grounded before, but I think we may have to. No TV and no hanging out with friends for the next two weeks," Dad added sternly.

I nodded. Without TeeVee, there was nothing I wanted to watch anyway. And thanks to our fight, Zara didn't want to hang out with me. My first time being grounded was going to be pretty much like any day this week.

"You can use the extra time to study, write that monologue, and get your grades up," Dad continued.

Mom put her arm around my shoulder. "Do you want to talk to someone, like Mrs. Espinoza said?"

I shook her hand off. "No."

"Then will you talk to us? To me?" she asked.

I kicked a stray pebble in the parking lot.

"I know circumstances at home are tough, Sonali," Mom said. "You always look so unbothered by it. But is that really how you feel deep down?"

I shrugged. "Yeah. I'm fine."

"See? I told you she can handle it," Dad told Mom. "She's strong like me. *And* she can handle tough news."

"Kirit," Mom started, but Dad glanced at me.

"Your mom has been taking extra calls when she's at the apartment," he said.

"Okay," I said, not understanding why Mom working extra hours at the hospital when she wasn't with us was bad news.

"No, it's not okay. We can't afford tuition along with running two households like this much longer," Dad said, unlocking his car. "Your mom shouldn't work extra hours to pay for your tuition if you don't do well at school." He opened the door for me.

"Kirit," Mom said again. "Go easy on her. She has a lot going on in her life right now."

Mom didn't know the half of it.

"Because of your decisions. The problem is we're always too easy on her," Dad said softly. "I'm sorry, Sonali, but you have until midterms to change your grades or else we'll have to make changes. Samji?"

I nodded. I understood. First the Bollywooditis. Then losing *Lockers*. Then the fight with Zara. Now possibly having to switch schools. Because of Mom and Dad's decision to separate, I was being punished yet again. Detention sounded one hundred times better than this.

CHAPTER 29

The rest of the week I had to spend every morning getting the cold shoulder from Zara in our car pool and every evening after virtual dance practice studying math with Dad. It was torture and I still didn't quite understand everything he was saying. I guess I should have just been thankful he wasn't singing the math lesson to me.

When Dad finally gave me a break from simultaneous equations to go help Ronak with his homework, I rushed through my house, which was now entirely Bollywood, with walls the colors of mangos and statues everywhere, and went to my room.

I put my math book on my desk and knocked into the pile of notebooks. I reached for my brainstorming notebook to try to figure out what the grand finale could possibly be, but the notebook's spiral was latched on to the faded green notebook from Dada. I pulled the dusty old notebook out and freed it from the metal. I went to put it back in its spot, but I could smell the faintest trace of Dada's sandalwood soap on it.

I opened it up and inhaled deeply, my eyes closed. I could almost picture Dada sitting right next to me, making me laugh when my parents got into a long argument about something downstairs. I hugged the book and felt my chest tighten as a slow version of one of Dada's favorite bhajans played in a flute solo on my score. He used to sing that prayer song to Avni Foi every night when she was sick, as she slept.

I quickly put the notebook down before I started crying from the memory. And then I froze. It had opened up to the page I had doodled on after Dada died. I saw all the "I'm sad"s after that. I turned the page, looking at a list I had written about everything I missed about Dada, from his laugh to the smell of his soap to all the movie trivia he taught me. I ran my finger over a spot where my teardrops had waterlogged the page, leading to a permanent, wrinkly divot. Before more tears fell now, I quickly nestled the notebook back into the leaning tower of notebooks.

I shook my hands, trying to shake the sadness, and grabbed my planner. I knew what would make me momentarily happy. I flipped to today's date and x'd off "study math." I looked at the dozens of "study math"s written across the days by Dad, and suddenly got an idea.

In one of the old Hindi movies Dada and I used to watch, the heroine crossed off days on a calendar, and over the course of a song, the month passes by. If my Bollywooditis could make my school and home look like a Hindi movie, maybe it could be powerful enough to make time pass in a movie montage.

I know I had decided to give up on finding a solution, but I had to give this idea a shot. So I grabbed a red marker and willed my Bollywooditis to come on as I began crossing off days in my planner while humming. I tried to make myself emotional, almost grabbing Dada's notebook, but I didn't want to look inside it again. I had crossed my way through March, but there was no change in the soundtrack, no magical wind, nothing. That meant no song was starting. And without the help of the magic, the days weren't going to pass any quicker than normal. I'd give myself an A for effort, since I definitely wasn't going to get an A in math, but as far as I could tell, my Bollywooditis wasn't here to help me.

It was here to ruin my life.

CHAPTER 30

The next day I entered the computer lab calmly, hiding how worried I felt, masking my worry. Davuth was dancing around his computer as Air, Mr. Raven, and the rest of the class typed to the beat and hummed in the background. Davuth spread his arms wide and threw his head back in a classic Shah Rukh Khan pose. "*Space bar. Shift key. Listen to me! I've got no hesitation as I make my presentation. My PowerPoint . . . is on point!*"

Mr. Raven high-fived Davuth. "That's the spirit!" Mr. Raven exclaimed. "I'm glad you're so confident in your PowerPoint presentation, Davuth. Now, let's take our seats. You've got one more minute before it's time to start coding," he added.

I headed down the aisle, sitting next to Davuth, who was still out of breath from his little number. Beside me, Air opened the coding assignment Mr. Raven had written on the whiteboard.

I started choosing commands to solve the questions Mr. Raven had given us, trying to code a little girl out of a room full of people turning into monsters from glowing stars an evil wizard was throwing. But I kept picking the wrong arrow keys, and the girl kept getting overwhelmed with the magic.

"Darn it," I muttered as the little computer girl grew fur on her head.

Air looked at my screen as the bell rang. "Everything okay?"

I took a breath. "Yeah. Everything is fine."

"Are you still grounded because of what you did in math?"

I nodded. "And I had to write an apology, and we all have to retake the test."

"Why didn't you just sing before class started, like Davuth just did?" Air asked, coding her girl out of the magic spell on her screen. "Was it because of the film magic?"

"Filmi," I said softly. Zara had told her. She had told Air when I specifically asked her not to tell anyone about it. She couldn't help but blab since she loved the sound of her own voice so much. And she wondered why I didn't open up to her. I paused and then slowly explained. "It's a Hinglish word. Half Hindi, half English."

Air nodded. "So, is it true?"

"What?" I asked her.

"That none of this is normal? Singing, expressing ourselves, the bright colors, none of it?"

What else had Zara told her? I nodded at Air.

"So, in the real world everything is dull and no one sings what they're feeling or expresses themselves?" Air asked.

I sighed, getting more and more annoyed at Zara for telling. And other kids were turning my way every now and then, trying to hear what she was saying. I recognized those expressions, like the kids couldn't look away but they also felt bad for me.

"How can I help?" Air asked, turning from my screen to look at me.

"What?" My fingers slipped off the keyboard.

Air shrugged. "I mean, I love singing and dancing and these colors. They're a part of my life and always have been. But I don't want you to feel bad. So how can I help you feel better about all of it?"

I blinked hard at her question, thinking about the notebook that had somehow turned into a journal when I was sad about Dada's death. I remembered how hard I had cried when I had written that list of things I would miss about Dada. I remembered how when I wrote about his guitar and how he had taught himself to play Hindi movie songs on it, I had really broken down and showered the page with my tears. I twisted my lips, suddenly remembering something else. I remembered how after I had written it all down, after I had finally expressed myself, even if it was just to a piece of paper, that heavy feeling weighing my heart down felt ever so slightly lighter.

I wondered if this is why Mom told Revati Auntie about Avni Foi being sick or Beejal Foi about the separation. Maybe she needed someone to help take the weight of it all off her shoulders. Maybe I needed someone to help me shoulder the burden too. But how would I just come out and start saying something to my mom, Dad, Ronak, Avni Foi, or to anyone after all these years of convincing everyone I was just fine?

"Maybe like a singing-free zone or something? Would that help?" Air suggested.

I gave her a small smile. I could see why Zara liked her so much. "I'm not sure," I said, wishing that a singing-free zone would make my Bollywooditis stop but knowing it wouldn't. "But if I think of something, I'll let you know," I quickly added, so Air wouldn't think I was being mean. "And maybe one day, when things get better, you, me, and Zara can hang out. She's been pretty quiet on our drive to school in the mornings," I said, trying to see just how much Zara had told Air about our fight, since she'd told Air all about my Bollywooditis.

"She's been really busy with practice," Air replied. "And she has dress rehearsal coming up. I'm sure once things calm down, she'll be back to her old self." Air stared at her screen. "Did I tell you I talked to my parents about how upset I was they made me take drama instead of mock market?"

I shook my head. "What did they say? Were they mad?"

"They actually felt bad," Air replied. "Can you believe that? I didn't even have to sing it to them. I just said it and they felt awful. My mom even found a tutor who had taught mock market before. She's going to teach me once a week so it will kind of be like I got to take the class."

"That's awesome," I said, feeling genuinely happy for the first time in a long while. "How did you convince them to do that?"

Air shrugged. "I just thought about what you said and decided to be honest about everything I was feeling." She clicked the mouse a few times, coding away. "I actually started crying when I told them how mad and sad I was about missing my only chance at taking the class. I think that's what did it. That's when they realized just how much it meant to me."

"I'm glad things worked out." I smiled, turning back to my screen and watching as the computerized kid I had neglected was overrun with glowing stars, the magic turning her into a monster.

CHAPTER 31

On Sunday afternoon, as Dad wrote practice math questions on the back of junk mail for me to solve at the flashy kitchen island, and Ronak enjoyed filling in a peacock paint-by-number canvas at the table, the doorbell rang.

"Is Mom early?" Ronak asked, quickly dropping his paint-brush to run to the door.

"She has the key. Why would she ring the bell?" I called after him as I heard the door open and the musty smell of the thick, humid air outside entered the hall.

My aunt stepped in with a large round Pyrex container full of food and the usual beaming smile on her face.

"Avni Foi!" I grinned, running to give her a hug while avoid-ing getting hit by the Pyrex in her hands.

"Guess where we went to dinner last night?" Avni Foi asked, stepping out of her shoes and walking us to the kitchen, where I had abandoned Dad and the math problems.

"A really good restaurant?" I asked, looking at Dad and his skunk wig, trying to remind him I hadn't eaten at a restaurant in ages, thanks to him and his rules.

"Nope," she replied, lifting the blue lid off the glass container.

The smell of daal dhokli, a lentil soup with squares of flattened whole wheat dough in it that I always found slimy but Ronak loved, filled the kitchen.

"You went to Ramila Auntie's and Pankaj Uncle's?" Dad asked, inhaling the aroma with a smile.

Avni Foi nodded. "She gave me the leftovers and I had to bring you some." Avni Foi washed her hands and opened the dark-purple cabinet door where our tiny stainless-steel bowls were. "Is Falguni here?"

Dad shook his head. Avni Foi pulled out three bowls.

"No thanks," I said, trying not to scrunch my nose up at the smell that everyone else loved. I may have been in the minority, but I'd rather do math than eat daal dhokli.

"Your loss," Avni Foi said, winking at me as she put my bowl back. She grabbed a small pot and poured the daal dhokli into it, simmering it on low on the stove to heat it up.

"I can't believe you all like this," I laughed, holding my breath as Avni Foi stirred the food slowly.

"I can't believe you don't," Ronak retorted, licking his lips in anticipation of the meal.

Avni Foi spooned the daal dhokli into the bowls. "You know, when I was going through chemo and nothing tasted good to me, this was the only thing I craved."

I looked at Avni Foi's twisted lips and furrowed brows. It was like she was debating whether or not she should even say what she was already saying. She didn't talk about her cancer very often, and Dad could hardly even say the word "cancer" after she got sick.

"Did you eat it?" Ronak asked.

Avni Foi shook her head, handing him his bowl. "I didn't want just anyone's daal dhokli. I wanted Pankaj Uncle's. No one makes it like he does."

Dad cleared his throat as he took his bowl from my aunt.

"So why didn't you just ask him to make it for you?" Ronak asked, taking a gross, loud, slurpy bite.

Avni Foi handed Dad a spoon and their eyes locked for an instant before Dad quickly looked down and began to stir his food.

"Pankaj Dada didn't know Avni Foi . . . was sick. We didn't want to reach out to him and Ramila Dadi during that time and involve them," Dad replied, using the terms for "grandfather" and "grandmother," even though they weren't really our grandparents but that's just what we called anyone from Dada's generation.

I nodded. Of course we didn't tell the whole world. Dad and Dada didn't want everyone gossiping about Avni Foi and how sick she was. Dad didn't want anyone to know things weren't perfect. I wasn't sure why. Maybe he just wanted to keep up appearances like he had since that poster-board moment, always stopping his bickering with Mom at parties so everyone would assume my presentation was just some childish nonsense instead of the truth. Dad had never really explained why he didn't tell anyone. It was just the way things were.

Avni Foi sat on the stool next to Dad. She twiddled her fingers. She squeezed her hands. She opened her mouth to say something and then closed it. She frowned. And then she sighed. "We should have," she said softly, putting her hand on Dad's.

I watched his Adam's apple go up and down as he swallowed hard, even though he had no food in his mouth. He turned to her.

Avni Foi nodded and then exhaled loudly, like she was tired of holding everything in. "I was so hungry. I was so full. I was so nauseous. I was so sick. I was so weak, and scared, and mad, and in pain, and lonely, and every awful feeling you could imagine."

I watched Avni Foi pour her heart out, putting everything out there like it was that easy to just share something you had buried deep down for a long time.

"I told you I was craving this. It was the one thing I wanted, and you and Bapuji wouldn't listen," she said, her voice cracking. "We should have told them, Kirit bhai. We should have told them. . . ." Avni Foi blinked back some tears, but Dad just pulled his hand out from under hers and took a bite of his food.

This obviously was about more than daal dhokli, but Dad seemed to have no interest in addressing it. Like all that work Avni Foi had just put into expressing herself was for nothing. But a part of me wanted Dad to address it. I remembered how awful she felt during chemo and her surgeries. Sure, Dad thought he was doing what was best for her, keeping her safe and protected while pretending everything was fine to the outside world. I thought it was the right thing to do then too, and lots of people in our community kept bad or tough things quiet, so it wasn't abnormal. But looking at Avni Foi's face, and thinking about Air and her parents, or Mom and Revati Auntie, I started to think maybe it wasn't the best thing to do. Maybe all it did was make my aunt get hurt.

"That was really good, Avni Foi," Ronak said, walking past her to put his bowl in the sink. "Thanks for bringing it," he added, trying extra hard to be sweet and make my aunt feel better.

Avni Foi got up from the counter and squeezed Ronak's chin while making a kissing noise. "Rony-Pony. You always know just what to say."

Ronak beamed. "Do you want to help me do my paint-by-number?"

"I'd love to!" Avni Foi said, putting on a smile like it was a Halloween costume concealing the truth and heading over to the kitchen table to Ronak's masterpiece.

A low rumbling thunder announced itself outside. I glanced at the window behind Dad, at the quickly darkening sky.

Dad didn't bother turning back to look. He was too busy staring at his daal dhokli, his eyes looking heavy and gloomy, like a rain cloud about to burst.

Only, it couldn't.

CHAPTER 32

With the weeks of dreary February rain finally over, I was hoping the crisp March air would bring along with it an end to the downpour of bad luck I was having. While Ronak was at his after-school art class, I was driving through Westwood with Mom, who was craning her neck in every direction, her knuckles white on the steering wheel.

"Why are there no pull-in spots left?" she asked, taking a sharp turn at one of the movie theaters in our neighborhood that hosted red-carpet premieres every month.

I held on to the handle above the door for the turn, the tabla beat racing on my soundtrack. "Mom!"

"Sorry. It's just so busy here today. Usually I can find a spot I can just pull into." She made a sudden left turn again. "We'll just have to park at the structure and buy something at the grocery store to get our parking ticket validated."

"So we have to go to the grocery store after getting groceries at the farmers' market so parking is free?"

"Yeah. Why not?" Mom asked, pulling into the dark structure.

"Maybe you can ask someone to teach you how to parallel park?" I offered, softly, unsure how my mom would take the suggestion. I was trying to be less harsh on her, less harsh on Ronak, after seeing how sad Avni Foi was the other day. Maybe their way of thinking was better than what Dad and I were doing. Like we both bottled things up so much, when the emotions eventually came out, they were super strong. And for one of us, they caused filmi magic to grow exponentially stronger.

"Maybe," Mom said with a forced smile as she got out.

We walked along the fig-tree-lined streets until we came to a row of colorful canopies at the farmers' market that shut down a corner of Westwood each week. A man by a juice stand was hammering a sign into a wooden beam above coconuts and pineapples that said, FRESH COCONUT WATER.

Mom paused. "Naliyer nu pani joiye chhe?"

I nodded, taking the green coconut with a blue-and-white-striped paper straw and sipping on the cool coconut water inside.

"You know, before I moved here in eighth grade, back in India, Ba would shred coconut into our pauva for breakfast," Mom said, talking about her mom.

I nodded, inhaling the smell of citrus as we walked past a table full of oranges, grapefruits, and limes.

"I used to help her break them open on the back patio, under the cool breeze from the wind blowing through the wet clothes hanging to dry on the lines above us."

Mom picked out a bunch of avocados, my dad's favorite. I thought about how he would make guacamole at home whenever we got take-out enchiladas, because it was more cost effective but also because he said no one could make guacamole like him. I thought about how Dad would have parallel parked with ease. About how different life really was with my parents apart.

"We would hit those coconuts onto a grinding stone to split them open, and when I was around your age, I smashed my finger by accident, and half my nail came off."

I began to feel a lump in my throat as Mom paid the farmer for the avocados Dad wouldn't be using. I swallowed it down fast, in no mood to do a farmers' market solo, just as the man hit the nail on his sign one last time with a hammer.

Suddenly the ground started to shake and ripple.

"Whoa!" I shouted, grabbing on to Mom's sleeve and almost falling forward. "Do you feel that? Is it an earthquake?"

Mom, who just stood there like it was no big deal, raised a confused eyebrow at me as everything became fluid like water was slushing across my eyesight. "Earthquake? Don't be silly; it's a flashback."

Apparently, I hadn't done a good job of shoving down those sad feelings about Dad.

Suddenly, everything in front of me and Mom changed from the streets of Westwood to the porch of a wraparound white bungalow. In India. Not only that, the image was yellowed and faded, like a really old movie.

Sad instrumental music began to play as I noticed a crying young girl in a paisley-patterned, cotton chaniyo choli, sitting cross-legged on the porch in front of a woman in a white sari. I recognized the woman. It was my grandmother. My mom's mom. That meant the little girl sitting before her, holding her bloody, nail-less finger, was my mom when she was younger.

"Ba! My nail!" she cried melodramatically, although I was pretty sure I'd be wailing like that too if I knocked half my nail off in a coconut-splitting accident.

My dadi shook her head, blinking away tears as she stared almost right at me. A whiny super old Hindi-music-style version of Mom's theme swelled from the soundtrack as she held her daughter's face. "You listen to me, you hear?" she asked loudly, like a very bad actor. "You'll miss out on much more in life than hitting a coconut if you let your fear rule you!" The music grew louder as Dadi's eyes grew resolute. "Don't let it win! Pick up that coconut."

Little girl Mom shook her head, crying. "I can't . . . I'm . . . so . . . scared!"

Dadi held another brown coconut and waved it around in a way that seemed seriously reckless and way too close to young Mom's head. "Pick it up, Falguni! You can do it! I believe in you! I. Believe. In. You."

The background score reached its crescendo as young Mom fought through the pain, groaning, sweating, crying, as she reached for the coconut with all her effort. She roared as she hit the coconut on the stone grinding tool, breaking it open triumphantly.

And just like that everything started to wiggle again. The bungalow and the porch and my young mother and suddenly-alive grandmother faded away like a distant memory, and everything in front of me was once again the streets of Westwood.

I felt my stomach go sideways from the rippling. As the undulating faded away, I swallowed down the urge to vomit. "I feel seasick."

Mom shrugged. "From what? From my memory?"

"Yeah. Just because you think this is how it's always been. It isn't true. I need time to get used to everything," I muttered, almost telling my mom more about the magic for the first time since the early days of Bollywooditis, when she thought I was singing about her marriage.

Mom put her arm around me. "I'm so glad you're finally opening up, Sonali. I want to give you all the time you need to get used to everything."

"What?" I frowned, feeling a little steadier on my feet. I took a sip of my coconut water, now that I was sure I wasn't going to narf it back up, and steadied my expression just in case I got hit with another nausea-inducing flashback. "I'm not talking about the two of you. I'm talking about the whole world shaking every time you have a memory."

Mom sighed. "It's brave to talk about feelings, Sonali. You know that, right?"

"Yeah," I replied as we walked toward a stall selling native plants, thinking about how it took a lot for Avni Foi to tell my dad what she was feeling. "And maybe you should be brave too. Like in your flashback?"

We reached the end of the street and watched as a teenager effortlessly pulled up to the spot Mom had to pass up, and parked in it.

CHAPTER 33

Back home after picking up Ronak, I was up in my room doing some last-minute cramming for the math test on Friday, and reading up on my homework for history, English, and science. I pretty much had to get above a C+ in math and all As from this point on in everything else to raise my average enough to make Dad happy, or I would have to switch schools.

Although a part of me wondered what I even was worried about missing out on, since Zara still wasn't talking to me other than an occasional shrug when I asked her a question.

I closed my math notebook and decided to be brave like Mom said, and attempt to write my monologue. I looked up at a poster of the famous old Indian western. I hadn't seen it in a while, since my parents didn't want Ronak seeing all that filmi fighting (just their own fighting). I remember how I had watched it with Dada when he was really sick in India, just a few weeks before he passed away.

I had crawled into his bed in the bungalow and snuggled up next to him as we watched the over-the-top bad guy almost defeat the good guys. Dada told me when his neighbors' kids were little and staying up way past bedtime, the neighbors used to tell them to sleep quickly or the bad guy from this movie would come get them. I laughed, telling him it was silly to be afraid of a fictional villain, especially one so exaggerated. But that night I had to sleep with the lights on because I was terrified that villain would come get me, so I guess the performance worked.

So as silly as the idea of portraying a werewolf seemed to me, I had to make it work too, no matter how many eyes were staring at me when I performed it.

I grabbed my pencil and with the soundtrack synthesizer playing tranquilly, began to scribble down a monologue: "I'm a werewolf. This is my tail."

Mom's cell phone rang in the hall, playing the peaceful flute music, and I heard her pick up. From the lack of joy in her voice, I knew she was talking to Dad and it was going to be anything but peaceful.

"Don't be ridiculous, Kirit!" Mom said loudly from the hall outside before busting out in super-fast Gujarati.

I covered my eyes like I used to when I was a little kid trying to block something out and sighed, trying to concentrate on writing the monologue. Ignoring the lump that was suddenly in my throat, I swallowed hard, put my pencil to paper again, and wrote: "I'm so furry. Howl. Howl. Howl. I love the moon."

"So what?" Mom said from outside, and my shoulders and back began to throb. "So this is supposed to be a secret forever? No friends can know. No family. We'll just hide the truth and bury everything and pretend we're happily married like we've been doing all these years? This is like Avni's cancer all over again."

I scooched my chair back, knowing I was feeling strong emotions, knowing what was next. As expected, the loud tabla beat was instant, covering up my mom's angry words, the strumming sounds of a sitar filled my room, and my hair began to blow. I caught my reflection in my darkened window. I had dramatic kajal lining my eyes like a Bharatanatyam dancer.

I spun out of my chair and began holding the pencil between my thumb and pointer, the other three fingers flickering like a furious fan to the beat.

Taandav dances were brief, instrumental pieces in old Hindi

movies with serious classical dancing. I had watched Sridevi and other actors and actresses dance out their anger, frustration, devotion, and even love through short Taandavs before and knew this number would be over soon.

Grateful no one was around to watch me dance out my frustration, I began doing classical dance steps. I guess the only good thing about doing a wordless song was no one could confront me about the lyrics, since there weren't any.

I danced rapidly to the corner of my room, my feet thundering on the floor. As the tabla rhythm got faster and louder, I spun furiously. Then I threw my hands into a modified two-finger a-okay classical dance pose, shaking them to the left and right, quickly, before a drumbeat sounded and I slammed the pencil down on my notebook triumphantly.

The sounds of my parents' argument once again filled my ears as I watched the pencil roll around uselessly on my notebook full of abandoned werewolf monologue lines.

CHAPTER 34

The next evening, after making sure I knew everything I would ever be able to know for the math test retake tomorrow (and wishing the Bollywooditis could make me as good at taking tests as it made me at singing and dancing), I sat on our back patio steps, a comforting breeze fluttering around me. I was trying to write my monologue when I saw Zara's patio door slide open. She stepped out in a teacup costume, for her role in our school's production of *Beauty and the Beast*, and not for a reenactment of our parents' favorite drink.

She didn't notice me as she danced from side to side, singing in a loud, clear voice, no signs of the nervous wavering I'd displayed when Zara tried to make me sing in public before Bollywooditis struck me.

"I'm a chipped dish but don't throw me out. We're all a little chipped inside. Some of us just show it better than others. Some of us talk about it to our mothers . . . ," Zara sang, looking like a glamorous teacup as the wind blew her hair back, and her face looked radiant, even in pain. *"Let it all out. It just takes a chip or a crack in that hard exterior to show what it is, in your interior. . . ."*

I watched her fearless performance, as she put her emotions on display for everyone in a way I never could. Maybe it was another form of bravery, like when Avni Foi told Dad about the daal dhokli, or when Mom told Revati Auntie about Avni Foi. I felt my chest sink a little, thinking about how I picked on Mom for the stuff she wasn't good at, like unclogging toilets and parallel parking, when she could show her emotions in a way I never could. We were all brave and strong in our own ways.

I felt guilty for how I treated Mom and awful that my aunt hadn't gotten the full support she could have used. I also felt annoyed that I could recognize how courageous Zara was with this performance, but she couldn't acknowledge how brave I was for not breaking down with everything going on in my life. My heart raced. I frowned and braced myself for another solo from these emotions. But I didn't sing or dance.

Instead, when the performance was finished, Zara's eyes met

mine. Magical sweeping music played all around me, and the dafli, another Indian drum, began to thump on the soundtrack. I was tired of fighting, so I shoved the feelings aside, tore a handful of weeds out of the patio garden bed, formed them into a bouquet, and raced toward Zara. But despite how hard I was trying to run, I was barely moving.

I gasped.

I was running in slow motion, like in a moving movie reunion.

I willed my feet forward, but it was like I was charging through water, or in zero gravity. I groaned, but that sound came out elongated and deep, like I was yelling in slow motion too. I pushed through, finally reaching Zara.

"Hi," I said, awkwardly, the magical wind tickling my locks.

"Hi," Zara replied.

We sounded as awkward as my parents. But Zara wasn't scowling as much as before. Maybe it was a good sign. "Is dress rehearsal tonight?" I asked.

"Why do you want to know? Or is it another secret?"

I dropped the weed bouquet and all the annoyance came rushing back. I was sick of Zara's accusations. And I didn't think she got to accuse me of anything after she blabbed to Air about things I had told her in private, even if she was lucky that Air actually wanted to help me instead of gossip about me like Zara was doing. "All you want to do is talk. Talk, talk, talk. Talk about everything," I added, realizing I was sounding like Dad again. "But maybe you talk too much. You told Air about the filmi magic. Why would you do that?" I yelled as the wind stopped flickering my hair.

Before I could figure out what caused the glitch in the magic, Zara spoke up. "If it's really true, wouldn't you want everyone to know, so everyone could work together to fix it?"

I paused. Maybe Zara was right. But my parents were so stressed from fighting all the time, I didn't want to add to their drama. And with the whole world loving their new Bollywood life, why would anyone believe me, when my best friend didn't?

Zara shook her head. "No answer. More secrets. Big surprise. Remember when I said we tell each other everything that first day in drama? I was wrong. *I* tell you everything. You keep it all inside."

I felt an invisible wall go up instantly, and the wind came back, throwing my hair back and then unraveling the bouquet on the ground. "You know I'm not the bad guy here," I said softly.

"You know, you always say 'you know' about all these things about you. But I didn't know you were afraid of snakes. I didn't know you lowered the windows because you were carsick. I thought you just liked the fresh air." Zara's voice began to rise. "And then you tell me about filmi magic and all these strange theories, but you can't tell me anything else about it but expect me to just believe you when that isn't our reality. Our reality is we sing. When we feel something, we let the whole world know. We show our emotions. Because we've been moved to do so. Literally. An internal force lets us express ourselves. That's how it has always been. If your magical condition is real, why does no one else know that? Why do we all only remember the world like this? When did it start? Why did it start? What was the big change?"

"For the millionth time, you know I don't know," I snapped, as a gazebo perfect for a romantic Bollywood dance in the rain popped up in Zara's yard, thanks to the magic. I didn't pay it any notice though. What I said was the truth. I didn't know why this started.

"See?" Zara said. "You said 'you know' again. You think I know all these things about you or all these things you're thinking, like I'm a mind reader, but I don't. I don't think I really know you at all."

My eyes began to sting a little. Was Zara right? Did I assume a lot but never tell her things? How would we have become friends in the first place if that was true? Maybe I wasn't the one putting the wall up. She was. After all, how could Zara misunderstand my intentions so badly? How could she say any of these hurtful things about me? She was my best friend. Correction, she *was* my best friend. Past tense.

Slow sitar music began to play. Our soundtracks weren't combining in disharmony this time though. This time they didn't even bother to try to come together.

My eyes narrowed at Zara. Maybe I was avoiding all the complicated feelings I was having about saving face and not showing the world your bad side and Zara not getting it when she should, but I was annoyed. "Maybe if you gave someone else a chance to talk once in a while, I wouldn't be this unsolvable mystery to you, who you ditched once you became obsessed with becoming best friends with Air."

Dishoom!

The word meant to mimic the sound effect used in physical fights in old Hindi movies, whenever someone hurt someone else, suddenly emitted from my hands.

Zara flew backward like I had punched her in a movie.

"Hey!" Zara shouted, her eyes bugging out like a bad actor's as she very dramatically pointed at me. "That hurt!"

My words hurt? "Very funny," I muttered, but quickly stopped, realizing we were fighting, and sometimes a big argument was the big moment, or the grand finale, of a movie before everything was resolved. Was this it? Was I about to have an irreversible Bollywood makeover?

Zara rubbed her heart like I had actually hurt her there. "It's not funny, and neither are you. You're just secretive and . . . and you're nothing like Air."

Dishoom!

The noise sounded again, this time from Zara, and I crumpled over, feeling excruciating pain in my gut. This wasn't the grand finale. I still remembered everything. And those memories of how Zara treated me hurt. I had had it.

"*You know* . . . ," I said on purpose, gathering myself as I got to my feet again. "I've been listening to you most of my life . . . and I'm done. Earmuffs."

I put my hands over my ears and walked away from Zara, every part of me in pain.

CHAPTER 35

Dad came over early Sunday evening for dinner. Mom had made spinach and corn shaak, rotli, and daal bhaat for dinner. She also had Ronak and me slice up some cucumbers and squeeze lime on top before sprinkling black salt on them, but the smell of the black salt mixed with citrus made me think of my lemonade song back in the early days of my Bollywooditis, and I sort of lost my appetite. How would I have even explained that song to Zara? How would I have repeated those awful lyrics I had sung? She was wrong to expect me to put the sadness I felt for the way I hurt my mom, the annoyance I felt at Dad, the anger I felt at both my parents for putting us through any of this in the first place, and the humiliation of Avni Foi witnessing everything, into words for her entertainment. I wasn't a senseless first grader anymore. I knew better now.

"I checked the portal," Dad said, sitting down at the table and ignoring Mom, thus sparing us those uncomfortable "hi"s they had been doing on Sundays. "You got a B- on your math test."

I breathed a sigh of relief, but I couldn't get over how upset I was with Zara. It felt like a tornado of emotions and I had to seek shelter. Or just stop the storm. I took a sip of water and closed my eyes for a split second, pushing the feelings down until the tornado was nothing but a little breeze.

"Great job, Sonali ben!" Ronak cheered, in between spoonfuls of his daal bhaat.

It took me a second to realize he wasn't applauding my emotional storm-fighting abilities. He was talking about my test.

"Ronak thinks that's awesome!" he added.

I frowned. The magic had struck again. Ronak was talking in the third person, like a kid in a Hindi movie who was supposed to be super cute but just came off as super annoying instead. But my parents, in their heavy makeup and skunk wig, didn't even flinch.

"Why are you talking like that?" I asked, even though I knew the answer.

"Ronak doesn't know what you're talking about," Ronak replied.

"Ronak always talks like that," Dad said, running his fingers across the white stripe in his wig. "So, let's get back to talking about you and your grade. It's better than last time for sure, but I want to see you do better on the next test. And you did well on your history project, English paper, and computer homework. But you're going to need an A on that drama midterm next week, or there will have to be some changes."

I nodded.

"Don't be so hard on her," Mom said, and I noticed a green bit of palak stuck in her front teeth.

Ronak looked at me, motioning with his eyes for me to say something about the spinach.

"You're too easy on her," Dad snapped.

"Well, soon you won't have to hear me say anything to her—"

"You have some palak in your teeth, Mom," Ronak said softly in Mom's ear.

She looked flustered and began to pick at her teeth with her tongue. "Thanks, dikra," she whispered to him.

"Since everyone's done, should we start the movie?" Ronak asked, with a flustered smile that gave away how eager he was for the fighting to stop. "Ronak thought maybe we could see a historical epic? In honor of Sonali's grade on her history project?"

"Before that, we have something to tell you," Mom said.

"Now? She still has a drama midterm to pass," Dad said, reaching for his water.

Mom frowned. "You didn't have any trouble lecturing her after we got out of the meeting with Mrs. Espinoza. There's never going to be a good time. Besides, how much longer do you want to keep this in? Or do you want to continue to bury this forever, like with Avni? I told you. We have to be open with our feelings for this to work."

"Do what you want. You always do," Dad said, midsip, so his angry words echoed in the glass.

I felt a little ill as I turned to Ronak. His eyes were getting bigger and shinier by the moment. Whatever this announcement was, it didn't sound good.

Mom put her arm around Ronak. "We love you both, and that will never change. But some of these changes we've been going through over the past few months have made it really clear that we're better apart. For each other, but more importantly, for both of you."

Dad ran his spoon around his empty bowl, trying hard not to make eye contact with Ronak or me.

"But you're already separated," Ronak said, his voice trembling as a flush of anger made its way across my cheeks.

Why were my parents doing this? But they should do this, shouldn't they? I didn't know. I felt confused and annoyed and a little alone as Mom gave Ronak's shoulders a loving squeeze.

"I know, dikra. But now . . ." Mom looked at me and reached across the table for my hand.

I slowly gave it to her.

". . . Now we've decided to divorce," Mom finished, squeezing my fingers.

Nausea crept up my throat. I swallowed hard, my stomach hurting, my back hurting, and maybe even my heart hurting.

"Dad is going to move into the apartment, and we will make sure you see both of us as much as you need. But I don't think we should do any more Bollywood movie nights together."

Ronak's lip shook. "But that's our thing! That's our happy time!"

Tears fell down Mom's cheeks. She looked at Dad. "See?" She turned to Ronak. "I told your father, our only happy time can't be when we're all silently sitting next to each other watching a movie. You and Sonali deserve better than this." She wiped her tears. "We all do."

I tried to act unsurprised by the announcement, but the tabla began to take on a fast, loud, ominous beat on my soundtrack, and I knew what was about to happen.

Dad cleared his throat. "Think of it this way, Ronak. We'll still do Hindi movie night. Just at two different times, with each parent, separately. So double the Bollywood. Won't that be fun?"

Ronak got up from the table, sobbing, and I went after him before I did a solo at the table. Double the Bollywood? No thanks. I wasn't sure I could take any more Bollywood.

CHAPTER 36

As Ronak buried his head in his pillow, sobbing, the magic made me wind up the old music box from India that Ronak kept on his bookshelf. Dada had given it to Ronak when he was a baby, and despite the fact that the song that came out of it sounded like something out of a creepy horror movie, Ronak loved it. But now, as the eerie lullaby played, Ronak cried harder.

"*Don't cry, little brother,*" I sang, although I did understand why he would want to cry after hearing my mom say she and Dad were getting a divorce. The magical Bollywooditis wind circled my hair, and the whole room began to glow in a soft focus that made everything seem childlike and sweet.

"*Don't cry about your mother.*" I crouched next to him and tweaked his nose, like I was singing to a child or a sibling in a little kid song in an old Hindi movie. The whole room suddenly looked dated, with a golden-brown tint, like a faded old film.

Ronak sniffled. "Ronak's sad. So of course Ronak is going to cry."

"Or even your father." I stood up and put my arms around him, swaying him back and forth.

"They're not worth our tears. If you have a problem, come to me. I'm all ears." I tugged Ronak's ears, thinking about all the times I had held him in his room when he was sad, when it felt like I wasn't alone, it was the two of us dealing with our parents' issues.

"And I'll tell you to get all your friends and dance and forget about your fears."

Remembering how I would read picture books to him in funny voices to make him laugh when our parents weren't getting along, to distract him like Dada had sometimes done for me, I danced around his room, grabbing all his stuffed animals, dolls, and action figures and took turns pretending each was my dancing partner.

I pointed at his carpet, where we could hear through the floorboards the muffled sounds of our parents arguing downstairs. *"Sometimes I think we're the grown-ups and they're the babies,"* I sang, wiping Ronak's tears in a way I hadn't done in years, ever since my mask had gotten so snug that I couldn't stand *my* emotions, let alone his. "*So I'm singing to you like a song from the eighties. Just because they can't stop their temper tantrums doesn't mean we should stop being kids.*"

I picked Ronak up easily thanks to the magic and swung him around. "*That doesn't mean we should stop having fun. That doesn't mean our time is done.*"

Ronak laughed as I set him down and jumped on his bed. "*That doesn't mean we can't have a magical, wonderful, oh so spectacular childhood!*"

I offered Ronak a hand and pulled him up. We both jumped on the bed as I sang. "*So forget about your tears, and let go of your fears! If you have a problem, come to me. I'm all ears.*"

I used my fingers to wiggle my ears before doing a somersault in the air, which I never could have done without the Bollywood-itis, landing on my bottom on the bed.

Ronak laughed again. "You're so weird, Sonali ben. Ronak has to admit it's funny." His smile suddenly disappeared and his eyes hardened. "But everything is going to change forever because our parents just can't grow up and get along. And there's nothing funny about that."

I shrugged, trying not to pay attention to the distant feelings of anger and resentment that were clawing at me, and focused instead on making Ronak feel better, like I used to. "Lots of kids have divorced parents."

"Ronak knows that." Ronak looked away, blinking fast. "I just . . . I can't believe this is actually happening . . . to us."

My mouth dropped. Ronak suddenly wasn't using the third person to talk about himself. But why? Was the filmi magic getting weaker? Come to think of it, hadn't the wind stopped blowing my hair dramatically the two times I fought with Zara? Didn't the magic want me to be overdramatic? But Ronak wasn't being overdramatic right now. I wanted to ask Ronak what had changed, but his lip was trembling and it just didn't seem like the time to interrupt his feelings to investigate.

"You're talking in first person again," I said hesitantly, afraid the magic would go right back to how things had been if I pressed the issue more.

"I don't know what you're getting at," Ronak replied. "All I know is I feel scared and lost. Like I don't know what tomorrow is going to be like. It's like that fill-in-the-story book you got me that one Raksha Bandhan. Do you remember it?"

I nodded, remembering the gift I gave Ronak on the holiday

celebrating the bond between brothers and sisters, back when he was in kindergarten.

"It made me feel strange, all those lines at the bottom of each unfinished story. Like all this pressure was on me to finish the story, and I didn't know the answers. That's how this feels. Where are we going to live? If Dad moves permanently to the apartment, how will we see him? It's one bedroom. Do we all sleep in one room there? Does this mean they'll never talk to each other again?"

"You ask too many questions," I said. "I'm upset too. I just don't let it ruin my day."

"Nothing ruins your day. You didn't even cry when Dada died."

A lump immediately formed in my throat, feeling heavy and hurtful.

"Sorry," Ronak quickly added. "I didn't mean that. I know you were sad."

"I *was* sad. He was like my best friend. Other than Zara. He taught me everything I know about Hindi movies."

Ronak nodded as I stood up and started putting all the toys back in their places.

"And I did cry." I hesitated and then ran across the hall to the desk in my room. I took the journal from the corner pile and brought it in to Ronak, who was in the middle of cleaning up.

He flipped through it, seeing the page where I had written "I'm sad" over and over.

"I cried every single day in the shower," I said, blinking away tears as I squeezed Ronak's cotton, handmade doll from India, which Dada had bought him when he moved back to Ahmedabad. "For months." I quickly grabbed the journal and tucked it under my arm before Ronak got to the next page with the list of what I missed about Dada, which felt too personal to share. "I just didn't want you to see it and feel even sadder."

Ronak suddenly gave me a hug, clinging to my waist like I was a balloon threatening to float away.

"It's okay," I said softly, patting his head, clearing my throat until my tears stopped before they could spill, thinking about how I used to hold him the same way when we were young, to make sure he had a happy childhood. "Everything is going to be okay," I said, although I wasn't totally convinced myself.

Ronak nodded, finally releasing his grip on me so I could breathe easier.

"Divorce is like spinach stuck in someone's teeth," I said. "It makes you uncomfortable, but you ignore it and eventually you forget about it and no one is bothered."

Ronak just looked at me.

"What?"

"You're kidding, right?" he asked.

"About spinach?"

"You don't ignore it. You bring it up. You talk about it. It doesn't make you weak to express yourself. It's as brave as it gets, like Mom always says. I mean, what kind of person wouldn't tell a friend they have food stuck in their teeth?"

I cradled the journal full of my thoughts and emotions against my chest and looked at my brother's teary eyes, knowing the answer. It was the same kind of person who was forced to make any feelings she had buried deep down come out as an over-the-top, exaggerated musical number whenever her Bollywooditis acted up. It was the same kind of person who was totally sick of feelings.

It was me.

CHAPTER 37

Zara didn't come with us to school Monday morning. It wasn't earth-shattering news. But I did feel the earth shake a little in the garage when Dad told me. It was just a small tremor, something we felt a few times a year in LA, and I normally would have grabbed Zara and screamed "bachao!" for someone to rescue me, like I was in a sexist old movie, while giggling. But Zara wasn't by my side. And she wasn't going to be. Uncle had called to say she had to be at school early from now on for the play. I didn't care that she wasn't coming with us though. I looked at the roller skates crammed in a box near our bikes. Zara might have been right about me not being open with her, but I had my reasons and she'd never understand them.

When it came time for drama class that afternoon, I took my

seat next to Air, giving her a small smile but not even bothering to make eye contact with Zara on the other side of her. Since the school makeover, Ms. Lin now wore bright-red reading glasses that she was lifting off her nose repeatedly as she looked over paperwork in the back of the room. And any time she moved the glasses, a synthesizer played a horn for comic effect, like in Hindi movies that had to use a sound effect any time something happened that was supposed to be funny.

"Can you believe *Lockers* ends this weekend?" Zara whispered, unfazed, as Ms. Lin took her place on the *X* onstage. "I hope there's another season."

"Don't you have anything better to talk about?" I muttered.

"Like what?" Zara glared at me.

"Like something that matters," I hissed back, as Air stared hard at her shoes like they were the most fascinating things in the world. I was crabby, and I didn't care that my mask was temporarily off to let Zara know it. She wanted me to express myself, didn't she? "Like the fact that Ms. Lin has a comic-relief sound effect," I muttered, even though really, at this point, the sound effect was just another instance of the magic flexing its muscle.

"That's not new for anyone living in reality," Zara said.

Ms. Lin clapped her hands before I could respond. "All right, class, this is it. Your last class to prep before your big midterm performance. For some of you, there's a lot riding on this. But no matter what, I want you to have fun." She raised her eyeglasses and the synthesizer gave a loud honk. "Becoming another character is a great way to release anything you've been holding on to, and to learn more about yourself and how you're growing and handling all that life throws your way."

I fidgeted in my seat. I may have had no clue what I was going to say in next week's midterm, but I knew there was no way pretending to be a werewolf was going to help me handle all that life was throwing my way.

That Sunday, instead of having our Hindi movie night, it was Hindi movie dance night. Parvati ben, Parshva bhai, Tejal, Sheel, Neel, and Shilpa came over to practice on our side of town for once, since Dad was busy finding and scanning pictures Avni Foi wanted for her reception slideshow next weekend.

"Did you feel the earthquake this week?" Sheel asked, stepping around the cardboard boxes Dad had put in the corner of every room for his move. "The water in our pitcher was shaking. Pretty cool."

"Ronak was scared," my brother chimed in, back to using third person.

I sighed, sad Indian flute music on my soundtrack. The little bit of hope my brother had given me when he briefly stopped talking in the third person had pretty much disappeared. There was no undoing this magic.

"Where's Falguni Kaki?" Tejal asked, as half the cousins exchanged "what were you doing during the 2.6 earthquake" stories.

Parvati ben cleared her throat loudly like a know-it-all sharing insider information with me and my brother.

Ronak looked at me. "Mom's . . ."

"At work," I said quickly, pretty sure Mom actually was doing an extra shift to cover our tuition before she came by to switch with Dad.

"Should we start?" Parvati ben asked, peeking in one of the moving boxes before giving me a sympathetic look.

I started to stretch a little, knowing I'd be dancing a solo soon, since Parvati ben seemed to somehow know just what to say or do to trigger the Bollywooditis.

"What if another earthquake happens when we're dancing at the sangeet?" Shilpa asked. "And what if it's bigger than two point six on the Richter scale? You know how the music is so loud at weddings, you feel the ground shake from the vibrations of the speakers?"

"Yeah, what if we don't know it's an earthquake and it's the Big One?" Sheel added, wondering about the big earthquake California was predicted to get at some point in the future.

"It's statistically going to happen in the next few years, so why worry about it?" Parshva bhai asked, acting like he was a seasoned earthquake pro.

"Okay, if we're done scaring ourselves, can we start the practice?" Parvati ben asked, pressing play on her phone to start the music. "There's just one week to go and this is the last time we'll see each other before the sangeet, so let's give it our all one at a time," Parvati added, shaking her hips as she began the dance. "Who wants to go first?"

Knowing I had a monologue I still needed to write if I wanted a chance at staying at my school, I raised my hand. I was kind of over the fear of everyone's eyes on me after all the solos I'd done with the magic anyway.

"You?" Parvati ben asked. "I don't want to put any more stress on you with everything that's going on. Like *everything*," she added, motioning with her eyes to my parents' wedding picture on the cabinet behind her, and then to the moving boxes.

What was she doing? Did she want to bring everyone's attention to the fact that my dad was moving out? My shoulders felt sore from the weight of this burden. Like my cousin was putting more imaginary rocks on them for me to carry. I gritted my teeth and was trying to shake the feelings off when a drum riff boomed from my soundtrack.

I knew it. I hadn't hidden those feelings fast enough. I suddenly began to jump on the floor, causing the statues to rattle. "*Is it a three-point-two? Or is it just you? Is it a two-point-three? Or is it just me?*" I sang.

My yellow top suddenly looked red for the next verse, and my cousins were suddenly in orange T-shirts and tank tops as they hummed and danced around me, in what Zara and I had coined a "quick change," when actors' clothes suddenly changed in the middle of their dances.

"*Is it the Big One?*" I sang. "*Or is it just a regular day? It's all shaky. So why worry about it? Why stress about it? Even if it's a little quaky. It's all crashing down around me.*" I nodded in agreement at the lyrics. It was all falling apart. My friendship, my parents' relationship, my world. I twirled behind the mass of my cousins and came out, my tank top now orange as theirs turned purple, in another quick change. "*Like the plate Mom broke. Like every time she and Dad spoke . . . to each other.*"

I did a cartwheel over to Parshva bhai, peeking my head out from behind him as he did a bunch of high-energy jazz hands. "*The warning signs were there. On the Richter scale.*"

My cousins and Ronak hummed and nodded behind me as I shook my hands in an interpretive earthquake dance. Why were they nodding? Why was Parvati ben giving me such a knowing look?

"*We heard the signs above,*" my cousins sang.

Were they referencing my dad yelling at me upstairs during that party in first grade?

"*About my parents' broken love,*" Ronak sang.

I was mortified. I wanted to tell him to stop before he accidentally told everyone about our parents' divorce.

"*We saw the glittery signs in your hand,*" my cousins sang, confirming they were singing about that fateful party.

Why couldn't the filmi magic erase their memory of that moment, just like it had erased their memories of a world without Bollywooditis?

"*The presentation didn't go as planned,*" Parvati ben sang, her arm around me.

I flung her arm off, worrying what else I was about to reveal to my cousins, afraid to be confronted with other memories they had from my presentation. Forget about thinking Mom was brave. It wasn't brave to show your feelings. It was horrific. I felt all the embarrassment I lived through the last time I was humiliated in front of my family. I didn't want to express myself any more in these lyrics. I wanted it to stop. I threw my arms up in the air and sang loudly, "*Quick change. I can't change if they won't change, but it's too much change all at once!*"

I shimmied over to my brother, my tank top once again yellow. "*The Big One is coming and I'm not prepared!*"

"Wow, that's some dance you're going to put on for Avni," Dad said, walking by us with a box full of pictures.

"Heck, yeah! Grand Villas, here we come!" Parvati pumped her fist, back in her normal clothes, and pulled me to the side. "I know our parents are coming to get us, but if you need to talk about what's to come with . . . your parents, call me, okay?"

I clenched my teeth, irritated at my know-it-all cousin who had no idea what it was like to have parents who didn't get along. And instantly the magic gave all my cousins makeovers, where the girls had long rippling waves and the guys all had dated mullets.

Parvati crushed all of us into a group hug, shaking us while shouting, "Earthquake!"

I forced a smile at my family. But something about what Parvati ben said wiped the smile off my face. The Grand Villas. *Grand.* Isn't that what Revati Auntie had said about the sangeet too? Sangeets were like huge musical numbers, like the kind that were sometimes big moments in Hindi movies. I would be singing and dancing there. Was the sangeet the grand finale the magic had been talking about?

In an instant, the framed pictures of our family on the armoire flashed a bright-blue light. I squinted at them. The picture of me and Ronak in life jackets with my parents on a whale-watching boat was suddenly a still of a group dance on a cruise ship in shimmering Indian clothes. The still of me in a dirt-covered UCLA T-shirt in Sequoia National Park changed into a shot of me in a mustard-yellow sari dancing around trees. Every picture was getting a Bollywood makeover.

I started to sweat. This was what the magic meant when it x'd out the BE KIND, PLEASE REWIND sticker. I wouldn't be able to rewind. I wouldn't be able to look back on my real memories. I'd just have fictional, Bollywoodized memories accessible through quaky flashbacks.

The picture frames began flickering, as if they were covered in tiny lightbulbs. Like the magic was telling me *ding, ding, ding,* everything I was fearing was right. If that was the case, I only had five days before the whole world would go completely Bollywood, and even I would stop realizing things had ever been different before. I know I had given up, accepted the magic, but if even I had the Bollywooditis makeover, I'd lose my memories of how things used to be, wouldn't I?

Sure, it wouldn't be bad to lose the recollection of my parents' arguments or my presentation and have them replaced with musical memories. But instead of remembering how Dada had shown me how to paint the circles at the top of a pine cone each a different color with bright pink, blue, and green paints, would I only remember Dada singing a song to me about coniferous trees? Like how Zara had replaced our true childhood memories with ones of us singing songs that never actually happened?

That memory gave me happy feelings. Feelings I didn't want to bury, even if the moment with Dada made my heart feel light and heavy all at once, because he was no longer alive.

If the whole world, including me, got taken over by filmi magic, I'd lose all those moments—the bad, but also the good. Despite all the Bollywood tremors I'd been experiencing, I definitely wasn't prepared for that.

CHAPTER 38

"Sonali ben?" Ronak asked, when the last carful of cousins had left. "What did you mean when you said, 'I can't change if they won't change, but it's too much change all at once'? Was that about Mom and Dad?"

I groaned, shutting the door. Why couldn't I stick to instrumental, wordless songs around my brother to avoid having to have a postgame analysis done on my lyrics? I had bigger things to worry about, like how I was going to lose all my memories after the sangeet.

"Look, I'm not controlling what I'm saying," I snapped, feeling like a broken record.

"Sure you are," Ronak replied. "We sing what we're truly feeling."

That may have been true, but I didn't want to share those thoughts with everyone, no matter how moved I was by the apparent power of my feelings to do a solo. "Well, I don't want to sing about it," I said, running my hand on the stair railing behind us. "Okay?"

Ronak shrugged. "Okay. Then talk about it. Like Mom said."

I paused, trying to figure out what I could tell him. He wouldn't believe that we didn't used to sing and dance our thoughts out into the world. He wouldn't believe that Mom didn't always cake on makeup or that Dad didn't always have a flattened stuffed animal on his head. He wouldn't believe everything was going to be changed permanently at my aunt's sangeet. But maybe he would believe me if I told him how I felt. Like if I did a postperformance review on myself, thinking about the lyrics that I had been spewing all these months. Could they actually be how I really felt? I opened my mouth, searching for the words.

"I . . ." I thought about how Mom and Dad's separation marked the beginning of all sorts of changes, like the filmi magic.

"I . . ." I thought about how it had spiraled and was now triggered by Zara, too, and was spilling over into every part of my world.

"I . . ." I thought about how sick I was of singing and expressing myself. "I don't want to talk about it," I said, passing the den and heading to the kitchen.

"You never do." Ronak sighed, walking upstairs.

I sat down at the dining table before my werewolf-monologue brainstorming notebook and began to write, not sure what I was really saying other than, "I'm a human and then the moon comes out and I become a wolf. Change is fun," which was pretty much the opposite of what I was really thinking with the divorce and the impending doom of the sangeet.

Although I didn't want my Bollywooditis to strike when I was at the sangeet and transform me once and for all, I didn't mind getting a boost from it tomorrow in drama class. I needed an A, and Ms. Lin seemed to really like how expressive I was when the Bollywooditis curse was active. "Owoooooo," I wrote in the notebook, adding a big exclamation point to emphasize my point. Whatever point that was.

I flipped a page and tried to come up with ideas to stop the sangeet performance from being my last dance before my memory was taken over by the magic. What if I didn't show up to the dance? I couldn't do that. It was my aunt's sangeet. Or what if I sat my parents down and made one last attempt to convince them filmi magic was not only real, it had transformed our lives and was about to alter everything for good? "Yeah, right," I scribbled sarcastically over the page. The Bollywooditis hadn't yet erased my memory of what had happened the last time I made a presentation to my parents. I drew a bunch of stars, symbolizing the magic. The magic had taunted me before, when I had done an Internet search. What if I wrote it a message on the computer? Maybe it would communicate back to me again.

I headed into the den, where Dad was sifting through boxes in the closet. "Can I use the tablet?" I asked.

Dad gave me permission, his voice echoing from inside a box, and I headed over to the tablet on his desk.

"Are you planning on taking over the world at the sangeet?" I typed into the search engine.

A bunch of websites with titles that said "yes" popped up.

My heart sank. I had already lost Dada once. I couldn't lose my real memories of him, too. And as mad as I was at Zara, I didn't want to lose the recollection of what connected us in the first place. Or lose all my memories with my parents, especially the happy ones, like when we'd take turns picking Hindi songs for long drives down the Pacific Coast Highway, the ocean on one side, windows cracked, feeling peaceful and alive all at once. "How can I stop this?" I typed, hurriedly.

The same dramatic pictures of the old Hindi movies from that first night with Bollywooditis flashed across the screen.

More clues. Or more confusion. This was like a riddle I just couldn't solve. And if I couldn't solve it in time, the world was going to be forever changed. *I* would be forever changed.

"Darn it!" Dad exclaimed as a box of pictures toppled over.

I rushed to his side and crouched down, handing him some loose photographs. "Need help?"

Dad shook his head. "No, it's fine. You can concentrate on your monologue." He sighed loudly. "You know what? Actually, yes. I do need help. That's what your mom would want me to say, right?"

I quickly looked down. He was putting me in the middle yet again. I hated this. But I realized with the divorce and the move, this might be one of the last disagreements they had. That should have made me feel better, but somehow it made me feel twisted up inside instead.

"Avni Foi wanted a picture of us at Raksha Bandhan," Dad said.

I sifted through some dated-looking pictures of Avni Foi and Dad in the middle of a song about a wooden hobbyhorse that was straight out of a Hindi movie. A false filmi memory for sure. I set them aside and picked up the next picture, of Avni Foi and my mom dancing onstage in a high school that looked natural and didn't seem to have had the Bollywooditis makeover. It must have been taken right after both my parents' families had moved here from India. The next picture was of Avni Foi when she was around my age, with my dad. She was tying a rakhdi, a red and yellow embroidery-thread bracelet, around his wrist for the Raksha Bandhan ceremony.

"This one?"

"No, not that one." Dad flipped through some more pictures.

"This one?" I asked hesitantly, holding up a picture from two years ago. I knew it was two years ago because when I was in fourth grade, Avni Foi was bald from her chemo.

Dad nodded, his wig shuddering. "Looks like I really did need your help. Your mom would be pleased. Or say 'I told you so.'" He stopped himself. "That was a joke."

"Okay," I said softly, feeling that tightening inside, almost like a lump in the throat except I felt it everywhere.

Dad stared hard at the picture. Avni Foi, without hair or eyebrows or eyelashes, stood in her chaniyo choli, the skirt and blouse sort of hanging on her thin frame, because she had lost so much weight from the cancer treatments. She was holding a silver plate with a lit divo, the flame making the round red chandlo between her eyebrows and her face glow in the most radiant, peaceful way. Dad was seated in the image, his eyes shiny, and the Raksha Bandhan ceremony was about to start.

"Your mom took that picture," Dad said, handing it to me as I waited for another dig at my mother. "I didn't want to remember that moment. Or talk about it. I wanted the cancer to go away and to put it far behind us and never have to think about it again."

His eyes started to look as shiny as Ronak's as he continued. "Can you believe your aunt wants to put this in her slideshow?"

I shrugged. "I think it shows how strong she is."

Dad paused. "You do?"

I nodded.

And then Dad exhaled loudly as he picked up the next picture in the messy pile. It was a shot of all of us at dinner at Raksha Bandhan. Our plates were empty or halfway there. But Avni Foi's was full, and she gave a weak smile for the camera. "Yeah . . . it does. I'm kind of glad she wants to put it in a slideshow for everyone to see."

I frowned. For everyone to see? Out in the open? Not a dark family secret? This wasn't like Dad at all.

"She didn't touch dinner that day. . . . All she wanted was . . . daal dhokli," he said, his voice wavering ever so slightly as I raised my eyebrow.

Was Dad getting emotional about food?

"I didn't even say sorry the other day when she told me what she'd wanted, when she told me how we should have reached out to the community, to our family." His head hung low as he released his grip on the picture. "I messed up, Sonali," he said, drumming his pointer finger on the floor nervously. "I messed up."

"Dad . . . ," I started, not sure what to say.

"No. I did. Look at her. Look at her plate. We should have been so proud of her. What were we hiding by keeping it all a secret and not even telling family friends or our relatives? What were we afraid of? Well, I know what we were afraid of. We were afraid of people gossiping about Avni Foi. We were afraid of her losing opportunities if they found out she was sick. But mostly we were afraid of losing Avni Foi."

I nodded. It was almost like how I had had to scratch the word "separation" out in my notebook because it made it real. Dad was afraid the more he talked about the cancer, the realer everything would be, and the more he would have to deal with my aunt's sickness and all the emotions tied to it.

"But we never talked about it," Dad continued. "*I* never talked about it, that's for sure. But maybe . . . maybe if I had talked about it, with Bapuji . . ."

His voice caught in his throat at the mention of Dada.

". . . or with my cousins, or even with Revati, maybe . . . maybe we would have had some help as we struggled to cook and clean and get her to appointments and take care of you and Ronak and do our jobs well. And maybe this weight on my shoulders would have been lifted."

I sat up a little straighter, knowing exactly what it felt like to carry that burden, and looked at Dad. His filmi toupee was gone, just like the wind briefly stopping during my fights with Zara, or when Ronak ever so briefly stopped talking about himself in the third person. Was this an error in the magic, like a computer program breaking down? Dad's thinning hair and bald spot were once again visible, like it was before the Bollywooditis struck. Was this a sign there was hope? That I could stop the magic before it made a permanent change in my entire world? That I wouldn't lose all my memories? I stared at Dad's head, knowing it wasn't the time to point out that the wig had vanished, and worrying that it would come back if I did point it out, as Dad continued, unaware anything had changed in his appearance. I had to figure out what Dad had said to stop the Bollywood makeover.

"Remember how stressed we were, trying to get healthy meals cooked for you two while taking Foi to chemo and appointments and surgeries?" Dad continued. "That's when this restaurant habit started. Remember how sad everything Avni Foi was going through would make your dada?"

I nodded, swallowing the feeling of wanting to cry as I remembered those dinners with Dada. "He would just leave his full plate at the dinner table, saying he wasn't hungry."

Dad nodded. "We were never allowed to waste food when I was growing up. Dada had seen too many hungry people when he was younger to ever take food for granted. But when Avni Foi was sick . . . he wasn't leaving the table because he was full. He was leaving it to go to the bathroom and cry. So none of us would see it and think he was weak."

Dad handed me an envelope to put the Raksha Bandhan picture of him and Avni Foi in.

"I felt like crying too," he said quietly. "But I never did. I kept it all inside. We would go to parties, weddings, concerts, Hindi movies, and just smile and laugh with our friends and family like nothing was wrong. But there was so much wrong," Dad's voice started to crack. "I was so scared my little sister was going to die,

Sonali. And your mom and I were arguing so much then because we were both so scared for Avni Foi. And your poor mom was working all day, coming home to take care of you and Ronak, and then rushing back to the hospital to take care of Avni Foi. All she wanted was help. She kept saying we need to tell our friends. We can't take this all on by ourselves, but I wouldn't listen. I was too busy being scared and worried and . . . and stubborn. I messed up. I really messed everything up."

Dad swallowed hard as he put all the other pictures back in the box they had fallen from.

"I wish I had listened more. But more than that, Sonali, I wish I had talked more. I wish I had let it all out, not just then, but for all these years. Maybe . . . maybe if I had, we wouldn't be in the position we are in now."

I couldn't take how sad Dad looked, and reached out to squeeze his hand. "Or maybe we still would be," I said, hesitantly.

"I can second-guess everything I did for the rest of my life and I'll never know. All I know is I messed up. A lot." A tear fell from his chin.

I felt my throat tighten, and gave Dad a hug, holding on tight, as a mournful wooden flute played.

"What's going on? Are you crying?" Ronak asked from the

hall, worried tears already making their way down his face.

Dad turned to me and whispered, "I know you think all that crying makes him a baby. I used to too. But I've realized, it actually makes him pretty strong the way he shows his emotions and talks about his feelings. It's okay to cry. I wish I could have told your dada that too."

I nodded as Ronak threw himself into our hug, and I couldn't tell whose tears were falling on my shoulders, my dad's or my brother's. All I knew was, they didn't make my back hurt. They didn't make my shoulders sore. They didn't weigh me down, or Dad. In fact, they seemed to help Dad sit up taller than ever before.

I looked at Dad. "You're strong too," I said softly, blinking fast so no tears would fall.

CHAPTER 39

I had woken up a little earlier than usual Monday morning, with no more answers for stopping the magic. Instead, I added a couple of more lines to my werewolf monologue. It was still way too short and meaningless to get an A, but it was short enough to memorize, so maybe I'd earn some points for knowing my lines. I still couldn't figure out what Dad had done to make his wig go away and how I could apply it to all the other magical changes.

I walked into drama to upbeat synthesizers playing on my soundtrack, reading my notebook, hoping I wouldn't have to change schools on top of everything else going on in my life. Even if Zara and I were fighting, I'd been going to this school for almost my whole life. It kind of felt like home. Just minus the arguing parents.

I sat next to Air, giving Zara the cold shoulder she was already giving me. There was a nervous energy in the bright-green room. Some kids had gone all out, appearing in costume, although Landon's looked more like a narwhal than the Loch Ness Monster he was supposed to be.

Ms. Lin shoved her glasses up and down her nose as a background noise honked. She looked at the clock on our wall as the period bell rang. She clapped her hands. "Okay, class. Today's the big day. You're being graded on your participation, and applying what you've learned so far this semester. Remember, acting is all about being brave enough to show your emotions." She smiled. "Now, without further ado, first up for their midterm monologue, and just days away from her theatrical debut, Ms. Zara Zareena Khan!"

Everyone applauded as Zara took a deep breath and headed to the stage.

I felt a nervous twinge in my gut. We may have been fighting, but I still wanted Zara to do well. And I knew she could. I had seen her reenact countless scenes from our favorite Hindi movies growing up. She could even make herself cry real Ronak-, or now Dad-, level tears.

Zara took a seat on the distracting checkerboard floor, flicking her feet together like a mermaid's tail as she sang, "*I have dreams*." She ran her hands across the ocean-floor stage and suddenly CGI waves began crashing all around her. I guess solos were now allowed and encouraged in drama after everything I'd done.

The sea spray twinkled all around her on a very obvious green screen as she continued. "*And I'm not talking 'I wanna be where the people are' types of dreams. I want to keep my voice*." Zara grabbed her throat dramatically. "*I'm not going to let a sea witch or anyone else take my voice. That's not love*!" she sang, holding the last high-pitched note, her eyes getting watery as magical wind blew her hair.

I looked down. Was Zara singing about when I said she talked too much?

"*Everyone's voice is important*," she added, looking at me before quickly looking away.

She was right. Everyone's voice was important. Maybe that's a part of what she was getting at when she was saying she wanted me to share my thoughts with her. Maybe she meant she wanted to hear my voice, even if at times she took control of the conversations so I never felt like I had to say much.

"*So I'm not going to change who I am. I'm not going to give up my fins for feet. No way. You will not silence me. I'm going to use my voice. No matter what anyone says or asks of me. I'm going to express myself. My dreams. My fears. My anger. My sadness.*" Zara began to cry real tears in front of everyone. "*Yes, my sadness. Because what you did made me sad.*"

I looked down. What she did had made me sad too. Maybe we both put up walls. Mine was from being a robot. Zara's went up after she couldn't get answers out of me.

"*But it doesn't matter. I've got a lot to say.*" Zara made a fist in the air and roared the last line of her song. "*And you're going to hear it all.*"

A lump formed in my throat, seeing my best friend—or former best friend or neighbor or whatever Zara was to me at this point—crying, and I clapped along with the rest of the class. If the whole world really was going to go Bollywood at the sangeet later this week, I wanted to remember what this moment made me feel before I forgot it.

"You were great," I whispered to Zara as she headed to Air with a relieved look on her face. But Zara didn't hear me. Or she purposely ignored me.

Next, Air did her monologue about being the rare unicorn in her family, and I knew it was really about how different she felt from her Hollywood royalty family. Despite not having the same career goals as her parents, Air didn't seem bitter in her performance.

She seemed happy, talking about how her family members now embraced the unicorn and how different they were from one another.

"Sonali?" Ms. Lin asked, raising her glasses up with her finger as the synthesizer honked.

My stomach dropped as I took the stage. I looked over at Air and Zara. Zara looked away, but Air gave me a smile and a nod, encouraging me to start. My shoulders were hurting from the invisible weight I seemed to be lugging around these days, and I felt like my insides were a bunch of emotions blending into a bad-tasting smoothie full of guilt and annoyance with Zara, nervousness at having to perform in front of everyone, and a dash of anger that I even had to do this assignment when my life at home was in turmoil. Despite it all, I smiled. Because those bubbling emotions, threatening to push the lid off the blender, could only mean one thing. It was Bollywooditis time. And once that kicked in, I would be guaranteed an A. If there was no way to stop the magic from taking over, I might as well give up and embrace it, right? Even with all my memories replaced with false, filmi ones, at least I'd get to stay at Oceanview thanks to the good grade. Maybe that was an okay trade-off.

I paused for a second, waiting for the soundtrack to change to a new, faster rhythm. But nothing happened. My Bollywooditis was triggered by my emotions. Why wasn't it working? Was it storing the magic up so it could do a full takeover at the sangeet?

"I'm a wolf," I began, before realizing I had already messed up. "No, wait. I'm a human."

Ms. Lin dropped her head down to look at me above the rim of her glasses. They slid down her nose and the sound of a tuba honked in the background.

"I'm not a wolf yet," I said, fumbling. I felt my forehead start to sweat and caught Zara's eyes.

She sighed, and despite whatever she was feeling for me, acted out taking a deep breath and breathing out slowly.

I followed her lead and took a deep, slow breath in through my nose and exhaled through my mouth, feeling slightly calmer.

Just slightly though.

"Do you want to sing what you're feeling?" Ms. Lin whispered across the stage to me.

Yeah, I did. But it wasn't starting. "I'm a human," I tried again. "But every time there's a full moon . . ." I pointed up, remembering to use my whole body to act. ". . . I start to howl, and then . . . I start to change."

I crouched to the ground to prepare for my transition from

human to wolf, like the transformation that would happen at the sangeet, and I saw Air and Zara exchange a worried look about me. A worried look that spoke volumes. Like the looks Zara and I used to communicate with. Like the looks my family exchanged about me before they started laughing all those years ago.

"Change," I repeated, eyeing the close friends. "Changes . . ."

I felt the class's eyes on me and reminded myself I was strong. The weeks of performing solos for my family and classmates had forced me to get over that fear. I almost wondered what would have happened back in first grade when I felt my family's stares. What if instead of running, I had just confronted it right then and there? What if Dad was wrong and Mom was right about sharing?

I thought back to my notebooks. To how I couldn't even write the word "separation" without scribbling it away. Would I be able to write the word "divorce" and not scratch it out?

"I'm going through some changes," I said, fumbling the words a little. "Yeah . . ."

The soundtrack grew louder and faster, moving from background music to the foreground. There it was. I was going to be saved by Bollywooditis. I just needed to find something else to say until it made me sing and dance. And after that, once it made me express some exaggerated emotions, I was sure to get an A.

"A lot of changes," I added, willing the singing to start. I opened my mouth, expecting a song to come out of my mouth, complete with outfit changes, but nothing happened.

"Come on. Just start," I said under my breath, as the magical wind dramatically twisted my hair in the air. "Show everyone my emotions."

I froze. Was that what the Bollywooditis had been wanting me to do all along? When I felt those emotions coming to the surface, I had two options. I could hide them behind a mask, telling everyone I was okay, like Dad. Or I could rip that mask off and show everyone what was really under it. All the pain and sadness and anger and confusion and jealousy and fear.

Had I been making the wrong choice all along?

I looked at Zara, who looked seriously worried for me, eyebrows scrunched, and it suddenly dawned on me. Only when I was in the middle of pouring my heart out to Zara and letting her know how I really felt, did the wind stopped blowing in our fights. It came back when I bottled everything up again. Ronak stopped using the third person when he was talking about his emotions. Dad's wig disappeared when he finally broke down and told me how he really felt and cried. Those weren't random errors in the magic. Those were clues.

Just like those images of super-emotional scenes from old Hindi movies on the Internet. More clues I just hadn't understood. The magic wasn't telling me to be a movie star.

My breath quickened. My Bollywooditis wasn't triggered by my parents' fighting or by my fight with Zara. It was happening any time I hid my true feelings. I wasn't an emotionless robot. I had lots of feelings. But every time they came to the surface, I pushed them away. I had to confront those feelings, but I didn't. That's why the filmi magic had to do it for me.

The answer was within me all along.

My palms got clammy. This was what I had been searching for. This was how to stop the filmi magic from taking over at the grand finale and cure myself and the world of Bollywooditis once and for all.

The background score's beats were sounding off faster and faster.

A magical force pulled me to my feet. Everyone in class began to hum, swaying together as I threw my arms in the air. I shook my head, desperate to regain control. It didn't matter to me anymore that the song would have given me an easy A on the midterm. This was my chance, maybe my last chance, to put a stop to the magic before it was too late and things couldn't turn back after the grand finale. The magic spun me around as I sang: *"Find me a shovel and dig out these feelings—"* I cringed, pushing my arms down with all my force, groaning in pain as I fought back hard against the performance the powerful Bollywooditis was intent on giving. I didn't care how strong it had gotten over all those weeks. I had stopped it once before. I knew it was way stronger, but I could do it again. I had to.

My right toe started tapping, but I grabbed my foot and squeezed it tightly. "No!" I shouted, dropping to the stage, my voice quivering as the song tried to burst out. "I don't want to sing and dance anymore!"

The class gasped, appalled that I wouldn't want to sing in this Bollywood world.

I steadied my voice. "I want to say something."

The magical wind suddenly stopped, dropping my hair back into place.

"I'm going through big changes at home," I said softly, looking at Ms. Lin and feeling like I might start crying, like Winnie did all those weeks ago. "These changes aren't once a month with the full moon. They started a long time ago. They started in first grade, when my parents started fighting."

I turned, my feet almost hitting the plastic jacaranda tree as I covered my eyes. "This is how I would sit in my bed, listening to their arguments as my little brother napped." I felt my eyes filling with tears. It was hard to talk about this. But I had to. "They would argue over the silliest, most unimportant stuff, like emptying the dishwasher and taking out the trash. And it made my insides feel like there was this permanent knot inside."

I blinked slowly, letting some of the tears fall. It hurt too much to hold them in any longer. "When I got older, I started ignoring it. I wasn't covering my eyes anymore, but I did pretend I didn't notice when they gave each other the silent treatment or when they said something rude to each other. It was just easier that way."

The soundtrack began to slow down.

I took a breath, meeting Landon's eyes as he stared at me. I looked back at him with a stony gaze. But then I realized that was like a mask too. So I softened, and I didn't even try to hide the fact that my lip was trembling a little. And then instead of laughing, Landon gave me a small, encouraging smile. As brave as I felt, I wasn't ready to look over at Zara while being so open. I was afraid I might start crying if I did, and then I wouldn't be able to get everything out that I needed to say. So I turned to Winnie. She was wiping a tear away and giving me heart hands. Those heart hands I had found so ridiculous at the start of the term. But now I thought, maybe Winnie's parents went through something similar when they split up. And I nodded at her, relieved and grateful for her support as I continued.

"Then, earlier this year, there was another change." I paused, reminding myself I could do this. I held my head up. "Two homes. Two households to run. Countless things to worry and stress and fight about. I feel like every time they argue or say something mean to each other, it sticks with me. I can remember all the times they told me the other person wasn't kind. I can remember so many days when they tried to get me to side with one of them over the other. And I can remember all the fake smiles they put on for the outside world, so no one would know how they really felt about each other." I looked over at Air, who was nodding at me, letting me know I could do this.

The soundtrack was getting fainter.

"But I don't remember when *I* changed. When I decided I would start being as fake as they were so no auntie or uncle could gossip about us. Or wonder what my grandparents would think if they were alive. So no one would think I was weak."

I shook my head. "I wasn't being totally honest that first day of class," I said, watching Ms. Lin. "I wasn't really digging deep. I hadn't done that in so long, I'd lost the shovel. But . . . I think I found it now. Because a few days ago, there was yet another change."

I stood up, finally having the courage to look over at Zara, who had tears streaming down her face. "See, the one thing you don't know about me is . . . my parents are getting a divorce." The soundtrack inside me was suddenly silenced for the first time since the morning after my parents announced they were separating. A sweep of color was suddenly drained out of the classroom, as the bright-green, glossy walls suddenly turned a dull gray, back to their old color. The red-and-black-checkerboard floor turned to white-speckled linoleum again. And Ms. Lin's bright-red glasses were black again, and she suddenly stopped pushing them up her nose with comic background noises.

At long last, the Bollywooditis was gone.

My voice cracked and tears began to fall down my face, turning my cheeks sticky and salty with all eyes on me, but I didn't care. "My parents are getting a divorce and . . . it's breaking my heart."

I began to cry, really cry, a snotty, messy, loud, gasping cry, my shoulders shaking.

But it was the first time in a long time they weren't hurting. It was like a weight had finally been lifted.

CHAPTER 40

Zara rushed to me onstage, throwing her arms around me as I sobbed for everyone to see. Ms. Lin came up to me and patted my shoulder.

"I'm glad you were finally able to get it out, Sonali," she whispered. "Do you want to step outside with Zara for a bit?"

"Yes, she does," Zara said protectively, before catching herself. "I mean, if you want to?"

I nodded, and headed into the hall with Zara, ignoring the stares from my concerned classmates. The hall looked as plain and boring as it used to before its Bollywood makeover. As the door to drama class shut behind us, Zara took her hand off my shoulder.

"I'm a bad friend."

I wiped my face with my sleeve. "No, you're not."

"I am. You were right. I do talk a lot. And I made everything about me." She handed me a tissue from a pack in her pocket. "I had it in case I cried too much in my monologue."

I took it and dried my eyes.

"I knew you weren't interested in the play. I mean, you always acted like you weren't. But then you were being so secretive. I couldn't understand why you weren't opening up and being a real friend. And I just started assuming the worst. Maybe you did want the spot in the play. Or maybe you didn't want Air to be friends with me. And when I confronted you about it, you didn't tell me what was really going on, so I just kept thinking the most horrible things. That was wrong of me, and I'm sorry. I had no idea what you were going through."

"No one does," I said, thinking about how different things would have been for Avni Foi when she was sick if we had had more help, or if she had gotten the one food she was craving. And how different dealing with all these years of my parents' bickering would have been if I had told Zara what was going on and gotten help from her. "I'm sorry I wasn't more truthful with you. I didn't realize I wasn't really being real by hiding so many things. And I couldn't understand why you would ever think I would try to break up your friendship or steal your spot in the play, so I started getting angrier and angrier at you. And then I was singing and dancing at the field trip and—"

"What?" Zara squealed. "*You*? You were singing and dancing? In public?"

"Yeah. You did too," I said slowly, realizing Zara didn't remember anything filmi that had happened, now that I had stopped the magic. "It was magic. Filmi magic, actually. My house had a Bollywood makeover, the school had a makeover, our cars had a makeover, my dad had a bad movie wig, Ronak was talking about himself in the third person, my mom wore a ton of makeup all the time," I said, hoping our home, cars, Dad's hair, Mom's face, and Ronak were all back to normal again. "The Bollywooditis got so strong, it was going to change everyone permanently at the sangeet . . . until I let it all out onstage, and told everyone what I was going through."

Zara's eyes fluttered to the left and right, like she was wondering if she should believe me or not. "Bollywood . . . itis?" she asked.

I nodded. She had finally gotten it right. "That's what I called it."

"I don't remember any of this," Zara replied, looking utterly perplexed.

Not again. My intestines felt like they were knotting up.

"But I believe you," Zara added.

I felt the tension suddenly release from my gut. "You do?"

Zara nodded. "Yeah. But you have to do a better job of filling in all the blanks for me."

"I will. Maybe over ice cream. Or a badminton game," I said with a small smile, thinking about those awful posters I hoped I wouldn't have to see when I got home.

Zara raised an eyebrow at me.

"I'll explain everything," I said.

Zara nodded. "And I'll do a better job listening. I'm sorry you have been feeling so alone lately. You don't have to go through stuff alone, you know. Like your parents' . . ."

"Divorce," I said, getting more used to the word. "My dad didn't want people to know. I guess, I didn't want them to either. I didn't want anyone thinking bad things about us."

"Anyone who does that isn't worth having in your life anyway," Zara said, her eyes glistening. "I love the sound of my own voice, but I can't be the only one who talks in this friendship. You have to tell me what's going on so I can be there for you. And if you're upset at something I'm doing, you have to tell me what you're actually thinking and not get mad at me for things I wouldn't know unless I could read your mind. I'm not trying to replace you with Air. I just like her too."

"I like her too, too." I gave Zara a small smile as I dabbed my nose with the tissue. "And I'm sorry. I think I let everything get so bottled up inside that when it finally came out, it was a disaster."

Zara shook her head. "What you did in there wasn't a disaster, Sonali. That was like a total A+ performance. Trust me, I should know, I'm Zara Zareena Khan, star of the stage and screen." She smiled, tossing her hair. "Okay, not the screen yet. And I'm actually more of a chipped teacup than a star of the stage."

I smiled. Zara was right. I wasn't pathetic for crying in there. Neither was Winnie for crying at the start of the semester about her parents. Neither was anyone who expressed themselves.

"And after you explain everything to me, we can work on how to get rid of the Bollywooditis," Zara said. "Filmi magic is great in movies but not in real life. Maybe we should watch so many old Bollywood movies, it gets scared off, or . . ." Zara paused, trying to figure out in a few seconds what had taken me two months to figure out.

"Thanks, but I don't think I have it anymore," I said, listening carefully for any signs of the background music.

"You don't?"

There was nothing but the sounds of two friends talking. I shook my head. "I think I out-Bollywood'ed the Bollywooditis in my monologue."

Zara smiled. "It was pretty dramatic. If the candlestick ever gets sick for one of our shows, I'll be sure to recommend your name to Ms. Lin for a stand-in."

"Please don't," I said with a small smile. "I'm going to do a better job of saying what I'm really feeling and thinking. Just . . . not onstage."

The door to the drama classroom opened, and Air came out, whispering, "You missed Kiersten's evil tooth fairy monologue. It was . . . interesting." Air shut the classroom door quietly behind her. "Everything okay?"

I looked at Zara. "Totally okay."

Air nodded. "I was thinking, maybe the day after Zara's show, you could both come over to my house and we could celebrate with a *Lockers* marathon? That way you can catch up, Sonali, and we can watch all the episodes together."

I didn't need a three-part harmony on our soundtrack to know this was a good idea.

"Holy caps lock. I'm in." I smiled at my friends. After all the splitting that had been happening, "together" sounded nice.

CHAPTER 41

It turned out I actually liked *Lockers*. After watching five episodes in a row with Air and Zara while eating popcorn and pizza on Wednesday, I had no choice but to appreciate everything. Jacob's parents' divorce was different from my parents'. But I still felt bad for him and understood how he was feeling, and I talked to Air and Zara about it too, instead of keeping it inside. And some scenes were actually really dramatic and funny, almost like an old Hindi movie, just minus the songs.

Back home, in my regular, non-Bollywood house, with the kitchen and my room back to their normal colors, the giant posters of my face making cutesy expressions gone, the pictures back to normal, and the million-dollar sports cars replaced with sensible sedans, our evening was spent getting all our outfits together for Avni Foi's three-day wedding celebration with the mehendi, sangeet, wedding, and reception, which started tomorrow.

Ignoring the sounds of repetitive flushes from the bathroom across from my room, I pulled out a green chaniyo choli from the back of my closet for the mehendi, the event on Thursday when we would get henna on our hands. I reached up to the shelf at the top of the closet to grab the plastic box I kept my hundreds of bangles in, and had plopped it down on my bed when Ronak entered, with what looked like four identical, light-gold-colored salwar kameez of his own.

"Which one should I wear to the wedding? This or this?" He held up two of the light-gold tops with gold embroidery.

"Aren't they the same?" I asked, reaching for a sparkling magenta, orange, and teal chaniyo with traditional mirror work for the sangeet.

Ronak looked offended. "No! This one has paisley embroidery, and this one has, like, vines or plants."

I shrugged, pointing to the one in his left hand. "That one."

"Thanks." He turned to leave but suddenly paused. "Wait, I'll translate. Beep, boop, beep."

"That's funny," I said, with a puff of air at Ronak's robot-sister translation.

"Is that your laugh?" Ronak deadpanned, before I could catch myself from doing my old habit.

I may have messed up just now, but I wasn't going to again. I was going to keep my promise and not bottle stuff up anymore.

"I think I need to apologize to you," I started.

Ronak laughed. "For what?" But then he saw my face and quickly stopped smiling.

I sat on the bed. "Sometimes I make fun of you for expressing yourself so well."

"You mean for crying?" Ronak asked.

I nodded. "I used to see it as a failure, sort of. Like how I would take you upstairs and read to you so you wouldn't hear Mom and Dad arguing or see them giving each other the silent treatment. I think I was resentful that after all I did to help you not see their issues, you were still affected by them. But I should have realized, of course you were upset. I was too. I'd just forgotten how to show it. So, I'm sorry for hurting you, and for not being there when you were hurting. I'm going to try not to be so much of a robot-sister anymore."

Ronak gave me a hug.

"I also need to be totally honest with you. Remember that day I came home sick from school?" I asked.

Ronak nodded, slinging the rest of his clothes back over his arm.

"Well, I wasn't sick. I mean, I *was* sick, because I was terrified of not being in control when I was singing and dancing because of the filmi magic."

Ronak shifted, the plastic hangers on his clothes clanking against each other, as he raised an eyebrow. "What?"

I shook my head, realizing I was not doing a good job of explaining myself. "I called it 'Bollywooditis.' It was like filmi magic made me tell the world my feelings in the most obvious way possible, through Bollywood numbers. And we all had our own soundtracks. Although I don't know what was on yours because it's considered rude to ask. Do you remember when my room was bright yellow and I had huge posters of myself all over?

Ronak looked utterly bewildered. "Why would you, of all people, have giant posters of yourself on your walls?"

He didn't remember. It seemed like no one remembered any of our real-life Bollywood experience. "You were talking about yourself in the third person, like, 'Ronak doesn't know,' and Dad had this really bad Bollywood wig on that looked like a skunk, and the kitchen was bright red and purple, and our cars were—"

"Is this an April Fool's joke?" Ronak interrupted. "Or like those funny stories you'd tell me to distract me when Mom and Dad were arguing?"

"No. I swear," I said, spreading the chaniyo out and watching the tiny mirrors sewn into it flicker as they caught the sunlight from my window.

I looked at my walls. Dozens of glistening specks of light were being refracted all over the movie posters and the carved elephant Dada had given me, and rainbow-colored prisms fell onto the edge of the journal he'd given me.

"See?" I pointed to the stunning scene, inhaling deeply so it was almost like I could smell the last remaining hints of sandalwood on the journal even though I was across the room. "Sometimes filmi magic is real."

Ronak stared at the twinkling lights dancing across the posters of movies we loved, and nodded. "Yeah. That's true." He sat on the bed next to my clothes. "Okay. I believe you. Do you . . . need to tell Mom about your Bollywooditis? Maybe someone at the hospital can help?"

I shook my head. "It's gone now. I do need to tell Mom something else though. I need to tell her about the spinach in her teeth."

As if on cue, Mom screamed from the hallway. "Ronak! Did you clog the toilet again?"

I took one look at Ronak's mortified face and burst out laughing. It wasn't a puff of air and a statement. It was a loud, squealing, almost choking kind of laugh that was coming from deep within me.

"Is that your laugh?" Ronak asked. "I'm being serious. I don't think I've ever heard that one before."

I wiped the happy tears from the corners of my eyes. "Come on," I said, standing up.

Ronak and I walked into the hallway to find Mom flushing the toilet after successfully snaking it.

"You fixed it?" I asked as she bagged up the end of the snake that goes in the toilet and washed her hands.

"I did." She smiled, confidently, her face back to normal, chapped lips and all, finally rid of the dramatic filmi makeup.

Dad, who had come by to pick out clothes for the wedding festivities and pack more of his stuff up, emerged from my parents' bedroom with a stack of boxes covering his face. "I just got your drama midterm grade in the parent portal. You got an A, Soni. Good job."

I felt my heart beat faster. This meant I could stay in school at Oceanview. "Thanks," I replied quietly as Dad dug through the top box.

"Where did you put my dad's guitar?" he asked Mom.

"I thought you gave it to Avni." Mom said, shrugging.

"Why would I give it to Avni?" Dad snapped, trying to balance the boxes.

"Stop fighting," I said softly, my jaw tightening.

"Why would you want to keep it?" Mom said sharply. "Avni knows how to play it. You don't."

Dad frowned, putting the boxes down. "You always know best right? I—"

"Stop fighting!" I shouted.

My parents and Ronak all turned to me.

"Just stop!" I said, even louder, a hot wave of anger flooding me as if the dam I had been building up over all these years had just burst and become that unstoppable waterfall Ms. Lin had told me about on the field trip. I thought back to when I first realized how angry I was at Mom right after I had sung about lemonade. Only I wasn't singing about lemonade. I was singing about my parents. About how very mad I was at them.

"Aren't you sick of all of this? You thought you were stuck?" I asked, turning to Mom, remembering her words at the tar pits weeks ago. "I was stuck in something too, but I figured out how to make it stop. You've figured out how to stop it, but you still can't stop. Well, news flash, I know I've been saying I'm okay, but I'm not okay. I've been hearing you two fight my whole life and I can't take it anymore!"

I ran into my room and slammed the door so hard, the poster of Aamir Khan tilted on the wall. I collapsed into tears on my bed. So much for telling my parents about spinach. After everything I had been through, it looked like I still couldn't get it all out. I clenched at the paisley sheets on my bed when a knock sounded at my door.

"Can I come in?" Ronak asked on the other side of it.

I stood up, heading toward the door. "Are Mom and Dad with you?" I asked, hesitantly, not sure I could face them after my outburst.

"Ronak doesn't know," my brother responded.

"No!" I gasped. Not again. I threw open my bedroom door to find Ronak standing there sheepishly with my parents.

"Sorry," he mouthed. "I did know."

I scowled at him and the fake-out. "Thanks a lot," I muttered, plopping on my bed.

Mom and Ronak took a seat on the foot of the bed and Dad

crouched on the floor by me, setting down the lone box he had left in his arms.

"I'm sorry we upset you, Sonali," Dad said quietly. "I found something of yours, when I was cleaning up my papers."

I didn't say anything as Dad reached into the box and pulled out a stack of mini poster boards, the top one covered in faded colored-pencil hearts. I didn't have to look twice to know what it was. It was my presentation. My ears started to burn.

"I don't know if you remember this. But when you were little, you gave us a presentation on why parents shouldn't fight. You researched all these facts with Mom's old science facts for kids books and—"

"I remember," I snapped. How could I have forgotten that mortifying memory when I worked my butt off trying to teach my parents how to be nice to each other, and Dad yelled, Mom practically cried, and Dada laughed in my face?

"You do?" Mom asked, looking like she might cry again.

"Yeah. Dada thought it was the funniest thing ever."

Dad shook his head. "He didn't, Sonali."

Ronak sifted through the poster boards, confused, since he clearly couldn't remember what had happened when he was four.

"He did," I said sharply, feeling humiliated all over again as

Ronak paused to look at a drawing I had made of my parents arguing and me crying next to them. "He said it was so sweet and laughed louder than I had ever heard him laugh before. It wasn't supposed to be sweet," I blurted out before I could stop myself.

Dad nodded. "I know. But Bapuji saw me getting mad. He saw Mom about to cry. And he didn't know what to do with the rest of the family there watching. He didn't want you to be sad. So he laughed and tried to play it down. He tried to hide the truth from everyone. But he knew why you made that presentation."

I sighed. How would Dad know what Dada knew or didn't know?

"He talked to us for a long time that night after the party," Mom said. "He said this presentation was clearly about me and Dad. And we had to learn to get along for your sake and Ronak's sake. He told us we had to stop fighting because it was hurting you."

My throat felt tight as my mind began to fill with dozens and dozens of jumbled thoughts. Dada wasn't laughing at me? He was trying to protect me by laughing? I didn't remember Dad getting mad or Mom about to cry during the presentation. Just their reactions after. But I did remember Dada's stinging, embarrassing laughter, which made me think maybe showing my feelings was pointless, even before Dad's lecture confirmed that theory. That laughter spread even quicker than filmi magic, as all my aunts and uncles and cousins laughed too. It changed me forever.

I looked down, trying to suppress my thoughts. Trying to stop myself from saying any of this out loud. My pulse seemed like it was pounding in my throat. But then I realized something else had changed me forever: the filmi magic. I remembered what Ms. Lin and Mom and even Zara's song had said about being brave enough to show what you're really feeling. And what Zara had said about not always going through stuff alone. I felt my family all around me, even though I didn't have the courage to look up. Maybe recognizing I was angry was the first step. And now it was time to take the next, and let it all out. It was time to throw the mask out once and for all and say everything out loud. "Can I . . . can I talk to both of you?"

"Always," Mom said.

I looked at my parents' expectant eyes. It felt weird having them stare at me like this, waiting to hear what I finally had to say. I wondered if Air felt like this when she'd told her parents that she wasn't interested in Hollywood the way they were.

My heart was beating fast, but there was no song and dance that would get me through this. The Bollywooditis was really gone. Now it was up to me to show what I was feeling.

"I'm mad," I said, my voice shaking.

Mom's eyebrows furrowed. "About what?" she asked gently.

"At both of you. I know I always say I'm fine, but I'm not. I've been really mad, but I didn't know why. Now I do. I'm mad that you let things get this bad. I'm mad you didn't know I wasn't okay. I'm mad that I had to spend practically my whole life hearing you both snap at each other and pull us into your arguments and treat each other in such a mean way."

"Sonali . . . ," Dad began, his eyes shifting as he searched for words.

But I wasn't done yet. "I'm also sad. I'm sad that Ronak feels so sad. I'm sad because *I* feel sad. I feel sad to see two people I look up to fight all the time or stew in silence. I'm sad Dada's not here to make us feel better about it. I'm sad because we won't have Hindi movie nights together anymore. I'm sad because we won't be going to India together every December. Or going to Hugo's for dinner together. Or just driving down the PCH together while Hindi music plays."

"I'm hoping we do get to a point one day where we can have occasional dinners together again, Sonali," Mom said softly, looking at Dad. "I wish it could be different now, but . . . it can't. I feel so terrible we put you kids through all this," she said as Ronak rested his head on her lap. "And I'm so sorry I didn't realize you weren't okay. I'm so strong at work for my patients. But at home, I had become this dependent person, relying on others to do so much for me. Sometimes I just made myself believe you were fine so I could lean on your support and strength."

I looked at Mom's teary eyes. I knew what it was like to depend on something, too.

"I am learning to trust myself again," Mom said. "To rely on myself. I wish my journey didn't include hurting you both like this, though. I'm so sorry for everything we have put you kids through."

I nodded, squeezing Mom's hand. I got what she was going through. I was learning to trust myself to express my emotions and deal with everything my parents were doing too, instead of relying on my mask and burying everything deep down.

"I'm sorry too," Dad said, a couple of tears falling freely down his face. "And I'm proud of you for telling us all of that."

I sniffled, thinking back to all those times I brought bad grades home that Parvati ben never would have and feeling like Dad would never be proud of me.

"I wish I had listened the first time, all those years ago when you made that presentation, instead of taking my anger out on you. But we couldn't stop fighting. And instead of encouraging you to tell us what you were thinking, I just believed you every time you said you were okay, even though obviously you couldn't have been okay."

I ran my toes along the grains of the hardwood floor below. Not only had I been hiding my feelings from outsiders. I'd been hiding them from my friends and family, and from myself.

"We call everyone in the community our family friends, but we don't really treat them like family, do we? Hiding things to save face." Dad looked down as Ronak gave him a hug. "I put all this financial pressure on you when we were the ones going through a . . . a . . ." He cleared his throat, like he couldn't get himself to say the word "divorce." ". . . That wasn't right," he finished.

"I know the divorce is the right thing though," I said softly, my burden-free shoulders shaking as I cried.

"Sonali ben . . . ," Ronak said as Dad's face fell even more than I thought it could.

"I do, Dad." I sniffled. "Because you and Mom deserve to be happy. We all do. I think a part of me was also mad at the separation, like you were giving up. But now I realize, it isn't giving up. Me bottling everything inside and pretending I was fine was giving up. This is fighting to save our family. Just a different version of it. And like I figured out earlier this week, change is scary and makes me nervous and worried, but I know this change will make us all feel better in the end, however sad or mad it makes me feel now." I paused. "I think . . . I think I'd like to talk to someone. Like my principal said. Maybe the school counselor?"

"That's a good idea," Mom replied. "Look at you. Look how much stronger we've all become this year," she added, giving Ronak and me a hug and looking at Dad with teary eyes.

"Yeah," I said, thinking if we still had background music, ours would be playing a four-way harmony right now with just a few out-of-place notes. "Dad and I are actually showing our emotions. You just snaked a toilet."

"And I learned how to parallel park at the apartment last week," Mom said with a small, satisfied smile.

"You did?" Ronak said. "I'm so proud of you."

"And you are the strongest of all of us," I said to my brother, wiping my eyes on my shoulder. "We're going to get through this, together. Even if that means sometimes we're apart," I said. And for the first time since my parents announced they were divorcing, I actually believed it.

CHAPTER 42

With the sangeet no longer in danger of being the grand finale of my formerly filmi life, I sat calmly with Ronak at a table with all our cousins next to the Grand Villas' outdoor dance floor. We were on a high peak of emerald green, and the mountains of Malibu could be seen in the distance. All around us, little solar-powered string lights flickered, spiraling around the palm trees on the resort property. And the centerpieces on our white tablecloths were an array of succulents in short, wide, rectangular glass vases full of gray pebbles.

Avni Foi and Baljeet Uncle, who would become "Baljeet Fuva" after the wedding, sat before the pale gray wooden dance floor in two elaborately carved gold seats that looked more like thrones than chairs.

Revati Auntie greeted us by pinching our cheeks and patting our heads in true overbearing auntie fashion. I watched her stop at my parents' table, and expected Dad to cringe a little when he saw her. But instead he smiled, and although the music was loud, I could make out Dad saying, "Falguni and I have something to tell you."

I turned from my parents' table as Sheel leaned over ours, grabbing the little chocolate party favors out of the colorful sari pouches at each place setting. "Did you feel any more earthquakes?" Sheel asked.

I looked at Ronak and smiled. "Nope. Not since our last practice."

"That one was so good," Parvati ben said next to me. "I think. I can't remember much except it was super energetic. I think we've had so many practices, they're all blurring together."

I nodded, knowing she didn't remember anything the filmi magic had made happen.

"Just make sure you bring that energy today, everyone." My cousin leaned over and spoke softly but loud enough for people to hear. "Are you okay? When are they going to tell everyone what's going on?"

"About what?" Tejal asked, swinging her legs by Parshva bhai.

"Our parents are getting a divorce." I eyed the framed picture of Dada and Dadi on a stand by the head table. It was a little weird saying it out loud in a Desi space for the first time.

"What?!" Shilpa squealed, turning back to look at the table where my parents were sitting side by side next to our aunts and uncles.

"Don't stare!" Neel chided.

"A divorce?" Tejal exclaimed, staring along with everyone else. "Why? They can't!"

"It's okay," I said, as Ronak tried to come up with an answer. "They're happier apart."

"You doing okay?" Parshva bhai asked.

Ronak nodded. "Yeah. We're sad, but it's okay."

"And mad and annoyed and scared and nervous, and pretty much all the feelings except happy and excited," I added. "But like Ronak said, it's okay. We've been dealing with it for a long time. For years. We just didn't tell you."

Parvati ben nodded, for once realizing the inside information she was privy to went back way longer than she knew. "We're here for you anytime if you need anything. A distraction. Another dance practice?" She gave me a small smile.

I laughed. "Thanks. I'll let you know."

Baljeet Uncle's older brother, Sukhwinder Uncle, made his way to the dance floor, microphone in hand, and got everyone's attention.

"Thank you all for joining us tonight to celebrate my brother and soon to be sister's big day tomorrow. We've got really great dances for you tonight. And I promise I won't sing, so you'll be spared that."

The crowd laughed, and Sukhwinder Uncle glanced at a piece of paper in his hand. "First up, Avni's nieces and nephews. Please welcome, Parvati, Parshva, Neel, Sheel, Shilpa, Tejal, Sonali, and Ronak!"

The DJ began to play a booming bhangra song, its dhol beat making the whole dance floor vibrate as we made our way onto the wooden tiles. I was nervous, but like Parvati ben had told me a few days ago, I could handle this. The magic was gone, and this wasn't a grand finale anymore.

More like a new beginning.

As soon as we got into position, the music changed to our medley, and we began to dance. I watched my aunt's beaming face as she clapped along, the little dangling beads on the gold teeko draped on a chain in her part and on her forehead, her nose ring, and her earrings shaking. I wanted to give her the best sangeet ever, so I dug deep, channeled my inner Bollywood, minus the "itis," and began stepping and spinning and jumping and twirling with all the energy I could muster, mouthing along to all the words I had memorized years ago when I watched the movies with Dada.

And as I reenacted all those songs, I made sure to make all the expressive Bollywood faces I wouldn't have ever done before the Bollywooditis forced me to. I smiled, I cheered, I tilted my eyebrows diagonally to show pain, I made my mouth into an *O* to show surprise, I blushed to show embarrassment. I did feeling after feeling in song after song until it was time for the grand finale—the non-world-altering one.

As "Dil Le Gayi Kudi Gujarat Di" played, Parvati ben pulled Avni Foi and Baljeet Uncle toward us, and the rest of the cousins ran to our parents, pulling them onto the dance floor.

Beejal Foi and Arvind Fuva were doing embarrassing, over-the-top garba moves. Tejal's parents were breaking out in bhangra. And I wasn't sure what Sheel's mom was doing, but it involved a lot of shaking.

Mom began to dance, awkwardly at first before she let loose, twirling her mendi-covered hands above us, a huge grin on her face. Dad stood there stiffly until Ronak grabbed his hips and made them wiggle.

"Don't act like you don't know how to dance. We saw the video!" I laughed.

Dad chuckled, finally giving in and dancing around me and Ronak.

As the sun dipped close to the mountains behind us, bathing us all in a pink glow that was straight out of a magic-hour shot in a Hindi movie, I watched my parents and Ronak dancing, trying to capture this moment in my memory forever, just in case my parents never got to that place where we did do things together again.

I knew the family was going to change over time. I knew our housing situation might change. I knew I would change. But despite all those changes, I knew without a doubt in my mind that as long as we all kept communicating and being honest with one another about our feelings, my parents were going to be fine. Ronak was going to be fine. And I was going to be fine too.

And just like in any good Bollywood movie, I wouldn't mind singing that from the highest of mountaintops.

Acknowledgments

When I was growing up, I never saw any books with Indian American characters in it. There wasn't Desi representation in American TV shows, movies, or even department store ads that came in the mail. What I did have, was Hindi movies.

Those movies shaped my life. They allowed me to see myself in their characters. My walls slowly became covered in posters of Aamir Khan, Madhuri Dixit, Sridevi, and others. I learned Hindi by watching three Hindi movies a week, rented on VHS tapes that did not have subtitles. When we went to India every couple of years, I would buy clothes based on what the characters wore in my favorite movies. I formed deep connections with many family friends and relatives over our shared love of these movies. And I learned to become a storyteller by watching these movies, one day even working in Bollywood and having conversations with some of the very people whose posters adorned my walls as a child.

None of this would have been possible without my parents. Thank you, Aai and Dad, for all those trips to the store to rent these movies, for the weekends spent in the movie theaters in Michigan, watching Hindi films, and for taking me to movie theaters in India to fully experience Bollywood in all its glory, and feel seen. Thank you for encouraging my love of Hindi cinema, for making it possible for me to meet all my childhood heroes backstage at concerts, in hotel lobbies, and even at the mall. And thank you for believing in me when I told you I wanted to become a screenwriter, and was going to work in Bollywood.

I'd been searching for a way to share my love for Bollywood and its filmi magic with my readers, and I'm so happy I could do just that in this book. Thank you to Karina Yan Glaser, for the Nerd Camp MI conversation that sparked this idea for me.

The seeds of this story were planted decades earlier when I was first considering a filmi career path. Thank you to the Barjatya family, Ashutosh Gowariker, and Ameen Sayani for your kindness. Thank you to Jim Burnstein, for all things screenwriting, and to Vidhu Vinod Chopra, for reading my paper twenty years ago and giving me a job in Bollywood.

Thank you to my incredible agent, Kathleen Rushall, for believing in this book. I'm so grateful to you for all these years of friendship, advice, and encouragement. Thanks for being on this journey with me.

To my brilliant editor, Jennifer Ung, thank you for making Sonali's story what it is today. I really can't believe how lucky I am to get to work with you. Every step of the process has been so much fun. Thank you for everything, (including, of course, the dog pictures).

To Krista Vitola, thank you for your guidance and for providing support in these final stages of the book hitting shelves.

To designer Laura Lyn DiSiena and cover artist Abigail Dela Cruz, thank you for the most gorgeous cover that captures Sonali and her filmi magic so perfectly. To the entire team at Simon & Schuster BFYR, including Justin Chanda, Kendra Levin, Dainese Santos, copy editor Lynn Kavanaugh, proofreader Beth Adelman, Sara Berko; Lauren Hoffman, Chrissy Noh, Lisa Moraleda, Shivani Annirood, Christina Pecorale, Victor Iannone, Emily Hutton, Theresa Pang, Michelle Leo, and Anna Jarzab, this book would not be possible without you. Thank you!

Thank you for the answers to my questions for this story,

Nishad Parmar, Rahul Kshirsagar, Kalpana Auntie, Ila Auntie, Dave and Andrea Turner, Simran Jeet Singh, and Adil Daudi. To Brynn Wade, Ali Standish, and Sarah Canon, for reading early drafts and for your incredibly helpful notes. To Raakhee Mirchandani, my Bollywood sister. And a huge thanks to the original Hindi movie screenwriter in the family, Dad, for all the Gujarati help. Any mistakes are mine alone.

Thank you to all the educators, booksellers, and librarians who have gotten my books into the hands of so many readers. And thank you to all the readers who have spent time with these characters and connected to their stories. You remind me every day that in addition to filmi magic there is also bookish magic.

Finally, thank you to all my friends, family, Limca, Cookie, Apoorva, Aai, Dad, Sachit, Zuey, Leykh, and Arjun, for your never-ending encouragement, support, and love. You mean the world to me, and I'd sing that from the highest of mountaintops any day.

About the Author

Born and raised in the Midwest, Supriya Kelkar learned Hindi as a child by watching three Hindi movies a week. She is a screenwriter who has worked on the writing teams for several Hindi films. Supriya's books include *Ahimsa, Bindu's Bindis, American as Paneer Pie,* and *That Thing about Bollywood,* and more. Visit her online at SupriyaKelkar.com.